BELIE

A SEAN COLBETH MYSTERY

SEAN COLBETH INVESTIGATES
BOOK EIGHT

CHRISTOPHER H. JANSMANN

Ephram Cotte
& Company
PUBLISHING

ISBN: 978-1-960914-28-6 (Kindle Edition)
ISBN: 978-1-960914-30-9 (Paperback)
ISBN: 978-1-960914-29-3 (Hardcover)

Library of Congress Control Number: 2025913109

Printed in the United States of America

For Paula:

My heart, my love, my everything is yours, always and forever.

Books by this Author

Chronological Order

Blindsided

Pariah

Outsider

Peril

Ditched

Bygones

Downhill

Duality

Focus

Bewitched

Requiem

Vengeance

Mirage

Solitude

Masks

Belie

Silenced

Sean Colbeth Investigates

Blindsided

Outsider

Downhill

Duality

Bewitched

Vengeance

Solitude

Belie

Vasily Korsokovach Investigates

Pariah

Peril

Ditched

Bygones

Focus

Requiem

Mirage

Masks

Silenced

Oliver & Vasquez

Reflection in the Shadows

Shorts

Snow Drifts

Baubles

Contents

Preface   ix

One   1
Two   21
Three   36
Four   50
Five   57
Six   69
Seven   79
Eight   96
Nine   105
Ten   115
Eleven   128
Twelve   137
Thirteen   149
Fourteen   159
Fifteen   172
Sixteen   184
Seventeen   192
Eighteen   203
Nineteen   213
Twenty   225
Twenty-One   234
Twenty-Two   244
Epilogue   256

Acknowledgments   265
About the Author   267

PREFACE

BELIE

verb (belies, belying, belied)

1. (of an appearance) fail to give a true notion or impression of (something); disguise or contradict
2. fail to fulfill or justify (a claim or expectation); betray

— *New Oxford American Dictionary* (2023 edition)

ONE

East Newberry was just one of many dying mill towns in Maine; that it happened to be located along the Penobscot River only made it slightly more notable, and even then, primarily because it was the de facto halfway point between Bangor and Windeport. Like many residents in that portion of the state, I'd passed through it on a number of occasions without giving it more than a fleeting thought. There wasn't much to consider, anyway; beyond the hulking mass of the long deserted late-nineteenth century textile mill crowding the banks of the Penobscot, what little was left of surrounding town couldn't have been more than a few blocks, if that. Windeport by comparison felt like a teeming metropolis, which was saying something considering we'd been in our own version of steady decline for more years than I cared to count. I'd seen an article some months back in the *Bangor Daily News* that a developer had proposed renovating the old mill into affordable housing; while it had been a laudable concept, with an ever-shrinking tax base, the town hadn't been in much of a position to fund the project. Coupled with the unwillingness of any commercial lender to underwrite something in the heart of one the most economically challenged counties of the state, the idea had died a horribly slow death; as I drove past the foreboding brick structures on a late Monday evening in November, I wondered a little bit about man's inhumanity to man — or woman, for that matter. Nearly thirty years after the mass exodus of manufacturing from my beloved state, we had yet to figure out how to plug the massive hole it had left behind; I had no idea just how many lives had been destroyed by corporate obeisance to increasing shareholder value but assumed from the size of the mill it hadn't been a modest number in East Newberry.

My thoughts continued along those bleak lines as I slowed to a stop at the fifth checkpoint; by that point, I'd somewhat adjusted to seeing my colleagues from the State Police in full tactical gear, touting semi-automatics far more appropriate for some overseas conflict area than a down-on-its-luck backwater county. Rolling down my window, I held out both my badge and official state I.D., then waited impatiently for the officer to radio in for verification. Tapping my fingers on the steering wheel of my unmarked SUV, my eyes shifted to the cruiser parked behind the sentry, its strobe lights flashing in time to a disco tune only it could hear. The red-and-blue flickers of light reflected dully from the aging brickwork of the giant mill just beyond, providing a weirdly festive vibe wholly inappropriate to the situation.

At length, the officer turned her attention back to me. "Sorry for the delay, Commander," she apologized as she handed back my badge and I.D. "They are a bit overwhelmed at the moment up there."

"I can imagine," I said, nodding. "Any word yet?"

"None," she replied, shaking her head. "Whoever did it seems to be in the wind."

Seeing a slight trembling in the hand holding the radio, I softened my look. "No one ever truly disappears, Sergeant," I said.

"With respect, sir, it's a big state."

I risked a slight smile. "That just means we have home field advantage. Where is the scene?"

The young woman nodded down the street. "Turn left at the next intersection; you'll see the lot for the river launch where everyone has been parking. The command post is a little further beyond the lot; you'll find Captain Roberts waiting for you there."

"Thank you."

She nodded and stepped back as I rolled up the window; starting down the street, I quickly found myself plunged into relative darkness after the brilliance of the lights from the cruiser at the checkpoint. By the time I'd reached the aforementioned intersection, my night vision had reasserted itself; turning, I discovered it didn't matter, for my destination in the distance was awash in the harsh white glare from temporary spots that had been hastily erected around the small, paved area. Pulling in, I realized the lot was nearly full of the ubiquitous silhouettes of vehicles favored by law enforcement; about the only distinguishing features among them appeared to be the varied logos of the Federal, State and local agencies that had responded to the all hands call that had gone out some hours earlier. One of the few trucks *not* bearing any sort of logo instead had the requisite canoe hanging over the edge of its tailgate, a stark reminder of the lot's true purpose; I snagged the spot just beside it and killed the ignition on my SUV. Pulling my gun from the safe in the glovebox, I slid it into the holster at my waist as I exited my SUV; given the circumstances, I found myself unusually comforted by the presence of the weapon — and the fact that I had aced my recertification on it just a few weeks earlier.

Slowly making my way down the crowded street, I wasn't all that surprised that the general air of malaise seemed to hang over even that portion of East Newberry. Having lived in Windeport for nearly my entire life, I'd had a front row seat as my Village slowly circled the drain; it wasn't hard to think the boarded-up store fronts, cracked concrete sidewalks and burnt-out streetlights might be a peek at our future. Pausing beside a Postal Service mailbox that had more rust than blue paint, I wondered what it might have been like in the days when that small stretch of downtown had been the vibrant heartbeat of the community; in the close darkness of that cold evening, it felt far more like the setting for one of the zombie apocalypse movies Vasily had made me watch a few years earlier.

There were a few signs of life, though; at the far end of the street, the bright lighted sign from a national chain pharmacy stood out particularly well against the unrelieved bricks of the other abandoned storefronts, a veritable traveling rose flourishing among the weeds. Adding to the evidence that East Newberry hadn't completely given up was a small twenty-four-hour diner straight out of a Hopper painting a half-block from the scene; the large window allowed soft white light to spill out onto the street, chasing a few doldrums away but little else. Movement behind the long counter caught my attention, and I watched for a moment as a short man in a tired-looking apron carefully put away a load of white mugs on an open shelf. My intrinsic desire to test drive one of those mugs with the brew from the impressive stainless-steel coffee pot beside them was overridden by the knowledge that there were other pressing matters to attend to — but not before wondering if the now-vacant pool hall next to the diner had been run by the same owners; if nothing else, the two businesses had used the same sign maker, one who had created beautifully crafted neon signs evoking the essence of what patrons would find inside. The large coffee mug outlined in dark neon for the diner was even animated slightly, appearing to have small plumes of white steam wafting toward the heavens every four seconds. Resuming my walk toward the scene, I thought perhaps the pool cue hanging over the now boarded-up business might have been as similarly eye catching, though it was extremely hard to tell at that point.

The portable command post had been parked along the curb of the already narrow street that ran parallel to the Penobscot River; sitting in front of the long row of brick buildings on that side, the shadowless white of the spots that had been set up along the sidewalk made it look more like a beached whale than the latest in crime fighting technology. Behind the RV, a small fleet of ambulances had been parked, almost as if they were staged to assist at some sort of sporting event; only one seemed to be doing any business, though, with its double doors open to reveal a patient on a stretcher being attended to by a duo of paramedics. The crimson stain on the white bandage wrapped about the victim's head was visible even from my distance, as was the pallid complexion that presaged a hasty trip to the nearest emergency room.

More troubling perhaps was the long line of hearses parked on the other side of the street, evenly spaced so the wide rear door could be opened sufficiently to slide in the small gurneys favored by funeral homes. They, too, appeared to be quiet, but judging from the calm patience of the clutch of morticians gathered just in front of the first somber colored vehicle, their expectation they would soon be called to action was nearly palpable. If what I had been told about the scene was even remotely accurate, I knew the Chief Medical Examiner was going to have her hands full in the coming hours.

As I approached the command post, one of the two side doors suddenly popped open and disgorged the form of Captain James Roberts, my friend of many years and now, as a result of a strange series of incidents over the previous summer, my superior; his face turned in my direction as he came down the short steps, and he paused to wait for me to arrive. Uncharacteristically, he was attired not in his usual Class A uniform but a weatherbeaten overcoat, jeans that had random paint stains on them and the standard footwear for most Mainers: the classic L.L. Bean Boot. Usually hidden from view beneath his Smokey Bear hat that seemed to be standard to those in upper leadership at the State Police, his salt-and-pepper hair looked unusually unkempt, as though he'd been running his hands through it. That suspicion was confirmed when he did just that as I came up beside him.

"Jimmy," I said, eyeing him carefully. Lines of tension had appeared around his eyes, lines visible even in the uneven temporary lighting. It made him look far older than he truly was; my stomach twisted slightly at what had done that to him.

"Sean," he replied. "I pulled rank and asked Norm to join us here in East Newberry. Someone from the County should have already replaced him at his checkpoint; I've also asked the County to add additional points along Route One north and south of Windeport. I suspect he's not too far behind you."

I nodded, for my number two had called me directly after the order had come through; I'd been privately skeptical that anyone fleeing East Newberry would head toward my hometown but had kept that to myself. "We're spread a bit thin, Jimmy."

Roberts looked toward the building we were standing in front of, then glanced at the yellow crime scene tape that was fluttering in the light breeze coming up from the river. I had never understood where the oddly specific scent of a river came from — or why it was just as distinctive as the salinity of the ocean I lived along. "It will have to do. New Hampshire has more troops on the way, and I think I can call in a favor from Massachusetts." He looked back at me. "They'll be too late to do anything worthwhile, of course, but at this point we have to consider the public relations angle in addition to the *actual* manhunt."

"In this age of online speculation, we do what we have to," I sighed.

Roberts looked back at the building; he considered the faded lettering over the tall plate glass windows for a long moment, almost as if he were steeling himself to face something unspeakable. The original call from headquarters hours earlier had been scant on the details of what had gone down in East Newberry other than a person of interest was now being sought — and that every major route in the state within two hundred miles of the town was being shut down. I'd wound up manning a checkpoint where I-95 intersected with Route 203, originally at the very limit of the zone of interest; Norm had replaced me when the summons from Roberts had come through a short time later, requesting my presence at the scene. As I took in the exterior of what was apparently Pizzeria Angelina, it felt as though I were back in Windeport staring at the pizza parlor that had been at the far end of Main Street for as long as I could remember. The red-and-white checkered doors certainly were the same, but the bloody handprints on the panels definitely weren't. My eyebrows went up at the crimson streaks trailing down the door, ending in a small pool of viscous fluid that spoke to how much time had already passed.

"First and second victims," Roberts said tonelessly as he nodded to the pool. "Sixteen-year-olds; both shot – we think -- while exiting the restaurant after eating."

My eyes went back to the puddle of blood, dawning realization washing over me. "Did they make it?"

Roberts shook his head. "Until the area was cleared, first responders were prevented from getting to any of the victims," he said as he reached for the door. He paused with his hand on a door handle shaped like a pizza paddle and looked at me. "You were never in the military, were you?"

"No," I replied. "You did a tour in Afghanistan, though, if memory serves."

"Just after 9/11," he said before nodding toward the interior of the restaurant. "What you are about to see in there is worse than anything I encountered that final year I was a Marine."

I felt my stomach twist even tighter. Between the two of us, we'd seen more death than anyone rightly should; while not entirely inured to it, there was a certain kind of callus that built up with each experience, a protection mechanism to shield what little might be left of our souls. The look I saw in Robert's face combined with the mix of despair and anger in his eyes told me whatever lay on the other side of those doors had breached the protective barrier he'd constructed — and quite likely would do the same to me. Taking a deep breath, I quickly nodded my head and steeled myself as my superior pulled open the door.

I wasn't all that surprised at the stench that immediately hit me as I stepped into the restaurant behind Roberts; there is a peculiar pungency to bodily fluids that have been exposed to the air that is hard to explain and equally as difficult to forget. We paused just inside a small vestibule that housed a coatrack full of winter jackets on one side and a cork board with local notices on the other; it was a heartbreaking indicator that business had been brisk that evening. There was an unusual pony wall separating the vestibule from the main part of the restaurant, wide enough to accommodate a thick growth of something green and bushy; it served as a visual break between the entrance and the restaurant beyond. I assumed it had been added to create some sort of welcoming ambiance but couldn't help but note that the four-foot-wide opening in the pony wall wasn't quite on center. It also served to make the vestibule feel far smaller than it was, enhancing the crowded, cluttered impression being given from the mass of winter jackets present. There was no way to miss the trail of bloody footprints on the dingy tile just beside where we were standing, nor the vibrant yellow crime scene marker that had been stationed near them; I tried not to think what it meant that the number showing on the small placard was in the quadruple digits. Pulling a pair of latex gloves out of my coat pocket, I snapped them on before accepting the paper galoshes from Roberts. Sliding them over my boots, I took a moment to brace myself before turning to face what Roberts had clearly been telegraphing was the scene of a brutal massacre.

When faced with an incomprehensible reality, the human brain — as marvelous as it is — will often go into a version of safe mode and instead focus in on the smaller details first, allowing adequate time to slowly absorb the overwhelming horror that would otherwise short out every synapse; without that protection, you'd likely wind up in the corner, curled into a fetal position mumbling incomprehensible phrases. My first few moments looking over the scene had the coffee I'd drunk on my trip up to East Newberry quickly burning its way through the lining of my stomach, an ominous sign that despite my many years in law enforcement, even a veteran such as myself could still be surprised when confronted with undeniable evidence of cold blooded, brutal violence wreaked upon the unsuspecting.

The pizzeria was a throwback to a different time; the decor might have once been intended to evoke a vague sense one was dining some-where along the Mediterranean but now felt as tired and dated as the lettering above the windows outside. Half-moon booths more appropriate to a Beverly Hills high end restaurant lined either wall, positioned beneath fading frescos of vineyards and beaches and classical Roman ruins; small tables set at an angle ran down the aisle between them. Every surface had a checkered red-and-white tablecloth mimicking the pattern on the doors just behind me; small vases held a faux bouquet of flowers possibly meant to look like a rose wrapped in baby's breath. Tiny, squat shakers of cheese or red pepper flakes were snuggled around the vase — at least on the few tables that had been undisturbed.

As the coatrack had foreshadowed, bodies were *everywhere*.

Most were slumped back against the cushions of the half-moon booths or draped in an almost casual way across the tables; more than a few were lying, face-down, on the bloody tile between the booths and the freestanding tables, arms thrown out in front of them as they were felled by the shooter. The pattern was eerily similar to something I had seen working a school shooting in Utah a few years earlier; then, much as now, those who had immediately tried to flee had been ruthlessly cut down in their flight, clogging any possible escape for those who remained. In essence, the diners in the booths had become easy targets after the first wave.

Swallowing back the sour taste in my mouth, it was harder than I expected to continue forward; it took a moment for the true carnage to sink in, and when it did, I felt myself beginning to shiver uncontrollably. Crime scene technicians from the State were methodically going through the space, doing their work alongside agents from the F.B.I. and A.T.F.; I watched in fascinated horror as a tech measured the distance between a victim's finger and a tipped-over baby bottle just in front of it. It took a long, long moment for me to realize there was small head covered in wispy hair and blood in her lap; my stomach flipped over, and I tasted bile at the back of my throat. Swallowing hard, I turned my attention to the long transaction counter at the rear; in addition to being where patrons placed their order, it also served as a barrier to the open kitchen, one where the flickering flames of a wood-fired pizza oven were still quietly going about their business. The plastic sanitary panel between the counter and the kitchen was riddled with a random pattern of bullet holes, spidering the material in a way that glass could never do; blood spatter against the cabinets and the pizza oven itself was a stark indicator that the staff were not spared the attention of the shooter.

Incongruently, the mellifluous sounds of instrumental Muzak began to invade my consciousness. Blinking, I realized a rather terrible piano version of *Ebony and Ivory* was drifting down from the ceiling. Looking up in disbelief, I tried to find the elusive speakers but only saw the lethargically spinning ceiling fans mounted against a pressed tin ceiling that had seen better days. Dropping my eyes back to the restaurant proper, I reluctantly began to count the bodies I could see before turning back to Roberts.

"How many?" I heard myself say.

"Nineteen, plus four staff members," he replied. "Coroner has already taken a wave to the morgue in Augusta," he added, nodding toward the empty space directly in front of us. "I expect the next wave will go within the hour."

"Shit," I breathed. "Was there some sort of party going on?"

"We don't know," Roberts said before nodding to the chaos. "Anyone who could have told us that is dead — save for the owner. He's in the ambulance outside."

"I saw him," I said. "Has he been interviewed?"

"Not yet," Roberts frowned. "Two bullets to the torso and some sort of head injury; he's lost a ton of blood, enough that the EMTs need to stabilize him before transport."

"All the same, if he dies whatever light he can shed on these events is lost with him."

Roberts smiled slightly. "Maybe you'll have more luck getting past the medics than I did."

"Worth a shot," I said before wincing at my poor choice of words. "How about the LEOs?"

"In terms of them knowing anything?" Roberts asked before

shaking his head. Pointing to a somewhat obese woman in a standard black police uniform, he continued. "That's Chief Shawna Tell. She's pretty much it for the law around here; her single deputy is a part-timer retired from the Army. The most she's been able to do is give Heather the names of the victims; as police administrators go, she's a bit more relaxed when it comes to the ins and outs of the job."

My eyebrows went up. "Meaning what, exactly?"

Roberts lowered his voice. "Meaning she spends most of her time at the Casino between here and Bangor," he replied. "That's where we found her after the shooting."

"Ah," I said. "Well, having names is a place to start." I paused for a moment. "How about the local leaders? Unless I missed them, they weren't at the edge of the crime scene tape, demanding answers."

"What passes for a city council is similarly thin," he said. "One is a snowbird and left for Florida already; the other two are back at City Hall getting ready for the inevitable press conference by making coffee." Roberts paused. "The mayor and her wife were the first bodies we took to Augusta."

"Damn," I sighed. "Who's left in charge?"

"I've got a team trying to determine that," he replied. "Hopefully we'll have someone in a suit by the time we get in front of the television cameras."

"Lovely." I nodded at the mess. "What's our working theory?"

Roberts actually managed a bit of a smile. "That's why *you're* here, Commander, seeing as though you run the Major Crimes unit and all."

"Ah," I said.

"So," he continued, "what do *you* think?"

"I'd remind you that I've only been here five minutes—"

"Humor me."

Catching the unusual tone in his voice, I narrowed my eyes at him questioningly but decided to acquiesce. I turned toward the vestibule. "Shooter came through the front door after taking out the teens," I said, glancing down at the tile. "And likely exited, too, if these prints are accurate."

Roberts nodded.

Gesturing toward the bodies on the floor, I glanced at Roberts. "Based on the blood patterns and the positioning of the victims, I assume this was the second batch of victims. We can probably infer exact timeline a bit from the liver temps."

Roberts nodded again; I was starting to feel like I was a rookie officer undergoing some sort of exam.

"Did the temps get taken already?" I asked.

"Yeah," he replied. "It gave us a rough window, which seems to be somewhere between seven and eight. That matches the first wave of 9-1-1 calls reporting gunshots, which was at 7:09."

I glanced around the room. "I don't see any security cameras," I said. "Anything on the exterior?"

"Not for the restaurant," he frowned. "There's an ATM just down the street that might have an angle on the front, but we won't know until the warrant comes through and we can scan the video." Roberts shrugged. "It's a small town with an even smaller LEO. We'll put out the standard call for anyone who saw something suspicious later; that might shake loose a tidbit or two."

"I won't hold my breath."

"Probably wise." Roberts.

I nodded toward the first set of tables in the aisle. "I suspect the team already pulled bullets from the ceiling above us; I'd assume there was a round of shots designed to stampede the patrons."

"Already bagged," he replied, then pointing to the gaps in the pooling blood where the first batch of victims had lain. "These had the coolest liver temps, so the science says they were killed first. Next came those behind, followed by the patrons in the booths."

I glanced to the kitchen in the rear. "That leaves the staff last," I murmured. "You said they were all killed, too?"

"Save for the owner. He managed to hide in the dry storage closet, though not before being wounded."

"Odd," I said. "Isn't there a back door? Some place where the deliveries are received?"

"Yes," Roberts nodded.

I felt the frown on my face forming. "And none of the kitchen staff used it to get to safety?"

"Apparently not," Roberts replied.

My frown deepened. "Even if we presume the shooter had a fully automatic weapon, there had to be enough time for *someone* to have escaped."

"People don't act rationally in these situations," Roberts reminded me. "You'll see for yourself when you check out the kitchen, but it's clear there were a ton of split-second decisions being made back there. One victim died a few feet from the door; another still had the handset from the landline and appears to be the one who made the 9-1-1 call from this number." He frowned himself. "And while the owner was hiding in the proverbial cupboard, at least one of his cashiers appears to have died protecting the other while huddling beneath the counter."

I looked at the kitchen in the distance; it couldn't have been more than ten yards from the front door to the kitchen. "It makes sense that the staff were killed last; that at least fits the timing of the 9-1-1 call you mentioned."

"Relatively speaking, yes," he replied. "Again, based on what limited observations we can make with field tools, it does appear the cooks and clerks were taken out with or just after the patrons."

"There were over twenty people in here," I said, then paused to let that sink in for a moment. "Our shooter had one hell of a weapon if they were capable of mowing down everyone nearly simultaneously."

Roberts glanced at the blood-soaked tables. "With fully loaded clips at the ready, yeah, that's our working theory. Shell casings have already been bagged for the lab, we'll know for sure in a few hours."

"And we think the shooter made a clean escape?"

"Yeah," Roberts nodded tiredly. "You saw the footprints on the tile back at the entrance; it's conjecture at this point, obviously, but whatever they drove to get here was likely parked on the curb out front. The timing is a bit tricky, of course; if we allow that it took maybe five minutes to wipe out everyone here, and the shooting started close to the first 9-1-1 calls, that gave the suspect a window of a few minutes to escape before the surrounding streets were locked down."

My friend of many years frowned again. "The deputy was first on the scene and knew he was far from capable of handling an active shooter, so that forced him to wait for appropriate backup before safely approaching the restaurant."

I felt my stomach twist again. "How long was the delay?"

"Long enough that our shooter has a significant head start," Roberts sighed.

"Hence the checkpoints, for all the good they will do at this point."

"Exactly."

I glanced at my Apple Watch. "Jimmy, it's nearly midnight now," I said softly. "Whatever trail you are expecting the team to find here has long since gotten cold."

"I admit it's a long shot at this point," he said before adding with a tired smile, "but if anyone can tease a clue out of thin air, it's you."

My eyes went to a lump of gray dura matter a few feet from my boots. Oddly, it looked a bit like undercooked oatmeal. *Something I won't be eating for a while,* I thought. "You might have more faith in my abilities than I do at this point; I'm not sure I'll uncover something the techs overlooked."

Roberts put a hand to my bicep. "One of my jobs as your boss is to remind you how brilliant you are," he replied.

"Jimmy—"

The muted sounds of the phone going off in his pocket had Roberts reaching for the device. "Ah," he frowned, "it's the Governor. She's gonna want an update."

"Then I'll take a look around," I said, knowing I truly didn't have much say in the matter.

"Good," he replied, then eyed me as his phone continued to sing. "I need your unique insights — perhaps now more than ever, considering we're looking at more murder victims in this room than we typically see in a full year."

I nodded. "Of course."

"Find me later," he said as he pressed the phone to his ear. "Madame Governor — yes, I'm at the scene..."

I watched for a moment as Roberts turned and exited the restaurant, clearly trying to appease a politician's worst fears as he spoke to the Governor. I'd met her briefly during one of my meetings at Headquarters; while I didn't know her personally, she was well aware of *me*, for I'd apparently worked a murder up in Fort Kent years earlier that had taken place on a potato farm adjacent to land her parents owned. Standing there in the middle of the blood-stained pizzeria, I found myself suddenly wishing I was actually digging through piles of manure on a backcountry farm looking for a murder weapon instead of stepping around internal organs that had been freed when their owners had been shredded by gunfire.

Turning back to the pizzeria, I felt myself shift fully into investigator mode; those strange senses I used when reviewing a scene made themselves known, allowing more details from the remaining victims seep into my consciousness. Slowly, I stepped through the results of the mayhem, taking in everything a second time as my eyes moved from one thing to the next. One half-moon booth held what looked like two senior citizens on their version of date night; the gentleman had on a suit that was three decades out of date, with a small flower pinned to his lapel. She had an ornate hat with a mock bluebird pinned to the rim; the half-eaten pepperoni pizza had been paired with a small bottle of wine that had been shattered by a bullet, mixing the pinot noir with the blood spatters on the woman's dress. The next booth had five lanky teenaged boys wearing matching basketball jerseys crammed behind the table; two were face-first on some sort of deep-dish, and one appeared to be missing the entire left side of his face. Stepping over someone in yoga attire, I took in what was left of a middle-aged guy in sweats leaning at an angle in another booth; the logo of a local private university was emblazoned on the front of the hoodie, a name I recognized from my collegiate swimming days. Two women were in the booth opposite, both slumped beneath the table; a large book of quilt patterns was on the dingy tile in front of them, upside down in yet another pool of blood.

The further I walked, the more the details became sharp fragments in a wider horror that was rapidly becoming incomprehensible in scope; each person had a story, had people who knew them — maybe even loved them — victims whose last moments had been unimaginable. I bumped into the long counter before realizing I had completely traversed the space, my thoughts lost in the tragedy that had befallen those who had randomly decided to eat out that evening.

There are few certainties in life, I thought, *but one of them is that you can grab a slice of pizza without fearing for your safety. What happened here has to have a reckoning — justice of some sort needs to be served.*

I touched the edge of the long, wooden counter with a gloved hand and found its solidity a reassuring presence. A few inches from my finger was a splotch of something biological, and beyond that, one of the point-of-sale systems the pizzeria had been using. Craning my neck around the counter, I could see the screen had been fractured by a number of bullets, though it was making a valiant attempt at creating a rainbow pattern from the remaining operational pixels. There was a small half-Dutch door at the end of the counter where I was standing; pushing through, I found a tech bending over the tangled forms of two clerks huddled beneath the register. Slumped sideways, it was still easy to see that they were barely teenagers, likely students in the local high school; the way one was holding the other spoke to a relationship beyond that of just being fellow employees, which drove a cold sliver of anger deep into my already aching heart.

Nodding to the tech, I continued my perusal. The pizza oven loomed large in the corner, and beneath it, the rotund form of a cook clad in institutional white with a flour-and-blood-stained apron. A handset for a telephone AT&T hadn't sold since the late seventies was in one hand, the cord stretched out to the base affixed to the wall beside the oven. Kneeling, I could see the guy had a literal death grip on the phone, so much so that the techs had simply wrapped a plastic bag around the hand in question to protect whatever evidence might be on the handset. A few feet from the body were a set of half-moon shaped glasses, the lenses cracked from having fallen, forcefully, to the ground. I waddled over to where they lay beside a yellow evidence marker so I could lean down and examine them; details were had to make out, but I could see enough to determine they were not of the variety you could pick up in any pharmacy; they looked surprisingly solid, speaking to having been prescribed and then filled at a moderately priced optician office.

Standing, I moved over to an open wooden door in the far wall and peered into what was the aforementioned storage closet; the small pool of blood indicated where the owner had been found, which was just beside a pile of debris from a set of shelves that appeared to have collapsed during the attack. Beside the storage closet was the door to a large walk-in fridge; pulling the handle open, I glanced inside and found several massive transparent plastic containers on one set of shelves holding a reddish-colored sauce; more shelves in the back held various bags of what looked like blocks of cheese (presumably mozzarella). Smaller bins of fresh vegetables and various other food items I didn't immediately recognize rounded out the space. Letting go of the handle allowed the springs of the hinges to quickly snap the door shut with an unusual sucking noise; I took a moment to scan through the posted food safety instructions before shifting my attention to the open pocket door between the fridge and prep counter still holding two in-progress pizzas.

Stepping through the doorway put me into a small storage area; it ran the length of the wall behind the kitchen and, as I'd suspected, also contained the corrugated metal door I'd assumed would be there. Not as well-lit as the kitchen behind me, it also appeared to be kept at a temperature far cooler than the main space. It took a moment for my eyes to adjust to the dim lighting, but when they did, I saw the slumped form of the final kitchen victim, leaning against a stack of fifty-pound sacks of flour just to the side of the exit. Possibly contributing to the cooler temperature, the garage-like metal door had been opened about a foot from the concrete, allowing a significant draft of cool night air into the pizzeria. The strange scent of the Penobscot River hung heavy in the air, intermixed with whatever bulk dry ingredients had been stored against the walls and on the various shelves covering every inch of visible wall. Just based on the level of inventory I'd seen in my short perusal, it seemed the pizzeria did a brisk business.

I was immediately struck by the strange positioning of the body, for I'd expected it to be more-or-less splayed out in front of the door, seemingly in the act of trying to escape. Instead, it looked like the cook had been on some sort of cigarette break and caught unawares — a virtual impossibility given the cacophony that had to have been coming from the front of the restaurant when the shooter began their rampage. Curiosity at the non sequitur had me examining the space a bit more closely; the second thing I noted was the dearth of those brilliant yellow evidence tents. Save for a handful around the body, the space was virtually barren in comparison to the restaurant proper.

Assuming the shooter stood in the doorway, I thought as I stepped back slightly, *he would have squeezed off a round or two taking out that victim. And yet...*

I looked down around my feet and didn't see any placards indicating that shell casings had been retrieved. Backing up into the kitchen, I confirmed I'd seen them there (with a small tag indicating the evidence had already been bagged). Stepping back into the rear storage room, I felt that frown forming on my face again.

No casings? That's not possible, unless the shooter took them. But they didn't bother out front…

Stepping closer to the body, I pulled out my iPhone and enabled the flashlight, and then more-or-less searched the wall and sacks of flour behind the victim, fruitlessly trying to locate bullet holes beyond the ones that had created the crimson stains on the formerly white apron the cook was wearing. When I found none, I stepped back with a furrowed brow; though it went against procedure, I leaned down and gently pulled the body away from the sacks of flower just long enough to confirm a growing suspicion.

No holes in the wall, no holes in the flour. Only the victim. Was he moved?

Turning slowly in a full circle, I found myself shaking my head.

This floor is immaculate — or as immaculate as a stockroom would be. With the amount of blood out in the main space, there would be evidence of someone coming in here; no way the shooter would have carefully stepped around that mess. I don't think the shooter got out here — nor do I think this victim dragged himself here from the kitchen; there's no trace of that sort of activity, unless the techs found something I'm not seeing.

I turned to look at the victim.

"You are an anomaly," I said softly as I knelt again beside the man. "How did you come to expire in this spot?"

Predictably, the victim didn't say anything — but it didn't have to; as I started to stand, my brain finally clicked into gear and froze me halfway. My eyes snapped to the long, white tag that was sewn into the top of the apron; that it denoted the size as *large* was less relevant than the strange fact it was on the outside of the garment. Except, of course, it wasn't.

Who wears an apron backwards? I thought. *Certainly not an experienced chef… hang on…*

Reaching down, I fingered the gold-toned cufflinks around one wrist, then realized the cook was wearing a tailored shirt more appropriate for a board room than a kitchen.

"Damn," I said aloud as I sat back on my haunches.

Two

As I exited the pizzeria to find Captain Roberts, it was hard to miss the ambulance that was providing treatment to the owner; in fact, it was now the *only* ambulance, as the rest had packed up and returned to duty elsewhere in the county. Interrupting my quest to speak with my boss, I redirected to the rear of the vehicle and waited at the bottom of the steps for a few moments, quietly watching as the EMTs went about their business. I had a deep respect for my first responder colleagues over on the life-saving side of the fence; while my own profession had its share of challenges, I presumed having to handle medical emergencies on a regular basis eventually led to some sort of burnout, or at the very least, ultimately tore a hole in one's soul.

The owner of the pizzeria still looked as ashen as he had when I'd initially caught sight of him, though the fact a slight bit of color had appeared in his complexion felt like an optimistic sign. That close, I had a unique perspective on the myriad tubes and cables running to his form, connecting him to lifesaving equipment that appeared to include an IV bag containing a dark red fluid. Having donated enough blood in my lifetime, I recognized an infusion was in progress though I wondered how many units the poor guy had taken. While his torso was bare —

exposing skin nearly as sallow as the bodies inside the restaurant — multiple wide strips of white bandages had been wrapped around him, nearly covering his entire chest. The crimson-stained wrap about his forehead I'd seen earlier was in the process of being replaced by the shorter of the two professionals; as she snipped off one edge of the strip, her dark eyes turned in my direction. I took it as the invitation it appeared to be.

"Commander Colbeth, Major Crimes," I said as I held up my badge. "How's he doing?"

"Better," she said as she placed the scissors she'd used down on the thin blanket covering the rest of the owner. "We finally have him stabilized, though we aren't entirely certain there isn't some internal bleeding we can't detect." She sighed as she nodded toward the equipment. "Even with all of this technology, there's no substitute for a full Emergency ward."

"Off to the hospital, then?" I asked. The name badge on her uniform said *I. Dominguez*.

"Yes," she nodded. "As Bangor General is slightly closer, we're headed there." She paused as she wrapped the extra gauze back up and put it in a small drawer behind the stretcher. "I presume you'll be following us there so you can interview him."

I smiled slightly. "I guess that answers my question."

"I've already told Captain Roberts that this gentleman is in no state to participate in an interview," Dominguez continued as she moved to the end of the stretcher and looked down at me. "He's already taken two units of blood and pumped full of enough pain killers he likely thinks he's on a European vacation."

"Fair enough," I said. "What can you tell me about his wounds?"

Dominguez looked at me thoughtfully. "In the absence of someone here with a medical power of attorney to approve the release of that info, I trust you'll consider what I tell you is privileged?"

I nodded. "I'd say 'Scout's honor,' but I never had the time to be a Boy Scout."

"That surprises me," Dominguez replied, a slight smile playing at her lips. "The patient took several shots to the torso, possibly from the back; we suspect one was a through-and-through based on the exit wound, while at least one bullet — and maybe two -- are lodged in the muscles around the ribcage."

My eyebrows went up. "That seems fairly lucky."

"It was," she nodded. "You've seen the scene and where we found him; my read on it is he was ducking for cover when he was hit, negating the worst of a possible direct impact. He's still lost a ton of blood and has some serious surgery in front of him, but it seems likely he'll pull through at this point."

"And the head wound?"

"Hard to say, exactly," Dominguez replied. "From where we found him, our best guess is that he was underneath the shelving that collapsed in that closet. His forehead bore the brunt of it, and he might also have a concussion as a result."

"Ouch."

"Exactly."

The other EMT spoke up at that moment. "Ready to go, Iñez."

"That's my cue," Dominguez said to me.

"I appreciate the time," I said.

"When will you get to the hospital? I can let the attending know so they expect you."

I looked at my Apple Watch. "Hard to say," I sighed. "Probably sometime close to lunch, but it depends on the Medical Examiner."

Dominguez nodded, then paused. "I hope you find whoever the hell did this."

"I will," I said.

Stepping back, I let the second EMT jump down and then watched as Dominguez pulled first one door, then the other shut; a moment later, the vehicle rumbled to life before trundling down the narrow street, headed for the Emergency Room in Bangor. Once the ambulance turned the corner, I found I had an unobstructed view of the many hearses still awaiting their cargo; it was a depressing reminder of the work that lay ahead. Suddenly desperate for a cup of coffee, I resumed my trek to the command center. I found Roberts at one of the long desks built into the side of the reconfigured R.V., tapping away on his laptop; happily, beside him was an industrial-sized coffeemaker that appeared to have just chugged to completion on a fresh carafe. Grabbing one of the paper cups stacked beside the machine, I poured myself a healthy amount and then leaned on the counter beside my boss, sipping at the delightfully hot brew while I waited for him to complete his work.

The age difference between us was starkly apparent in how he worked the small keyboard on his device. Where I was a fluent touch typist, borne from the necessity of doing my high school and college papers on a word processor, Roberts appeared to be from the hunt-and-peck school of thought, carefully depressing each and every letter with the tip of his index finger before ensuring the same letter appeared on the screen. After a few moments, it became an ever-increasing agony watching him toil away — enough that I nearly volunteered to take dictation for him in the hopes he might complete his sentence sometime that century. Trying to distract myself, I sipped from my brew and looked around the cramped quarters of the command center, marveling again at just how well funded the State was when compared to my old gig in Windeport. A half-dozen officers were scattered at various consoles, monitoring one of many aspects of our nascent investigation; monitors mounted to the wall were tuned to the handful of local television stations in Maine, all of which were currently broadcasting breathless around-the-clock coverage of a manhunt I was nearly certain would never come to fruition. One particular screen showed a live shot of a reporter just outside the final checkpoint I'd crossed to get into the scene; they seemed to be speaking to a member of our public relations team and not getting the sort of answers they were hoping for. Glancing to the bulletin board beside the monitors, I could see a formal press conference had been scheduled for seven A.M.; with luck, I'd be on the road by then and able to avoid what was certain to be a media circus.

Harrumphing, Roberts smashed one final key before looking up at me. "I thought we were promised artificial intelligence that could write our reports for us," he said as he closed the lid to his laptop.

"Be careful what you wish for, Jimmy," I said as I sipped at my coffee. "First A.I. will write your report, then it will wind up running the department."

"Now *that* is a scary thought," he said as he stood and reached for a cup. "Sorry I didn't rejoin you in there," he continued as he poured himself a slug of caffeine. "The Governor demanded a status report."

"Didn't you give her that over the phone?"

"You've not been with us long enough to have noticed she's something of a stickler for procedure," he sighed. "Which is another way of saying, if it's not written down, in her mind, it didn't happen."

"I'm a bit surprised you're the one interacting with her," I said. "Shouldn't Colonel Rivers be doing that?"

"She's out of state at the moment," Roberts said. "I've spoken with her, though, and she's already on her way back to Maine and should be at the press conference."

I wasn't surprised; the head of the Maine State Police was entirely capable of moving heaven and earth when the moment demanded it. I'd met Judith Rivers for the first time that summer during a Professional Standards inquiry into my conduct of the Brogan case; while I'd been impressed by her, the ruling by the board had directly led to my now being employed by the State of Maine instead of the Village of Windeport. "She'll handle the press, then."

"Thank *God*," Roberts breathed. "Not my thing. Not by a long stretch."

"I thought working the press core came with the rank," I smiled slightly.

"*Hers*, yes," he replied as he tore open one of those pink artificial sugar packets and dumped it into his mug. "I presume you tried to talk to the owner before you appeared on my doorstep."

"He was still under," I nodded. "The EMT filled me in on the details of his injuries, though. I'm surprised he made it this far; I'll run up to Bangor General in the morning to get a full statement."

"I figured."

"What's the story on the victim in the rear storeroom?" I asked.

Roberts gave up looking for one of those plastic stirring sticks and swirled his mug instead. "Same as the rest," he replied. "At least, until the forensics come back. Why?"

I set my paper cup down on the small counter and retrieved my iPhone, then tapped on the photo of the cufflinks I'd taken. "These seem a bit over the top for a pizzeria cook."

Roberts squinted at the photo before his eyes widened. "Holy hell. Those look like fourteen carets."

"That was my guess, too," I nodded. "And at the risk of making something out of nothing—"

Roberts rolled his eyes. "*Seriously*? Aren't you the cadet that once told me even *nothing* could be a *something* when it came to investigations?"

"Modesty forbids," I said dryly.

"Sure it does. What is your *nothing* this time around?"

I slid to the next photo on my phone and held it out. "The apron is on backwards."

Roberts put his coffee down and took my phone for a moment, tapping at the photo to enlarge it. "I suppose it is," he said as he handed back my iPhone. "Contrary to what I just said, I'm not sure I see the relevance."

"Me either," I replied, "other than it's an oddity. Along with the cufflinks."

"Well," Roberts said thoughtfully, "maybe we can clear that up by looking at the list of employees."

"Is there a warrant already in progress?"

"Yes," he nodded. "Our staff in Augusta started working on the usual list of items about an hour ago; financials for the firm, phone records, the usual. I'll make sure they add tax and payroll records to the list before it gets sent to the judge."

"Good," I nodded, "for I really want to see the list of who was employed at this pizzeria."

Roberts eyed me. "You think this one victim is important in some way?"

"My gut says yes," I replied, "though I don't know why. Yet."

"Far be it for me to go against your gut," he said, "but we have a restaurant full of people who have perhaps just as much a connection to the shooter as the one with cufflinks. Hell, he's probably the brother of the owner; maybe he makes pizza on the odd night after putting in a long day as an accountant."

I had the strangest feeling I was being upbraided by my boss; more startling perhaps was how out of character it was for Roberts. "I wasn't implying we should focus all our resources on that particular victim," I said somewhat defensively. "Only making the observation that they don't fit the wider pattern."

"I know," Roberts nodded. "And I appreciate it. I just want you to keep the bigger picture in mind."

Wondering for the first time if the pressure of dealing with what was soon to be a national news story was getting to my friend, I prudently let the issue go with a curt nod. "Of course. I'm going to head back in; Norm should be here by now."

"Sounds good. Just as an FYI: there is an all-hands meeting scheduled for this afternoon."

"Here?" I asked. "Or back at HQ?"

"Probably hybrid," he answered. "The time and link to the virtual conference room should be in your email."

I nodded before draining the last of the now tepid coffee from my cup. "That works; I'm not sure where I'll be, exactly, by the time the meeting rolls around."

"Hopefully somewhere with internet," Roberts advised with a slight smile. "Or at least good cell coverage so you can dial in."

Resisting the temptation to pour another cup of coffee — and tamping down an unusually sarcastic response to my boss, I simply nodded and pushed open the door to the RV. Stepping down the metal staircase to the ground, I idly noted the temperature had dropped a few more degrees while pondering why I was having such a visceral reaction to Roberts. He had been my friend for more years than I cared to count, and that seemed to be making it difficult for both of us to transition into our new professional relationship. As Chief of Police for Windeport, I had, essentially, been his peer; now, I was just another department head among many he was responsible for. Perhaps that was slightly unfair, for I knew I had a certain level of dispensation others in our organization didn't enjoy; still, it was clear at least one of us was chafing slightly — and it wasn't him.

Growing pains? I wondered as I slowly walked back to the faded cheer of the restaurant's facade. *Or is this a warning sign?*

Pausing on the edge of the grimy sidewalk, I realized it wasn't the first time that I'd experienced a version of buyer's remorse with respect to my new gig. Slightly more than two months in, I would have expected to have hit my stride, and yet, I couldn't help this nagging feeling I wasn't firing on all cylinders. Glancing back at the command center RV, I knew intrinsically it had nothing to do with my friend and longtime mentor; Roberts had been nothing but accommodating, welcoming both me and the rest of the former Windeport Police Department with open arms.

So where is this coming from? I asked myself. *This sense that I'm not where I'm supposed to be, that I've made a colossal error in accepting this new assignment? I don't usually doubt myself like this.*

Folding my arms against my chest, I had a sudden moment of clarity, one where I understood exactly what Vasily had been going through that summer, I'd pressured him into rejoining my staff. To say it had been a disaster would be to put it mildly; I'd ignored the warning signs that he'd not fully recuperated from his assault in my zeal to get the world reordered as I'd once had it. His subsequent second departure for

California had been a clarion wake-up call that all things change — *must* change, must *grow* — in order for the universe to continue moving forward. Whether I was facing the same moment of reckoning was hard to say, but this time around, I was loathe to ignore my instincts.

Maybe it will pass once we both find our way. One can hope.

My moody introspection was interrupted when a pair of headlights swung around the corner at the end of the street, then turned into the same lot where I'd parked the SUV. A moment later, the form of my number two appeared on the sidewalk; like me, the unexpected call to duty had pulled him from the normal domestic activities of a mundane November weeknight, and he was dressed accordingly in navy blue wind pants, a grey hooded sweatshirt and a ball cap on backwards. A surprising amount of hair was spilling out from beneath the hat, a nod to how Norm Thomas had begun to explore the freedom of being, well, Norm Thomas. It hadn't hurt that the arrival of a certain National Park Police Officer in his life had gently encouraged him to step out from behind the shadow of the man he'd been while living in Southern Maine; between him and Vasily, I'd begun to wonder if I was inadvertently running some sort of side hustle connecting people with their true callings out of my office in Windeport.

"Hey," Norm said as he approached me. Now that he was closer, I could see the strap from his backpack over a shoulder. "Sorry it took so long; getting through the checkpoints was not pleasant."

"Everyone's a little bit on edge," I replied. "Including our boss."

Norm glanced over my shoulder at the command center. "I can imagine."

I started to say something else but paused when I thought I caught a shimmer of something over one of Norm's eyes; looking closer, I was startled to realize my partner was wearing a dark eyeshadow with glitter. It took another moment to realize it complimented the eyeliner; there was also a strong possibility his lips weren't normally as deeply red as they now appeared. My expression must have telegraphed my surprise

— another indicator that I wasn't myself — which led to Norm smiling sheepishly.

"It was Drag Queen Story Hour at the Windeport Public Library," he said with a half shrug. "I didn't have time to wash off everything."

Well aware that Norm was gay, this was still news of a sort. Wondering how to extricate myself without insulting my number two, I cautiously spoke. "I had no idea—"

"I'm not," he quickly said as his cheeks began to flame a deep crimson. "Totally *not* my thing. But your cousin can be damn persuasive when the need arises; her regular reader couldn't make it, and I had the unfortunate luck of both answering the phone *and* being the right size for the costume."

"Ah," I said, coughing while somehow being strangely relieved. "That sounds like Charlie. Now you understand the pain I endure each Halloween as Chat Noir."

"I do," he nodded. "Truly."

I waited a beat. "Honestly, the color of the eyeshadow suits you—"

"*Fuck*," he groaned. "You know what? Maybe I'll run back to the truck and grab my sunglasses before we go in."

"Too late for that," I smiled slightly. "Besides, I think everyone will be more focused on the crime scene than your cosmetic choices this evening."

"*Fuck*," he breathed again. "I'm so going to change my number after this."

"Charlie will still find you," I laughed despite the gloom around us. "I learned a long time ago you can't run from a librarian. They know too many ways to locate things."

"Sound advice," he sighed as he pulled a pair of latex gloves from a pocket of his sweats. "What do we have?"

I took a few moments to bring Norm up to speed on what we were about to step into; by the time we were standing in the small foyer area together, his face had taken on the grim expression I knew I'd been wearing myself. "Until we know more about the shooter, the manhunt portion of the investigation will remain a joint operation between us and the Feds," I continued. "Captain Roberts has tasked Major Crimes with sorting through all of this and try to make some sense of it."

Norm frowned as he looked over the mess. "That's a tall order, even for us."

"I know," I nodded. "But we start with the basics. I'm going to drive down to Augusta in a few hours to go through whatever her team finds during the postmortem with Lou, then circle back to Bangor General to speak with the owner."

"He survived?"

"By hiding in a closet back in the kitchen, yes," I nodded again. "Though 'survived' might still be a premature status; the EMTs had a hard time stabilizing him before heading out. I'm hoping there is still someone to talk to when I get to the hospital."

"No kidding," Norm replied.

"Heather Graham is somewhere around here," I continued. "According to Jimmy, the local Chief of Police gave her a first round of identities for our victims. I'll want those verified as quickly as possible." I caught a slight smile on Norm's face. "You're already working on that, aren't you?"

"I may have made some calls on the way up," he said. "Caitlyn already has access to the case file and is working through that angle now. I've also asked Detectives Napier and Smart to tackle the flood of information that the warrants on the business will bring in. They've been assisting the admins down in Augusta to try and speed up the filing."

My eyebrows went up. "Not bad."

"I had a good mentor," he smiled.

Those same eyebrows went into a deep furrow. "'*Had?* Past tense?"

"My bad," he smiled again. "Do you want our team to walk the scene, too?"

I thought about that for a moment. "Not yet," I replied. "I've already walked it and will do it again; I want you to go through it as well with a fine-tooth comb. It's not likely either of us will locate something the combined brain trust currently here missed, but you never know."

"All right," he said. "Where do you want me to start?"

I hesitated, for at some level I wanted validation that what I'd found in the storeroom was an anomaly; having him start there might prejudice his view, though, so I opted for a traditional approach. "Front to back," I answered ultimately. "Find me when you are done."

"Got it."

Norm took a moment to retrieve his tablet from the backpack and then began to methodically work the room; despite the fact he was slightly more than ten years my junior, it still amazed me how much easier it had been for him to adjust to the paperless ways of the State Police; while I'd never been a huge fan of the classic detective notebook, I'd neither been one to carry around something as bulky as an iPad when working a case. Between my trusty MacBook and dependable iPhone, I'd not felt the need to change how I did my thing. Sadly, that meant my State-issued iPad had been languishing in a desk drawer since starting my new gig.

Seeing the iPad also triggered a reminder that my trusty MacBook had, in fact, been acting rather erratically over the past couple of days; I'd had a devil of a time coaxing it awake the prior morning, though once it *did* finally let me log in, it proceeded to behave. Privately, I'd assumed the IT geeks back in Augusta had done something to it prior to the device being issued to me in August, revenge for my heretical request that the internal State network be rejiggered to support anything other than a Windows-based computer. I'd come to something of an icy detente with the Director of Information Technology, but only after Captain Roberts had interceded on my behalf — making me more than certain the professional nerds were just waiting for something to crash as an excuse for yanking back the fleet of MacBooks that had been shipped to my team in Windeport.

Lost in my thoughts, it took a gentle tap on my arm before I realized the lead crime scene tech, Heather Graham, was standing at my shoulder. "Commander," she said. "I've got some preliminary results for you if you have a moment."

"For you, Heather, I always have time." I nodded toward the room. "This is a bit hard to take in, though."

"Yeah," she replied. After waiting for a respectful moment, she glanced down at her tablet. "I imagine Captain Roberts already gave you the broad strokes."

"He has."

"Then I'll skip to the next act," she continued. "Shell casings and what bullets or bullet fragments we were able to pull from the walls and furniture have already been sent to the lab for analysis. Initial eyeballing by my team and the lead from ATF makes us think they are mostly from the same weapon."

"Mostly? That's not a term you usually use."

Heather sighed. "The sheer volume of what we collected is pretty overwhelming, but a few casings recovered in the rear of the pizzeria didn't match the majority tagged."

That frisson I felt when something important dropped into my lap hit my gut. "Where, exactly?"

She nodded toward the kitchen. "Back in the storeroom," she said. "There was a single victim out there, clearly suffering multiple gunshot wounds; the casings were in the vicinity, but I'll be honest, Sean, we're having trouble making the angles line up. That, and the casings *seem* to be the only evidence of gunfire in that space."

I nodded. "The victim might not have been shot there?"

Heather pressed her lips together. "I'm not quite ready to say that. It's worth noting, though, that we didn't locate any bullets in that space; I'm hoping they are in the victim still." She nodded toward the restaurant. "The problem with that is most of these folks are showing clear evidence of a powerful weapon, one unlikely to leave a bullet inside a body."

"That's one way to put it."

"Yeah." Heather paused again; I'd known her long enough that I recognized the level of distress hiding just beneath the surface. "Nothing else stands out so far; the victims in the main dining space all appear to have been shot within moments of each other. Liver temps more or less confirmed that pattern, with the staff just behind; the only notable exception is the victim in the rear."

I nodded again. "The ambient temperature in the storeroom messed up your measurements, I'll bet."

"They did. We'll have to wait for Lou's team to do a chemical analysis instead, though I have no reason to doubt it will place the victim in the same ballpark as the others."

I was starting to feel otherwise on that point but decided to keep that observation to myself for the moment. "Preliminary ballistics?"

Heather frowned. "We've sort of stepped out of the way for the Feds on that," she hedged, "so other than what we've recovered from the victims, I don't have much more than general observations."

"I'll take your general observations over anything formal from our Federal brethren any day," I smiled.

She considered me for a moment, long enough that I got the impression she was reluctant to put voice to something that was bothering her. "I guess the only thing I would point out is that the positioning of the victims isn't entirely consistent with the shooter having been at the front of the restaurant. I'll wait until I see the angles the FBI comes up with, but I suspect we'll find some shots were fired from the rear."

I glanced back at the victims and nodded slightly. "I think I registered that myself without realizing it," I said before turning my eyes back to hers. "People normally rush *away* from the gunfire, not toward it."

"Exactly."

"Two shooters, then?"

Heather shook her head. "Like I said earlier, the shell casings speak to a single weapon; hard to say without running a full analysis, but to my eye, I'd say no."

"So," I sighed, "I've got an unusual body in the stock room and a scene that doesn't make any sense with the current theory. You're not making this any easier, Heather."

"I know how you love a challenge," she smiled quickly. "We have soft IDs on the adult victims," Heather continued, "based entirely on what we found in various wallets and purses. Most were locals, though a handful were from the surrounding area."

"All right. Anything else?"

"Not at this point," she replied, shaking her head. "Photos and commentary will be in the system by the morning; it will take a bit longer for the FBI and ATF observations to trickle in, given how notoriously slow our integration with the servers in Washington are."

"I'll take what I can get. Thank you as always."

"Of course." She paused again, taking a long look at the remains of the pizzeria. "This looks like it was the lifeblood of the town. I suspect none of these people thought twice about going out for pizza last night."

"Likely not," I sighed.

"Hell of a thing." Heather looked at me. "What's your next move?"

"A visit with Dr. Hamilton, I think," I replied. "And, hopefully, a few answers."

"Amen to that," she said.

THREE

ome hours later, I was sitting in a twenty-four-hour Dunkin'
Donuts just off of I-95 in Augusta scanning the case files while
sipping on my second extra-large cup of coffee. Something the
menu had promised was a sausage, egg and cheese bagel sat a few inches
away from the paper cup; two bites in, I'd realized my appetite was non-
existent. While not altogether unexpected given the kind of day it had
been (already), as an athlete it was exceedingly rare for me to pass up an
opportunity to replenish calories. Glancing again at the bagel, I felt
something in my stomach turn when my eyes fell on a small glob of
cheese that had dribbled out of the bun and down onto the paper wrapping. Looking a bit too much like something better suited to the scene
at the pizzeria, I quickly wrapped what was left back up and carted it off
to the trashcan in the corner before returning to my perusal.

Tapping at the keyboard to move the text, I stared at the data, still
not quite believing that I was attempting to dispassionately review two
dozen lives that had come to an abrupt end. Over my career, I'd had the
random double or triple homicide; the closest I'd come to a mass casualty event like the one in East Newberry had been the school shooting
I'd consulted on, an experience after which I had prayed I would never

have again. Scrolling through the photos that had been downloaded from the Department of Motor Vehicles, I found myself experiencing a version of PTSD as various semi-smiling visages came and went. When the face of the young teenaged cashier appeared, I realized I needed a break and quickly closed the lid to my MacBook.

The strange beeping the device made at the action had me immediately open it back up; to my horror, instead of displaying the case system, vertical lines of various color hues filled the screen randomly before flashing white and then going dark. Tapping at the keyboard netted me absolutely nothing; after a moment, I depressed the on/off switch and was rewarded by seeing the Apple logo appear. My joy was short-lived, however, for the logo was immediately replaced by a small circle holding an exclamation point; beneath that icon was a web address in a font so tiny, I had to squint just to read it. Not that it mattered, for a fraction of a second later, the screen went dark once more. Pressing the on/off button a second time netted me absolutely nothing other than a sense this was some sort of foreshadowing of how the rest of the case was going to go.

Sitting back in the uncomfortable plastic chair, I found myself pondering what to do; loathe as I was to call for help from the IT department, I realized it was a stroke of luck the MacBook had died while I was just a few miles away from the actual Helpdesk. On the other hand, given where I stood with the Director of said department, I was unwilling to see just how much of a detente we actually had at that point in our relationship. Pulling out my iPhone, I scrolled to the support app and quickly confirmed Apple had yet to build a retail store any closer than the one in Portland; sighing, I booked the first available appointment they offered for Wednesday morning and then glared at the sullenly quiet MacBook just for a good measure.

Now ruing the fact I'd left my iPad in Windeport, I slid the MacBook into my backpack and stared out into the parking lot of the Dunkin' Donuts, somewhat at loose ends. Technically, I could badge my way into a cubicle at the Headquarters building and continue my review of what the various teams had so far collected, but a significant part of me saw the crashed laptop as a chance to regroup. I knew from having reviewed the file that Lou wasn't expecting me at the morgue until close to eight; smiling slightly, I realized I had the perfect excuse for how to spend the next couple of hours.

It took me about ten minutes to drive over to the local YMCA, and another five to check in with the pool monitor and rent a locker for the morning. I rarely left the house without my swim gear in the back of the SUV, mostly due to the fact that I typically bookended my day with the same Olympic-caliber workouts I'd been doing since competing in 2008. Going more than a day without hitting the water gave me the same sort of symptoms of withdrawal I was sure any self-respecting drug addict tried to avoid; besides, I always found my mental acuity was far better when I consistently got in a few thousand meters. Snapping my lock on the metal door, I was in the process of pulling on my swim cap when I heard my iPhone begin to ring. Frowning, I quickly dialed in the code for my lock and then dug through my neatly folded clothes to locate my phone; I frowned further when it turned out to be a number I didn't recognize.

Scanning the locker room to ensure I was reasonably alone, I tapped the answer button. "Commander Colbeth."

"Is this Sean Colbeth?" The male voice at the other end was clipped and professional.

"Yes," I confirmed. "To whom am I speaking?"

"Chief Ryan Bartram," was the prompt reply. "Glenn Hills Police Department. Is this a good time?"

Something in my chest squeezed. "Glenn Hills? New Hampshire?"

"Yes," Bartram replied. "Do you have a moment to talk?"

Looking down at the goggles hanging from my hand, I smiled wryly. "You caught me on the way to the pool," I said.

"When I brought up your profile, I wondered if you still swam," Bartram said.

"Twice a day," I replied, though my chest tightened further at the notion this guy had done some research on me. "What can I do for you, Chief?"

"Do you know Leslie Hammersmith?"

I found myself sinking down to the plank bench in front of the locker. "Not personally," I replied carefully. "Assuming we are talking about the same person, I believe that is the ex-husband of my girlfriend, Suzanne Kellerman."

"I think you know that we are," was the reply.

"What is this about?" I asked, though something in my gut told me I already knew.

"When was the last time you visited Glenn Hills, Commander?"

Sitting there in nothing more than my Speedo, I wondered at just how many more curves I'd be thrown that Tuesday. "I likely went through it on the way to a swim meet in Laconia back in October," I said. "The New England Regionals were held at the high school there this year."

"Yes, and you broke an age group record in the butterfly while you were at it."

"I did," I replied, feeling slightly unsettled. "Clearly, you know my movements, Chief. Would you mind explaining why this is of interest to you?"

There was a long pause. "So, you know where Glenn Hills is, then. Did you make a stop here? In either direction?"

Alarm bells began to go off in the back of my head. "What happened, Chief? For this feels a lot like the kind of call I would make to a person of interest in a case I was working."

"Your reputation is clearly well deserved," Bartram said. "Let me ask you this, then. Can you confirm you requested and then received extensive background information on Hammersmith back in September? Both from the Feds as well as the New Hampshire State Police?"

Now it was my turn to pause; while I'd not done anything to hide my inquiries into Suzanne's ex-husband, neither had I thought I'd drawn any attention to them, either. The fact that I *had* concerned me;

sure, it was something of an ethical gray area, but given the circumstances, one I'd been willing to wade into. Discretion — and limited honesty — felt like the best approach, so I let out an audible sigh as I pressed a hand to my forehead.

"I didn't realize I'd triggered something," I finally replied. "His file was flagged?"

"So, you admit to receiving the data?"

The use of the word *admit* brought me up short. "I'm sure there are courier records to support that I did, Chief. You probably even have my signature on them. What is this about, exactly?"

"I'm not at liberty to discuss an open investigation," Bartram said. "Why did you request the files?"

"I can't speak about an open investigation," I countered, parroting his own answer.

There was a long pause again. "If that is the case, perhaps we should compare notes," Bartram said. "Bring me what you have, and we can see what sort of overlap exists."

Every single fiber of my being was screaming that something serious was going on — and that I had somehow landed in the middle of it. I managed to keep my voice level. "I'm afraid we're dealing with a mass casualty event up here at the moment," I said calmly. "Once we get past the initial stages, I can have my office reach out and set up a Zoom meeting."

"It might be best to do this in person."

"I simply don't have time to drop everything and drive five hours for a meeting. Not in the middle of a situation like this."

"And yet you appear capable of carving out time to take a swim," he countered.

"Only because I am waiting for the morgue to complete the first round of postmortems," I said. "From your tone, though, I get the distinct impression you might want a signed note from the medical examiner as confirmation."

"It might help your cause, Commander," Bartram replied.

I felt my eyebrows go up. "I'll take that under advisement. Is there anything else?"

"Yes," Bartram said. "Where were you a week ago Sunday? Specifically, between the hours of noon and three p.m.?"

"That question sounds suspiciously like you need me to supply an alibi, Chief," I replied icily.

"Why would you think that?"

"It's the same sort of question I would ask a suspect," I replied. "*Am I suspect?*"

Bartram seemed to consider his words. "Let's just say you're a person of interest."

"Even better," I said. "In what, exactly?"

"Are you refusing to answer?"

"As much as you seem to be," I observed. "It appears we are working at cross purposes."

"Perhaps."

"Should I also presume the entirety of this phone call is being recorded?"

"New Hampshire is a two-party consent state," Bartram reminded me.

"So it is," I said, nodding to myself. "It's been nice chatting with you, Chief."

"We'll be speaking again," Bartram replied. "Soon."

"Of that, I have no doubt," I sighed before hanging up.

I stared at my iPhone for a long minute before slowly standing and putting it back into the locker; resting a hand atop the grilled door, I found myself completely unsettled by the call. It didn't help knowing that was the entire *point* of Bartram calling in the manner he had; it was a standard investigative technique that I had used to great effect many times myself. The broader question was *why* he was using it against me — though, as I stood there in the locker room, I thought I had a pretty damn good idea. Pulling my iPhone back out of the locker, I switched to the browser and did a quick internet search; my heart sank when the top six entries confirmed my suspicion. I tapped the link for the first one and then began to read the news article from the *Laconia News and Sun.*

Man Found Dead Under Suspicious Circumstances

GLENN HILLS, NH: According to authorities, local man Leslie Hammersmith was found dead in his home Monday after missing a board meeting at the company where he is currently chief executive. Hammersmith, 49, has lived in Glenn Hills since moving there from North Conway nearly three years earlier. Investigators have not ruled on a cause of death, noting only that they are still reviewing evidence collected at the scene...

Shock had me sitting down on the bench once more. Had someone walked into the locker room at that moment, they would have seen my jaw on the ground; staring at my iPhone's screen, it took three shots for it to register that the Monday in question noted by the article was, in fact, the day after the swim meet I'd attended in Laconia. As to whether I'd been in the area, there was no point in reviewing Apple Maps to confirm what I had already told — *admitted* — to Bartram: my route to the meet from Windeport had literally taken me through the small town of Glenn Hills. If I were truly a person of interest, someone over in New Hampshire was likely already pulling my phone records and location data for the window of time in question, making it an exceedingly wise decision to have not tried to duck that part of the interrogation.

So, I thought bleakly, *they seem to have already established opportunity; my pulling Hammersmith's records appears to speak to a motive. All that's missing is means... which I suspect they probably already have, hence the* invitation *to come in for an interview.*

Holy shit. I need a lawyer.

Tapping a finger on the cold wood of the plank bench, I ran through my analysis a few more times and came up with the same conclusion: I wasn't *just* their person of interest. Reading between the lines, I could easily see how it might look like I might have used my position on behalf of my girlfriend as some sort of avenging angel; about the only thing I had going for me was a decades-long reputation that countered such an image, but then again, there had been far too many instances where a upstanding member of law enforcement had been unmasked as a bad actor.

Shit, I thought again as I tapped at my phonebook searching for a specific name. *Shit, shit and double shit.*

To my great relief, I'd not removed Arabella Steinman out of my contacts; I'd not seen the lawyer from Fort Fairfield since the Professional Standards review, I'd been forced to endure back in August, so I was a little concerned that she might not pick up the phone. My mood lifted slightly when I heard her distinctive voice. "Sean! What a pleasant surprise. I was just thinking of you, actually."

"Really?"

"Yes," she replied. "I'm on my way to Portland to teach a three-day seminar to some first-year law students and am swinging through Windeport to deliver some papers to Caitlyn. I thought I'd poke my head into your new office and see how things had worked out." Arabella chuckled. "I suppose it's not really new, is it, if you are essentially where you were as Chief?"

"It feels like a fresh start to me," I said. "So, I'll go with new."

"Good."

"Unfortunately, I'll probably miss you. I'm working that mass shooting in East Newberry."

"Oh, *fuck*," she breathed. "I wondered if they'd pull you into that. How's it going?"

"Early days," I said, using the standard phrase that meant both everything and nothing.

"Ah." There was a bit of a pause. "That's not why you're calling, is it?"

"No," I replied. "Actually, I... you know, I guess there's no easy way to say this. I think I need a lawyer."

"Good thing you know one," she laughed. "What did you do this time? Piss off a senior citizen that was double parked?"

Her good humor was infectious. "I wish," I said, a slight smile on my lips. "I fear it might be far, far worse than that. Can anyone in your firm handle a possible criminal case?"

"It's not our specialty," Arabella replied slowly, "but we do take the occasional referral."

"I hope this is one of them."

"It might be best if we meet in person to discuss this," she said. "Where are you now?"

"Augusta," I said. "I've got to deal with multiple postmortems this morning, and then I'm driving to Bangor to interview an eyewitness." I paused, a sudden thought hitting me. "I do have to be in Portland on Wednesday, though. My MacBook is in need of some love, so I've got an appointment at the Apple Store."

"That works. I've got a two-hour break for lunch starting at noon; can you meet me at the law library at USM?"

I thought about that for a moment. "That's downtown now, right? Off of Commercial?"

Arabella laughed. "Technically, it's off of Fore Street, and has been for a while now."

"That's what I thought. How do you feel about snagging a table at DiMillo's instead?"

"I wouldn't say no to some lobster macaroni and cheese, if that's what you're asking."

"Then that's where I'll meet you."

"Good. And Sean?"

"Yeah?"

"If anyone reaches out to you about this situation in a legal capacity, refer them to my office in Fort Fairfield. Under no circumstances are you to talk to *anyone* without me being there."

"That makes it sound like you've taken me on as a client," I said as I felt my face flame. "One who may have already broken that rule."

"You've never stopped being my client," she reminded me. "Who did you talk to?"

"Chief of Police for Glenn Hills, New Hampshire."

There was a long string of expletives, followed by another. "Send me their contact info," Arabella finally said, her tone making clear her unhappiness with me. "And turn off your phone from this point forward."

"As much as I can. I am working a major case at the moment."

"I'm serious," she said. "Turn it off and leave it somewhere. A glovebox, for example. Or a box under your bed back in Windeport."

It finally dawned on me what she was saying without saying it. "Will do. And I'll see you tomorrow at USM."

"Sounds good."

Hanging up from my call with Arabella, I realized any desire I'd had to get in a workout that morning had pretty much evaporated. Unwilling to completely give up on it, though, I carefully replaced the iPhone in my rented locker, grabbed the rest of my swim gear and made my way out to the pool deck. Considering the hour, I was pleasantly surprised to find an entire lane open at the far end of the deck; I quickly made my way across the cold tile and dropped my gear at the edge, pressed the goggles to my eyes, then pulled my cap on before quickly slipping into the water. Bobbing on the surface for a moment, I took a deep breath to help focus on the workout I hoped to get in. I'd been a swimmer long enough that I had quite the library of favorite workouts, so plucking one from the virtual shelf wasn't hard; a few moments later, I was doing an easy warmup set of freestyle, intent on clearing my mind of any conscious thought.

Normally, I used my workouts as a way to gnaw on a thorny problem, but that morning I had no other agenda than trying to restore some semblance of peace to my soul. The mass shooting had eroded much of the emotional shielding I wove about me for protection while working my day-to-day career as a law enforcement officer; thus weakened, the second hit from some unknown police chief on a wild fishing expedition had lowered them further, opening me to recriminations and self-doubt on a level I'd rarely experienced. The strange gurgling noise as I sliced through the pool's surface was reassuring in ways hard to explain to a non-swimmer, a welcome embrace of normalcy for someone such as myself who had spent most of his life submerged in heavily chlorinated water. By the time I hauled myself back out of the water nearly an hour later, I was both pleasantly exhausted and more emotionally centered than I had been in some time.

The showers in the locker room were predictably better suited for someone far shorter than my six-foot-plus frame; somehow, I still managed to successfully run through my ablutions only to find I was still nearly forty minutes early for the first of the postmortems I was to attend. Thus handed an excuse to return to Dunkin' for another cup of coffee, I tossed my gear back into the SUV and started it up, intent on my next caffeine hit. I'd barely pressed the start button on the truck before my iPhone sang out the merry ringtone I'd long ago assigned to my beloved.

"Hey," I said. "I'm glad you called — it's shaping up to be an exceedingly long day. I'm not sure I'm going to make it—"

"He's dead," Suzanne interrupted.

I didn't have to guess who she was talking about, which in turn was its own reminder that I'd not followed Arabella's instructions with respect to my phone. "Who's dead?" I asked, deciding it might be wiser to let Suzanne fill me in on the details than to have to explain how I already knew myself.

"My ex," she replied. "I just got the call; they found him in the house he bought after we split."

"Oh shit," I said.

"Yeah." There was a pause. "I won't lie, there were more days than not that I found myself wishing for this; now that it's happened, I'm far more emotional than I expected."

"You were together for a long time," I reminded her. "I'd be surprised if you didn't still have some feelings there."

"I suppose," she sighed. "I've got to go to New Hampshire; despite everything we went through, it seems I'm still listed as the executor to his estate. Ironic, isn't it? The woman he wouldn't trust with our finances will now be responsible for disposing of them."

"Now that is quite a twist."

"I guess none of the women who came after me measured up enough for him to change anything." Suzanne sighed again. "Anyway, I know you're in the middle of something big; otherwise, I'd ask if you'd come with me. I think I could use the moral support."

"I'll come down as soon as I can get away," I replied.

"Cool."

As I committed myself, I wondered if it would be wise to cross the state line before knowing more about what Bartram was up to; while I wasn't one prone to jump to premature conclusions, I couldn't deny the conversation I'd had with the police chief had me concerned about what could be waiting on the other side of the border. That little difficultly paled in comparison to the far thornier issue of never having disclosed to Suzanne my little side investigation; now, as the silence stretched between us, I realized it would be far better she hear it from me first before the inevitable phone call from Bartram reached her. Fervently hoping no one was listening in on our conversation — while wondering where this tin-foil-hat side of me had appeared — I sighed and plunged ahead into uncharted waters.

"Suzanne," I began, "you should know before you leave that I was looking into your husband."

There was a startled pause. "Looking into... *Leslie*? Why?"

"I wanted to understand the man that had treated you as badly as he had," I replied honestly. "And how he had, frankly, gotten away with it."

The pause was longer this time. "Sean," she started carefully. "What do you mean, exactly, when you say *investigating*?"

"Just what it sounds like," I answered. "I did what we often euphemistically refer to as a background check, then traced his movements for the past few years; it probably sounds like a terrible invasion of privacy, but it's actually a rather standard process."

"If you're looking into a suspect," Suzanne said, immediately landing on the thorniest thorn. "Which he wasn't, since I never pressed charges against Leslie."

"Well, there's that," I allowed. "Still—"

"Isn't he just a little bit outside of your jurisdiction?"

"He is," I grudgingly admitted, "which is why I seem to be in some hot water with the Chief of Police for the town where your ex was living."

"Oh *shit*, Sean," she breathed. "Not a good look for you, coming off of that Professional Standards thing this summer."

"Tell me about it." I paused. "I probably should have run this past you first—"

"You think?"

"—and in retrospect, it was probably not the wisest of things to do." I smiled slightly. "When it comes to Milady, I don't always think straight."

"Yeah," she replied fondly. "I could say the same about my kitty. Still, it's not like you had to defend my honor or anything; the divorce was final years ago at this point. I'd have preferred to have just scrubbed out his memory at this point, replacing them with ones of you and me."

I wasn't entirely sure how to explain that I felt it *was* a huge matter of honor, at least for me; the hurt and pain Suzanne had been dealing with since leaving her ex had nearly derailed our own happiness together. It had taken far longer than I'd hoped to get us back to where we'd been prior to her second abrupt departure to Portland in August; the scales of justice needed to be balanced, and I'd thought digging around in Hammersmith's past might have provided the avenue to do just that. Now it was looking like I'd made a serious miscalculation, one with real-world consequences I'd never considered. Staring out the window of my SUV, I wondered a bit at how I would extricate myself from a situation I'd created without destroying everything I'd fought so hard for. Deciding it might be best to simply rip the proverbial bandage from the still-bleeding wound, I sallied forth once more.

"When I spoke with the Chief this morning — his name is Bartram

— I got the clear impression Leslie might not have died from natural causes."

Suzanne immediately understood where I was going. "That's why he called you."

"I believe so, yes."

"You didn't have anything to do with his death," she said. "You couldn't have! From what they just told me, Leslie passed away a week ago Sunday."

"The same weekend I was at the swim meet in Laconia," I replied softly.

"Where you were on deck from, like, six in the morning to nine at night. And won a few medals, too, if I recall."

"True."

"Then I don't see how that—"

"You have to go through Glenn Hills to get there," I said. "Or to return to Maine."

"That's nuts," Suzanne said. "I mean, sure, it looks kinda bad that my current boyfriend was running some sort of off-the-books investigation into my ex, but *seriously?* Besides, I was with you the entire time — we never stopped in either direction."

"True," I said, "and it's likely you'll be asked about that. Unfortunately, as you have already observed, I am your boyfriend. Any sort of alibi you might provide is likely to be viewed with suspicion."

Suzanne swore. "You really think they're coming after you?"

"I need to assume they are," I replied. "Fortunately, I know a good lawyer."

"Thank God." She paused. "You're certain about this?"

"Yeah," I replied.

"Fuck. Just, *fuck,*" she sighed. "And so typical of Leslie — messing with my life even from the grave."

Four

Suzanne and I sketched in a few additional details about her trip to New Hampshire before I hung up and continued on my quest for more coffee; having been on the clock since seven the prior evening, my sense of time had become skewed in the strange way it could when you began to suffer the first effects of sleep deprivation. Injecting another dose of caffeine into my veins would take the worst of the edge off, but I knew from years of experience it would begin to become a case of diminishing returns; like any good junkie, there would come a point where I could literally swim in a vat of coffee and it wouldn't do much more than let me drown, albeit happily. The honey-glazed donut that seemed to jump into the order was easier to rational-ize, given the workout I'd just put in at the YMCA.

The parking lot at the Chief Medical Examiner's office was unusu-ally full when I was waved through the security gate; it wasn't difficult to understand why, especially when I saw not one, but *three* hearses parked at the receiving dock for the facility. As I circled to find an empty space large enough to accommodate my SUV, I was reminded again that the sheer volume of victims from East Newberry represented nearly a full year of homicides for the State of Maine; that they had all came in on the same day was something else entirely. Slipping into the final slot beside the dumpster, I paused long enough to turn my iPhone off and shove it into the bottom of my swimming backpack; as much as it pained me to be without my trusted Apple device, my lawyer was right in assuming I was already being tracked. Disabling the phone would only provide a momentary frustration, though, for all state vehicles had little GPS gizmos far easier to stalk — and with less legal overhead than my phone.

Locking up, I strode across the lot toward the side entrance favored by those of us in law enforcement; I waved at the receptionist before using my ID to open the door to the inner sanctuary, yet another perk of being on the State payroll. I figured it was a good sign that it still worked. Stepping into the locker room, I was suddenly struck by the eyebrow windows that were just above the far wall; for all the post-mortems I had attended over the years, it was literally the first time I noticed how elegantly they framed the sky outside. Sparse but puffy white clouds popped against the brilliant blue Maine sky, several vibrant shades lighter than the flag that had been flying beside the building. For a November day, it was looking to be a ten — something to treasure as we braced for the dark days of winter that were just ahead.

Swapping my polo-and-jeans combo for a set of light green scrubs, I pulled the paper cap over my extremely out-of-control curls and then took a moment to stare at my reflection in the mirrors over the sink. The tired visage of a man with too much on his plate was a bit surprising, but then again, not; between losing my job in August, losing Suzanne briefly and then being asked to rebuild the Major Crimes department for Jimmy, I'd been on the run nearly constantly for months. Swim meets like the one in Laconia had been about the only brief respites I'd allowed myself; frowning, I couldn't remember the last time I'd taken any vacation. About the only downtime I'd had was my enforced sick leave after the shooting back in February, and even then, I'd wound up wiggling my way into a case Vasily had been dealing with at the same time. Placing my hands on either side of the dated tile for the sink, I knew myself well enough to see the early stages of burnout on the outer periphery.

Something else to be dealt with — later, I sighed as I tied the mask on and exited the lockers.

Finding Dr. Louise Hamilton turned out to be more of a challenge than usual; to my surprise, she wasn't in her normal exam room, though two very surprised-to-see-me medical examiners were. After several additional false starts, I discovered Lou in the oldest part of the building and a room so far from the entrance I feared I'd never find my way back out to daylight ever again. The Chief Medical Examiner turned in my direction as I pushed through the metal swinging door; from the way her eyes crinkled, I suspected there was a sly smile hiding beneath her face mask.

"I see you survived the quest," she chuckled.

"Barely," I replied as I moved over to stand at the end of the exam table. The body of an older man was present, though as unmarked as it looked, it seemed that Lou might not have started. "I didn't realize how many exam rooms you had in this place."

"It didn't hurt that the renovation back in '09 doubled our size," she said. "Though what that means in terms of us *needing* that much space is something I'd prefer not to dwell on." Lou paused for a moment. "On days like today, especially."

"Yeah," I nodded. "Full house and then some."

"We had to make space in the freezer," she said. "And I'm not sure we've had the final delivery from the scene yet, either."

"I figured as much."

"Along those lines, if you're here as the attending officer, I should warn you we've already completed a number of exams. Given the volume, we couldn't wait."

My eyebrows went up. "I wondered about that. The note in the file about the time—"

"Was before we knew the full extent of what was coming our way," Lou sighed. "On the other hand, I can save you a bit of time; my staff and I have cleared six of the victims so far and managed to identify four of them. If anything else of interest pops up, we'll flag it and give you a call, of course, but at this point — so far — it's been pretty cut and dry."

"Death by gunshot?"

"Exactly," she replied. "In far too many of the cases, *multiple* gunshots."

"Our working theory is that a semi-automatic of some sort was the weapon of choice."

"Ballistics will likely prove that out for you," she said. "The lab is backed up — no surprise there — but I expect the results on that no later than this afternoon."

"Good." I nodded to the cadaver. "So, who rated the attention of the Chief Medical Examiner herself?"

"Meet Kirk Nevelson," Lou said as she walked around to the head of the table. "Thirty-six, single and hailing from Concord, Massachusetts."

My eyebrows went up. "*Concord*? He's not a local?"

"No," she shook her head. "And to answer your question, he landed on my table because his fingerprints immediately came back; this young gentleman works at First Beacon Insurance as one of their investment managers. Part of that position included undergoing a rather deep background check that kept his prints on file with the Feds."

"Is that normal?"

Lou shrugged. "I suspect it depends on the firm. You'd have to talk to First Beacon, but I imagine their portfolio is valued with more zeros than either of us will ever see in our paycheck."

"Good point," I nodded. "Sounds like I'll need to make a trip to the big city."

"Lucky you," Lou chuckled.

"That, alone, can't be why he's on your table."

"Not entirely, no," she agreed. "You walked the scene, right?"

"I did, yes."

"So you know that the vast majority of the victims we've received were pretty ordinary lower-to-middle class individuals."

"That was my impression," I replied. "Save for one person. There was a guy with gold cufflinks—" My eyes widened and then turned toward the cadaver. "This is the guy from the rear storeroom?"

"Yes," Lou said. "In addition to those little gems — and they are on the table back there for you, ready to go into evidence — his clothing was also exceedingly high end. Shirt and pants were clearly tailored; shoes were expensive handmade loafers we already traced to Nordstrom's. The only thing missing was the silk tie and a suit jacket from the same material as the slacks."

"I'll call back to Norm and have him begin the hunt," I said. "When I saw this victim *in situ*, he was wearing an apron, though it appeared to be on backwards."

"It was. That's bagged for you, too. There was flour on it that we've sent to the lab."

"He didn't initially strike me as one of the cooks. I'm still waiting on the employee information, but from what you're telling me, I can't see him both working in Boston and also moonlighting at Pizzeria Angelina." I paused. "Certainly not with such expensive tastes in clothing."

"Not unless he liked a really, *really* long commute."

"Doubtful," I said thoughtfully. "Any connection to the owners?"

"Not that we can tell," Lou replied before waving in general at the building around us. "But, honestly, we've not had time to do the sort of deep dive we would normally do when we get a verified identity."

"Understood. I'll have someone on my team finish that." I tapped a gloved finger against the cold metal of the exam table, idly thinking that dead bodies probably didn't care about the chill. "I see three gunshot wounds," I observed as I scanned the naked form. "I don't want to make assumptions since you've not opened him up yet, but it seems obvious that might be what killed them."

"I agree," she said as she moved to the far side of the table and then pointed at the first chest wound. "This looks to be the kill shot, dead center mass; the CT scan confirms it was a through-and-through, more or less shredding the major vessels in the process."

"There should have been more blood around the body, then," I murmured.

Lou didn't seem to hear me and kept going. "Two more shots to the lower torso, which somehow managed to miss any of the major organs. Not that it mattered."

"It sounds like you're suggesting an order to me here," I said. "Can you truly tell?"

"More like informed conjecture," she replied. "Based on my understanding of human nature."

"I'll take whatever I can get at this point," I replied.

"Then you'll like this," Lou continued. Moving over to the computer sitting on a portable cart at the head of the exam table, she quickly tapped at the keyboard and then read something on the flatscreen monitor. "On a hunch, I had the lab run one of the newer processes we have for estimating time of death."

My eyebrows went up. "I've heard about that test, but I didn't think it was admissible in court."

"It's not mainstream yet, and honestly, I'd be unwilling to go on the stand and testify as to the validity of the results without running our more traditional analysis against it, but I thought it might prove interesting." Lou turned the monitor toward me and pointed with a gloved finger at a chart on the screen. "As I suspected, it contradicted the on-site liver temp results."

"That's not entirely surprising," I said as I wandered closer so I could look at the results. The font on the damn display was small enough that even squinting, I was hard pressed to see what she was referring to. "How the hell do you work with a resolution that tiny?"

"You truly need to get bifocals," Lou said. "Or a pair of cheaters from the local drugstore."

"I *have* those," I replied testily. "I just don't need them enough to carry them around like some senior citizen trying to read the lunch specials."

"Uh huh," Lou said, barely able to hide the rolling of her eyes. "The new test says this victim died far earlier than the rest."

"By how much?"

"I say this with caution," she began. "However, the chemical analysis of the DNA decay tells me between nine and ten A.M. on Sunday morning."

I felt my eyebrows go up again. "That's more than twenty-four hours ahead of the shooting."

"Exactly." Lou shifted the screen and displayed something else that apparently I was supposed to see; I couldn't, so I just nodded as she continued. "We dismissed the liver temp readings due to the ambient temperature in the storeroom, but that actually can't account for such a disparity." She looked at me. "This points to the body being stored somewhere for a while, somewhere cold enough to arrest decay."

"Like a walk-in fridge," I said, thinking back to the pizzeria.

"Exactly."

I glanced back at the corpse before looking at Lou. "I have to admit, I had a sense that this victim didn't die where we found him. There was a decided lack of evidence that a gun had been fired in the storeroom, aside from the obvious wounds in the body."

"Wherever he *did* die, based on lividity, I'd say your victim was in a similar seated position, if that helps. But it does seem pretty clear he was shot elsewhere and then moved."

"Wild," I breathed. "Is it actually possible someone was trying to hide a murder beneath the mass shooting?"

"I know they were," Lou said as she tapped at several small Petri dishes beside the computer's keyboard that I'd missed. "I was able to fish out a bullet from one of the lower abdomen wounds; it's consistent with a smaller caliber weapon — and doesn't match any of the ammo recovered from the restaurant."

I felt the beginning of a headache coming on. "Lou, you are seriously complicating my life."

"We aim to please," she chuckled.

FIVE

As a rule, I generally departed Dr. Hamilton's presence when she began her more detailed interior observations of a corpse; while not particularly squeamish, I'd had enough biology courses during my college years to know that I would never have a desire to get up close and personal with things that strictly speaking should never see the light of day. After grabbing the evidence bags Lou had stacked up for me and running through what passed for showers in the locker room, I was back behind the wheel of the SUV slightly ahead of eleven headed north to attempt an interview with the owner of the pizzeria. It wasn't a long jaunt from Augusta to Bangor per se, but it *was* one of the most unremarkable stretches of Interstate 95, showcasing seemingly endless miles of pine tree-lined pavement as though you were stuck in some sort of perverse version of purgatory designed by the Maine Turnpike Authority. Typically such mind-numbing blandness allowed me to shift my brain into investigator mode, providing much needed time to ruminate on the case. Owing perhaps to just how long I'd been awake at that point, the normal Zen-like state I usually found myself in proved elusive; when I reached the outer edges of metro Bangor and saw the massive sign for Dysarts on the horizon, I gave up entirely and took the next exit to refuel both the SUV and my rather loudly rumbling stomach.

Somewhat shocked at how much it cost to fill up my vehicle, I found a vacant parking spot in front of the restaurant and pulled in, locked up and then wandered inside. The famed truck stop had been doing business in that same spot since the late-1960s, and in many ways the interior still reflected the aesthetic from that time. Despite not being a full-time resident of the area, the elderly hostess behind the check in stand greeted me as though I were one of her regulars

"Afternoon, hon," she said warmly as she grabbed a plastic-covered menu from beneath the counter. "How is it someone so handsome is dining alone on such a fine day?"

Her smile was infectious and managed to pull me ever so slightly out of my self-induced funk. "That's the warmest welcome I've had all day," I replied, suddenly feeling every ounce of the weariness I'd been ignoring for the past few hours. "Do you greet all of your guests that way?"

The hostess smiled wider and lowered her voice. "How else do you think we keep our reputation for stellar customer service?" she chuckled. "Right this way."

Despite it being well past the lunch hour, the dining room was predictably full of diners; I didn't stop as frequently as I could on my travels to Bangor, but when I did, I never failed to find the place busy. It was a testament to both the food and the service, especially since I knew the drivers of the massive semis that dominated the parking lot were an exceptionally choosy bunch. Sliding into a booth with hunter green cushions and a nice view of I-95, I accepted the menu from my guide and had barely started to scan the menu when a massive ceramic mug appeared at my elbow, one that was immediately filled to the brim with steaming hot coffee. Looking up in appreciation, I caught the slight wink from the waitress as she sailed away from me to top off others.

Taking a sip of the brew, I found myself nearly closing my eyes in ecstasy; either I was far more tired than I'd realized, or the chefs at Dysarts had a direct line to some of the finest coffee beans I'd ever tasted.

Drinking a bit more, I was inclined to believe the latter and suddenly began to understand why there appeared to be a single waitress roaming the room with a pot of coffee. Picking up the menu again, I decided breakfast-for-lunch seemed appropriate and settled on a nice Western omelet with a side of toast made from their handmade molasses oatmeal bread. While I waited for the order, I stared out of the large window and idly watched the traffic on the interstate as it whisked by; thus pleasantly disengaged from everything, my brain sneakily dropped into investigator mode and finally began contemplating my next steps.

Tapping a finger on the warm side of the ceramic mug, I tried to unpack what it meant that we had, essentially, an extra body among the dead at the pizzeria. Assuming that Lou's analysis held up, it seemed clear whatever transpired to land Kirk Nevelson in the morgue had been well in advance of the mass shooting, but it was also hard not to feel it an unusually odd coincidence that his death would *happen* to take place mere hours before a far larger tragedy unfolded. Since I was not one to believe in coincidences, that lead me to consider two possibly unthinkable options: that whomever had killed Nevelson had known what was coming and planned to use it for cover, or, alternatively, had no clue about the mass shooting but *still* had the presence of mind to stage Nevelson's body in the midst of the mayhem. Shaking my head at the slight reflection of my face in the window, neither option felt solid — at least, not without more evidence. Considering how long the case system's list of what had been collected was, I suspected digging through that might prove illuminating, though thinking of *that* reminded me I was short one laptop at the moment.

The smell of something savory momentarily broke the trance, and I looked down to find my brunch had quietly arrived. Spreading a bit of orange marmalade on the toast, I chewed thoughtfully while I shifted to how I wanted to handle my interview with the owner. I was cautiously optimistic I'd be able to speak with him, mostly because I'd yet to be told he'd not survived the trip to Bangor General. The original set of questions I'd wanted to ask seemed less relevant now, though, in light of this strange second murder; knowing my time was likely to be at a premium with the lone survivor of the mass shooting didn't make it any less difficult choosing an appropriate approach. Sighing inwardly, I decided to pluck a card from Vasily's deck and, frankly, wing it; while I preferred to be completely prepared when speaking with a witness, I'd found over the years I'd worked with my best friend that occasionally fortune favored the foolish.

May today be such a day, I thought to myself with another sigh as I shoveled another forkful of egg into my mouth. *Of all days, may today be such a day.*

I made short work of my meal and lingered for a moment longer over one last mugful of coffee before settling with my waitress and decamping for the SUV. The day had become pleasantly warm, an unusual outlier for November that often presaged the bitter winter just over the horizon; still, I thought I'd enjoy the weather while I could and rolled down the windows as I pulled out of the massive lot for the truck stop. Merging into traffic on I-95, I kept one ear on Siri's gentle navigation pointers, all the while trying not to smile each time she warned me about a speed trap along the route. My semi-regular jaunts to Bangor generally revolved around competitions at the Olympic-sized pool on the campus of University of Maine, though that was actually a few miles north of the city; more recently, I'd begun to poke my head into the district court building checking in on cases that fell under my purview as head of Major Crimes. The wider metropolis remained something of a mystery to me, so it was always an adventure when Siri diverted me from I-95. In this case, she had me take the Hammond Street exit, placing me on one of the larger arteries that cut through the heart of Bangor. Traffic was pretty light that early on a Tuesday afternoon, allowing me time to appreciate the eclectic style of a city that had been built on the back of the lumbering and paper making industries; much like East Newberry, it felt to me a bit like an echo of an era long past that refused to fade gracefully into nothingness. Smiling slightly as I turned onto State

Street, it occurred to me that Windeport had been on track to suffer the same fate, right up until the cruise industry came calling. I guessed it disproved that old adage the past belied the future; maybe Bangor had a second act lurking in the winds that none of us had yet guessed was there.

Bangor General was in many ways the spiritual twin of Maine Medical Center in Portland, a vast, sprawling campus constrained only by the city to one side and the wide Penobscot river on the other. It took a moment for me to locate the visitor parking lot, and then a few more finding a spot large enough for the SUV. Locking up, I headed for the larger of the tall brick buildings and entered into the main lobby area; in this age of cutting personnel expenses, the traditional grinning receptionist had been replaced by a series of automated kiosks that allowed you to hunt-and-peck your way through a floorplan to locate the department you were likely already twenty minutes late getting to. I'd never found such software to be all that user friendly, and true to form, it took longer than I'd wanted to chart a pathway to the intensive care unit.

After only making two wrong turns and getting off the elevator on the wrong floor, I found myself in front of a pair of red double doors, beside which hung an old-fashioned wall-mounted phone. Picking up the handset, I heard it immediately ring an extension on the other side of the portal. A husky woman's voice answered promptly.

"ICU, this is Ginny."

"Ginny, I'm Commander Sean Colbeth, Major Crimes—"

"Ah," she said, her voice dripping with disapproval. "I imagine you're here to speak with Leon Angelina."

I blinked, for it occurred to me it was the first time I'd heard the name of the owner. "Yes. Is that possible? I only need a few minutes—"

"You probably should have called in advance," Ginny replied. "It might have saved you the trouble of driving out."

My heart sank. "Damn," I said softly into the receiver. "My day has been rather fluid given the situation in East Newberry; I wasn't able to get here any sooner." *That and the EMT pretty much told me not to follow them, too,* I thought to myself. *Looks like I should have pressed harder—*

It took a moment for me to realize Ginny was talking, interrupting my internal condemnation. "—lucky for you, he's just had lunch and is therefore awake."

"He's *alive*?" I heard myself blurt.

"Wouldn't be in my ward otherwise," Ginny replied drolly. "Give me a moment to come and get you."

"Okay, thanks," I said as she hung up.

Replacing the handset on the phone, I stepped back and took a moment to consider the small waiting room just outside the ICU; the threadbare couches looked as tired as I felt, and the flatscreen television mounted in the corner of the ceiling was giving a dark blue hue to what looked like some sort of courtroom drama currently playing. Someone had tried to liven up the space by adding a potted plant that was a veritable forest of green fronds. Suspicious of the slightly artificial looking color, I had just enough time to wander over and test my theory before hearing the automatic lock clicking open behind me. Turning, I watched as the doors slowly swung open to reveal a matronly woman in navy scrubs; my eyebrows went up slightly at the not-of-this-era traditional nursing cap perched atop a hairdo straight from the big hair styles of the mid 1980s.

"Commander," Ginny said as she folded her arms against her chest.

"I do apologize for the intrusion," I said as I moved toward the door. "Today has been the epitome of extraordinary circumstances."

"That much I'll buy," she replied with a slight softening of her expression. "This way."

"I realize you can't disclose much, but in general, how is he doing?" I asked as we moved down a pretty standard industrial hospital corridor.

I'd spent many an hour in my full Chat Noir getup working a similar hallway down in Portland, trying to cheer up the kids who had landed in the Barbara Bush Children's Center. It wasn't lost on me how there seemed to be a global constant to such places: the indeterminate white of the walls, the soft bleating of medical equipment, the half-moon safety mirrors mounted to the ceiling at every intersection — small pieces, when combined, that fairly screamed *we know you're in crisis, but we've got it covered.*

"I think it's fair to say the road to recovery for Mr. Angelina is going to be quite long."

Ginny turned left at the first major intersection, leading the way into the main area of the ICU. The standard semicircular nursing station stood watch in the center of a box-like space ringed with glass-walled patient rooms; most rooms were dark, speaking perhaps to how busy they happened to be at the moment. My guide stopped at the desk and twisted a monitor around so she could scan what appeared to be telemetry coming from the occupied spaces. Nodding to herself, she turned the monitor back and then headed toward one of the few rooms where the curtains had been drawn back.

Sliding the glass door open, Ginny stepped inside and then motioned for me to follow her. As the room had no outside window, the only illumination came from the fixture mounted above the bed, and that appeared to have been turned to the lowest setting. Far more equipment than I'd expected to find had been crammed into the space, with the commensurate number of tubes and wires and other sensors running down to the figure on the bed. It took a moment for my eyes adjust to the semidarkness, but when they did, the man propped up on the bed looked to be in far worse shape than when I'd seen him in the back of the ambulance. His head was turned slightly to the right, the mouth hanging slightly open in repose; the clear tube for the oxygen had been carefully woven over his ears so it could fit snugly beneath his nostrils, which flared every now and then. Most striking, perhaps, were the strange gray eyes that had been watching me from the moment I entered the room; slightly glassy-eyed due to the drug cocktail being pumped into his veins, they nonetheless appraised me with a sharpness that belied any notion that the owner of Pizzeria Angelina wasn't clearly in the moment.

Ginny moved to the omnipresent computer workstation and used her employee ID to unlock the system with a deft tap that spoke to her longevity at the hospital. Scanning the screen briefly, she turned to me and nodded slightly. "Five minutes, Commander. Then I'm going to have to ask you to leave so my patient can continue to recover from surgery."

"Of course," I replied with my best Downeast retail smile.

Five minutes was barely enough time to discuss the weather, let alone the intricacies of the situation Angelina had found himself in, but the duty nurse didn't seem to be someone I wanted to cross. At least, not yet. She nodded again before closing down the computer and withdrawing from the room. I waited for the soft *clunk* of the door latch before turning my attention back to Angelina.

"I'm Commander Sean Colbeth, Maine State Police," I began. "I run the Major Crimes department and am taking the lead in investigating what happened at the Pizzeria."

Angelina nodded; with the oxygen tub, it seemed a bit like a caricature of the movement. "Nice to meet you, Commander," he replied, his voice a bit raspy.

"I'm sorry it's under such circumstances," I continued. "Are you up to answering a few questions? Ordinarily I would wait until you were further along on the road to recovery, but as you've probably guessed, we're on a bit of a clock."

Those strange eyes widened. "You haven't found him yet, then?"

I pulled out my notebook; without my iPhone, I was reduced to recording my conversation the old fashion way; as I scribbled away on the white-lined paper, I wondered if I'd be able to read my handwriting later. "No."

"Damn."

"I take that to mean you had a good look at the shooter, then?" I asked, deciding to skip over the normal niceties of my interviewing script.

"Yeah," Angelina nodded again. "I was behind the counter finishing up a transaction for a customer when I heard gunfire out on the side-walk." He paused. "Not the sort of thing I'd ever have expected to hear in East Newberry."

"I imagine not." Something in what he said caught me. "Did you serve?"

"Vietnam," he said. "I was in the first of my four-year hitch with the Army." A rueful smile appeared on his face. "I enlisted to get away from the pizzeria only to come right back to it when I got out."

"Not the first time I've heard that from someone," I said. "Infantry?"

"Ayuh," he replied using the catchall Maine phrase that, in this instance, indicated affirmation. "I still have nightmares."

"I can imagine. How long have you owned the pizzeria?" I asked, temporarily tacking away from what I knew would be a more difficult question.

"I bought out my parents in the late-1970s," he replied. "Dad started the place in '65, back when East Newberry was still thriving." Angelina smiled slightly, which looked odd with the oxygen tube. "Or as thriving as a dying mill town could have been back then."

"Kept it in the family, then?"

"Had to," he nodded. "I ain't got any siblings, so there wasn't really much of a choice." That strange smile came back. "My daughter don't feel the same obligation, though. It'll end with me."

"You're married?"

"Widowed," Angelina replied. "I lost Beryl in '88."

"Is your daughter local?"

"Cape Cod," he sighed. "Got as far away from Maine as she could. Married up to a Boston Banker."

"Do you want me to contact her?" I asked, acutely aware there didn't seem to be any family present. "At the very least, let her know you survived—"

"No," Angelina replied firmly.

There was a weird undercurrent there, but I was reluctant to dive in;

it seemed clear Angelina wasn't on the best of terms with the rest of his family, so I decided to gently probe the shooting a bit further. "So you were behind the counter when you heard the first shots; what happened next?"

Angelina took a deep breath and winced as he did so, speaking to his injuries. "Took me longer than it should to recognize what I was hearing; by the time I did, the guy had already come through the door, guns blazing."

"He had more than one weapon?"

"Maybe?" Angelina shrugged. "From all of the noise, it was hard to tell, but it felt like he had more than one."

"Did you recognize the shooter?"

"No," he replied instantly. "I did get a brief look at him before I was hit, though."

"Can you describe the shooter, then?"

"Ayuh?" he breathed, using the term as an interrogative. "Medium height, I guess; he was coming around the coatrack at the front when I saw him, and his head was just above the hooks. I had to repair them last year, so I know they're mounted at five feet from the floor."

"Good," I encouraged. "Anything else strike you?"

"Black," he said after a moment. "He was clothed in unrelieved black from head to toe."

I nodded, thinking that would be the perfect outfit for fading into the night afterward.

"Goggles," Angelina said thoughtfully. "He was wearing goggles, too."

My eyebrows went up, but I was careful not to prompt him. "What sort of goggles?"

"Round," he replied. "Like the kind you would wear while skiing."

"I see. Any facial hair? Mustache, beard?"

Angelina shook his head. "I don't know," he replied. "I only had the one look, and even then, it wasn't a good one; I was more interested in getting out of there than taking notes."

"As were your patrons," I observed before I had a chance to check myself. With my latest infusion of caffeine waning, I couldn't help expressing my irritation at his drive for self-preservation.

"Yeah, it was pandemonium," he continued, seemingly oblivious to the undertone of my comment. "At least, in the early moments. With a weapon like that, it didn't take long before the screams stopped."

"Like what?" I asked, something tickling at the edges of my brain. "Did you recognize the gun?"

"No," Angelina answered before glancing toward the glass door behind me.

A moment later, I heard the click of the latch as it opened. "Commander?" came the husky voice of my nurse minder.

"Thank you for your time," I said to Angelina. "I might have some follow-up questions as we sift through the evidence at the scene, but those can wait until you're back on your feet."

"Whatever I can do to help," he replied.

I started to fold up my notebook then paused. "Just one more thing," I said. "We found one of your staff members in the rear storeroom, but we're having trouble identifying him. Who was on duty that evening?"

Angelina's nostrils flared for a moment. "I didn't get back there," he answered. "I had all I could do to get into the closet and barricade myself."

My irritation bubbled up again, for it was clear Angelina had been in a classic every-person-for-themselves mindset during the shooting. It wasn't especially unusual but coming from a proprietor of a restaurant in a small town where he likely knew everyone who had been dining there that evening, the sentiment felt especially galling to me. Tamping down my feelings as best as I could, I faked a smile and slid my pen inside the spine of the notebook.

"Thank you again," I said. "I hope you have a speedy recovery."

Angelina simply nodded.

Stepping around Ginny, I waited just long enough to see if I was to be escorted out to the waiting room; when it became apparent I'd have to find my way to the exit solo, I smiled slightly at the implied rebuke and began walking to my waiting SUV. The interview hadn't been especially revealing, not that I had expected it to be; still, something about it *was* troubling, and I was just tired enough that I couldn't put my finger on it. Only as I unlocked the door to the driver's side did it finally dawn on me what it might be. Sliding behind the wheel, I flipped through my notes I'd just made and scanned through the last portion of my conversation.

"With a weapon like that, it didn't take long for the screams to stop."
Frowning, I read it again, then backed up to earlier in the interview.
"The guy had come through the door, guns blazing."
Sitting back in the seat, I wondered why my subconscious had flagged it for it wasn't all that unusual for eyewitnesses to have faulty recollections, especially in as violent a situation as the one that had gone down at the Pizzeria. Still, the fact I felt like I couldn't dismiss it outright as an odd inequity felt significant, though the reasons for feeling that way were eluding me at the moment. As I started up the SUV, I knew I'd built a reputation for paying attention to such small things, for they often belied just how important they were to the overall investigation.

Only time would tell if my gut was right on this one.

SIX

I began the long trek back to Windeport after a brief detour into another Dunkin' for an extra-large cup of coffee. At some point, Suzanne had finally given up trying to break me from my caffeine addiction; honestly, I sort of missed the witty back-and-forth we'd had, another casualty perhaps of the break in our relationship back in July. As the city gave way to the more rural pine-tree-studded portion of the route, I thought a bit about how we had evolved as a couple; while there was no question I still loved her with a fierceness that nearly hurt, no small part of me worried constantly that I'd do something to cause Suzanne to bolt one final time. The fiasco I was trying *not* to think about in New Hampshire was the most recent leading contender, one more bad decision that was coming back to roost. In a striking moment of clarity, I realized despite everything, at my emotional core I'd never truly gotten over Deidre leaving me, nor had I ever fully addressed my role in her departure.

Well, that wasn't entirely true, I thought to myself. *I know now I was still mired in my mother's death; Suzanne helped me to see that. And in truth, De and I had begun sailing away from each other after that fateful conversation we'd had about having children.*

I sighed again as I came up behind a slow-moving logging truck. *Hindsight is twenty-twenty for sure, as that conversation I had with Suzanne about moving in together had nearly an identical outcome. I sure can be clueless at times, can't I?*

The logging truck slowed and then turned; I sped back up again and set aside personal thoughts for rumination about the case; that triggered a reminder that I'd wanted to revisit the scene in East Newberry to confirm something that had been nagging me since the postmortem on Kevin Nevelson. Adjusting my route at the next intersection, I raced the sun as it began to sink low on the November horizon; at that point in the yearly calendar, darkness fell far earlier than I liked, presaging the dark months of winter yet to come. Only when I pulled around the corner of the old mill and slid into an empty spot in the same parking lot I'd used hours earlier did it occur to me I'd not had to pass through any checkpoints; getting out of my SUV confirmed my suspicion that the situation had changed since the prior evening, for the mobile command center was no longer parked in front of the pizzeria. A small fleet of unmarked State vehicles were still present, though most appeared to be from the Crime Lab; from the flow of equipment coming out of the restaurant, it was clear the tide had turned, though I wondered why I'd not been notified.

I was halfway to the Pizzeria before remembering I'd turned off my phone and locked it inside the gun safe of my SUV; grimacing slightly, I wondered how many irate text messages I might have missed and decided it might be best to let that particular sleeping dog lie for a bit longer. Grabbing gloves from my pocket, I pulled them on as I waited for another tech to exit, then nodded at the officer who was stationed just inside and noting the various comings and goings of personnel. Despite the removal of all of the victims, the stench of what had taken place was still very much present; the small yellow evidence markers that had sprung up like crime scene mushrooms had all disappeared, presumably along with the evidence they had been denoting. Still, I was acutely aware of the fact I was in an active crime scene and carefully picked my way through the main restaurant toward the rear.

And then I stopped and turned back around. I'd seen the coatrack on my first visit, of course, but bereft of the bulky winter jackets it had been holding at the time, it was nearly unrecognizable; what I'd assumed had been some sort of standard set of hooks mounted to the wall was actually something altogether unexpected. Stepping closer, I ran a finger along the hand-turned wood that framed a wide wooden plank three feet wide and maybe half that in height. A staggered set of Shaker pegs were mounted in an offset manner to maximize the number of coats it could hold; the entire piece was stained a dark mahogany color that made it feel more like a fine piece of furniture than something as utilitarian as a coatrack. Considering the rest of the faded decor, this particular item felt quite new, which supported Angelina's assertion it was installed relatively recently; glancing at the rest of the pizzeria, I wondered why such care had not been taken on the rest of the restaurant.

My focus shifted from the overturned tables to the figure of Heather Graham heading in my direction, toting a small toolbox in one hand and her omnipresent tablet in the other. Smiling slightly when she realized I'd seen her, she paused beside me for a moment. "I wondered if we'd see you again."

"I spoke to the lone survivor a bit ago," I said by way of explanation, "and decided another walk-through might be helpful to match what he told me with what I thought I'd seen the first time."

"Sounds like you," she nodded. "And that explains why you seem to have fallen off the face of the planet. Captain Roberts has been trying to reach you since noontime."

"Ah," I replied. "You know what cell coverage is like in this part of the state."

"I do," she replied, then waited a beat. "You might want to turn your phone back on."

"Then how would I get any work done?" I asked with a forced smile.

It was hard not to groan at the fact I'd been so worried about Chief Bartram tracking me, I'd completely forgotten my own boss could do the same. "I'll call him back as soon as I'm done here."

"Good." She glanced at the coatrack. "That's a fine piece of art right there."

"I agree," I nodded. "I've been thinking it's hand done, possibly from Sabbathday Lake."

"You might be right," Heather replied.

"Does it strike you as odd in any way?" I asked. "I mean, to me, it doesn't fit the aesthetic of the rest of the pizzeria."

"Such as it is," Heather replied thoughtfully. "What are you thinking?"

"I'm not sure, yet," I said before eyeing her toolkit. "You have a hammer in that thing?"

"No," she replied. "But there's one in the truck." Heather paused. "Why?"

"This might sound odd, but I want to see what's behind it."

"There goes that gut instinct of yours again," she smiled. "Give me a moment."

"Sure."

While I waited for Heather to return, I ran my gloved fingers all the way around the perimeter of the coatrack, looking for and failing to find any sort of hardware connecting the piece to the wall. Returning my attention to the face of the coatrack, my eyes immediately fell on four small, recessed holes at the corners that had been plugged by a small dowel. I reached for the lowest one and gently began to twist it; to my relief, the dowel popped out easily, revealing the head of a stainless-steel screw. By the time Heather had returned with a slightly larger toolkit, I'd managed to wrangle the other three dowels out and had them carefully lined up on the grimy tile at my feet.

Quickly catching on to what I was about, Heather put down her kit and snapped the locks open; pulling the lid up, she rustled around inside the metal container and ultimately retrieved a small battery-powered screwdriver. Standing up, she handed it to me. "I presume you want the honors?"

"I won't stand on ceremony," I smiled. "Grab the bottom, would you? I think this might be heavier than it looks."

"Good thing I've been working out," she laughed as she reached up to hold the wood.

I made short work of removing the four screws; it took a bit more effort to pry the entire rack from the wall, for despite how new it looked, it appeared that the wall around it had been painted after it had been installed. A few gentle insertions of a flathead screwdriver at key points managed to break the tension of the dried paint, allowing us to carefully lower the entire thing to the tile. Standing once more, I examined the rectangular patch of differently colored paint that had been exposed by the rack's removal; glancing to the main space of the restaurant, it wasn't much of a stretch to assume it was the original color of the space.

What didn't appear to be original were the two dimples in the exact center of the rectangle.

"Can I borrow your flashlight?" I asked as I leaned closer to the wall.

"Sure."

It took a moment for her to retrieve the small tubular light and hand it to me; pressing the button to turn it on, I held it up to the dimples and immediately saw they were fairly typical patches to the drywall. Having had my own occasion to patch-and-repair walls in my bungalow back in Windeport, it was easy to recognize a job that had been done in haste and with materials purchased at a local hardware store. I stepped back and looked at Heather.

"What do those look like to you?" I asked as I handed her the flashlight.

She leaned in, shining the bright LED against the wall. "Definitely some sort of repair," she murmured. "Made from something that was incompatible with the older drywall of this wall — that's why it's pulling away from the surface like that."

"Do you get the sense that this coatrack was put there to hide that?" I asked.

Heather looked at me askance. "That seems like a lot of effort when you could just get someone to patch-and-paint the wall instead," she replied.

"True," I nodded, "unless you don't want to draw attention to *why* the wall has to be repaired."

"Okay," she replied slowly. "I see where you are going with this. Hang on."

Kneeling once more, she sorted through the smaller of her toolboxes and came up with a rectangular device that looked a bit like a stud finder. Tapping at it once, the gizmo beeped pleasantly; reaching up, she began to wave it in front of the two dimples on the wall. The first one didn't register anything on the small display, but the moment she hit the second one, the indicator lit up all four lights and began bleating.

"Huh," she replied thoughtfully. "Let me get some photos and then do a little bit of surgery." Heather looked at me as she put the device back into the toolbox. "This might take a few minutes...?"

"Then I'm going to leave you to it and circle back."

"Sounds good."

Unsure of exactly what I had just uncovered, I nonetheless felt the same frisson I always did when clues began to appear in a case I was working. I'd long ago learned to listen to my instincts, for they rarely led me astray — Suzanne's ex-husband notwithstanding. Slipping behind the counter at the rear of the pizzeria, I couldn't help the slight sense of anxiety I felt each time I thought about the New Hampshire situation; pushing it aside was becoming increasingly harder as the day progressed, making me think that a late-evening workout might be on tap to try and take the edge off.

Folding my arms against my chest, I tried to look at the space behind the counter as though it were the first time I'd been there; thinking back to what Leon Angelina had told me, I tried to picture him behind the cash register and turned so I could stand there about where I thought he might have been. To my surprise, I discovered that the greenery planted in the pony wall between the vestibule and the main dining area was tall enough to hide all but the very top of Heather Graham's head as she worked on where the coatrack had hung. Looking at the vestibule space more critically, I realized there was no clear shot of the front door no matter where someone might have stood behind the counter.

He might have heard gunshots, I thought to myself, *but it's nearly impossible he saw the shooter enter. And even less likely he would have been able to see him standing next to the coatrack. Interesting.*

Filing that little tidbit away, I pulled out my notebook and scanned my notes; tapping at the page with a gloved finger, I tried again to picture how Leon would have had to have stood in order to get shot the way he described. While I didn't have the diagram in front of me for where his wounds had been, I'd seen him in the back of the ambulance and knew that he'd been hit in the lower torso. The head wound had come later, when he'd been hiding in the closet.

Those shots would have been low, I thought with a frown as I knelt and looked under the counter. *There are plenty of bullet holes here to support that possibility, which also explains why the kids died here. I* paused with a start. *Those two kids were running the registers...?* I thought as I stood up again.

As there were only two point-of-sale systems, I felt my frown deepen.

Three people behind the counter taking orders, on a Monday night? Two staff and the owner? That seems... like a lot of money to spend on labor for a non-Friday, non-weekend date, but maybe the pizza business is like that...

I looked up again at Heather.

No, I thought, *no — something is off on this. These pieces don't fit.*

Tapping at the notebook again, I figured another trip to Bangor was in my future — or wherever Angelina wound up recuperating. Turning, I slowly moved over to the walk-in pantry where Angelina had taken cover and found myself pausing again. The storage space was directly behind the pizza oven, a monolithic thing comprised of a few tons of metal. While it was definitely riddled with bullet holes, it seemed equally as likely it had served as a bit of shield for anyone taking cover behind it. Eyebrows now firmly raised, I scooted around the edge of the oven and ducked into the storage area; the pool of blood where Angelina had been found was still there, as were the debris from the shelf that had collapsed. The smell of spices that should never be mixed filled the air; in the far corner, two massive metal canisters bearing an uncreative tomato icon stood watch over everything. Without the measuring app on my iPhone in hand, it was hard for me to confirm my suspicion that the shelf was *above* the top of the pizza oven, allowing a stray bullet or fifty to shred the supporting hardware. Squatting slightly, I felt myself nodding as I examined the lower portion of the wall.

No bullet holes, I thought. *None.*

Just to be sure, I shifted items around on the shelves that were still standing but found no evidence that anything had come into the space below about the five-foot mark on the wall. In short, it was an amazing stroke of luck for Angelina to have hauled himself into the safest spot in the pizzeria. Standing again, I considered the pool of blood once more and thought maybe that *particular* luck may not have continued had the EMTs been delayed any longer than they had.

Stepping back out into the kitchen, I moved over to the walk-in fridge and pulled the massive door open; the gust of cold air was as unwelcome as ever, but I soldiered on and stepped inside after making sure the portal wouldn't lock behind me. I'd only had a quick look inside the first time, enough to convince myself there wasn't anything to see. This time around, I began a methodical search, starting at the end of the shelving closest to the door; I wasn't entirely certain what I was looking for, but found it anyway three quarters of the way around the perimeter. That portion of the fridge had a set of long, vertical drawers with translucent material along the front; on first glance, they looked as though they contained vegetables, but when I pulled the top one open, I found only two heads of lettuce pressed up against the front of the drawer. Turning, I realized there were shelves I'd already gone through full of things like peppers, onions and other various produce; turning back, it seemed like a non sequitur to me that the drawers would *also* be in use. Stepping back, I felt that frisson again for the drawer seemed to be about six feet in length and maybe three wide — almost, but not quite coffin dimensions.

Shit.

Pushing the upper drawer closed, I pulled open the one below it. As before, a smattering of lettuce had been pressed against the translucent front of the drawer, but unlike earlier, a small pool of something red and viscous had accumulated in the rear — about where it was nearly impossible to reach with a towel. I knelt on the cold metal floor of the fridge and peered into the drawer, wondering if I was truly seeing what I thought I was seeing; I'd have to have Heather do the actual measuring, but I was reasonably certain I might have found where the body of Kirk Nevelson had been stored.

Slowly pushing the drawer closed, I found myself shaking my head. *This case is not what it seems,* I thought as I stood and exited the fridge. *I'm more certain than ever a murder was covered by a massacre, yet I'm no closer to understanding why.*

Heather was just snapping her toolbox closed when I returned to her in the vestibule. Looking up, she caught my thoughtful expression and frowned. "Uh oh. You found something else, didn't you?"

"Maybe," I nodded. "How about you?"

She smiled and retrieved a small plastic bag from her pocket. "Small caliber bullet," she said as she handed it to me. "It was buried deep in the two-by-four behind the hole we found. I suspect the other hole held something similar, but whoever tried to do the patch was able to remove it."

I held the evidence bag to the light, such as it was. "Why remove one but not the other?"

Heather pointed to a piece of wood on the floor. "Because they would have had far more than a simple plaster job had they tried to get it out," she said as she then drew my attention to the now sizable hole in the wall. The square box she had cut from it did a nice job of showcasing just how deeply she'd had to dig. "Doing the patch, paint, and hang a coatrack option supports the idea whoever did this was trying not to draw attention."

"The coatrack feels like it would have been plenty visible," I countered.

"Maybe," she allowed, "but not as much as having to patch, prime and then repaint this wall. That would have taken *days*, where patching and mounting might have taken an afternoon."

I looked back at where the fridge was. "Or a long, long overnight."

"Exactly," Heather nodded. "You think this ties into the shooting?"

"That depends," I hedged, "on what you can tell me about a drawer in the fridge."

Heather groaned. "Good thing I'm already into overtime," she sighed. "Let me get my things..."

SEVEN

Unlocking the door to my bungalow was a reminder that Suzanne was once again absent; it wasn't truly a surprise since she'd already told me she was heading to New Hampshire to deal with her ex-husband's estate, but still, it was something of a shock to have to fish out my key. I routinely left my home unlocked — the byproduct of having lived in a small town my entire life, and something that drove my girlfriend to distraction, a point she tended to drive home whenever she was the last one out. That evening, pushing the door open also brought with it memories of the last time she'd left Windeport; despite repairing our relationship during the time we'd been together on Carpenter's Island, it had still taken weeks before Suzanne had felt comfortable enough to resume overnighting at my place. Having her MIA again was something of a jolt to the system, one that I wasn't liking in the least.

Tossing the keys down on the small side table by the door to the carport, I kicked out of my boots and shrugged off the jacket I'd been wearing; I decided to keep my unruly curls, still damp from my workout at the UEM pool, beneath the beanie I'd pulled on for the trip home. Dropping the takeout containers from *Millie's* on the sideboard in the kitchen, I did a quick roundtrip to the laundry room to unload my workout gear and restock for practice in the morning, then returned to begin the process of re-warming my dinner. Four cheese lasagna had been the unexpected special of the day, along with a side of dinner rolls brushed with garlic butter; I slid both aluminum containers into my oven and set the timer, then realized I was pretty much out of things to do. With my laptop out of commission and the Red Sox off until Spring Training, I was, literally, alone in an empty house with not much more than a radio for company.

Moving into the living room, I snapped on the small Bose Suzanne had given me the prior Christmas and tuned it to the soft rock station broadcasting from the top of Mount Washington. It was about the only music station I could routinely get in Windeport, save for the all-classical public radio channel out of Portland that happened to have a tower fifteen miles north of town. I thought of myself as more of a contemporary jazz fan, but other than the satellite radio in the SUV, my options were few and far between; running a finger along the small shelf of CDs I'd collected, I considered putting in the latest from Norman Brown but decided I truly wasn't in the mood for something so up-tempo. Sitting down in my favorite recliner, I found myself eying the wireless handset for my landline and decided it was worth the risk to hear my girlfriend's voice, Bartram be damned. Plucking the device from its charger, I dialed Suzanne's number from memory and waited impatiently to hear her lovely voice.

"Hey," she answered. "I'm glad you called; I've just checked into the motel."

"I don't remember many of those in Glenn Hills," I replied.

"Yeah, there aren't any," she sighed. "I'm down in Laconia, the closest place I could fine. Which isn't all bad — the courthouse is here that I need to go to, as well as the lawyer Leslie retained."

"Have you talked to them already?"

"Only to set up an appointment for tomorrow," she said. "That's in the morning, and then I'm going over to the house to check out what's there." Suzanne paused. "I've asked the lawyer to accompany me, as Chief Bartram will also be in attendance."

"Probably wise," I said, still very cognizant of the strange situation we were in. "When do you think you might be back?"

"I'll have a better sense by tomorrow afternoon," she replied. "I've managed to get coverage for the practice through the weekend, but I truly have to be back by Monday at the latest."

"Then I'll make sure your plants at the apartment get watered," I said.

There was a long moment of silence. "Kitty, I've seen what you do to anything green—"

"I didn't say it would be me," I chuckled. "Raphael has something of a gardener's bent, so I thought I'd beg him to do it."

"Oh," Suzanne replied, the relief plain in her voice. "Yeah, that will work."

"I thought it might," I laughed. Just then, the doorbell to my bungalow rang out. "Oops — looks like I have a visitor. I'd better run."

"At this hour?" The concern was equally as plain in her voice now.

"I'm expecting Norm to crash my little pity party with info on the case," I replied. "Can I call in the morning?"

"Only if it's not at that ungodly hour you head to practice," she said.

"Cross my heart. I miss you already, Suze."

"I miss you too, Sean," she said softly. "Virtual hugs and kisses will have to do until I see you again."

"Ditto," I replied as I hung up.

I plunked the handset back down into the charger and pushed myself out of the comfortable recliner, then made my way over to the front door. For whatever reason, despite Major Crimes occupying the very same offices we'd had while I'd been running the Windeport Police Department, it just didn't have the same base-of-operations feel it once had. Much of that was due to the fact the *actual* base of operations was, of course, now in Augusta, underscoring just how much local control I'd ceded with my decision to join the State Police. My optimism at being able to work as I always had within the far larger bureaucracy had faded in direct proportion to the number of video conference calls added to my calendar; by early October, I'd begun to wonder if Captain Roberts had hired me more for my managerial skills than my detective chops. It had gotten so bad, I'd begun to block off sections of my days as a defensive measure just to ensure I had time to actually *be* an investigator; it was also one of the major reasons my senior staff had informally begun dropping by my place on random evenings to talk shop. For whatever reason, they felt far more comfortable doing so at the bungalow than back at the former Public Safety building.

Norm was by far the most regular guest at the bungalow, so I wasn't entirely surprised when I pulled open the door and found him standing on my front porch. What did surprise me was the rather summery shorts-and-sandals look he was sporting, the only nod to the chill of the November evening being a thick sweatshirt bearing the smiling visage of Mickey Mouse. "Hey," he said as he stepped into the living room. "You kind of fell off the radar today."

I smiled a bit sheepishly. "The day got away from me," I said as I closed the door behind him.

Norm looked at me for a long moment as he put his backpack down beside my loveseat. "Did you break your iPhone or something? 'Cause each time I called you, it went straight to voicemail."

"I need to have it looked at," I hedged, though I was certain the slight shading of embarrassment on my cheeks telegraphed my guilty conscience.

Folding his arms against his chest, my number two actually narrowed his eyes at me. "It wouldn't have anything to do with a certain Chief Ryan Bartram, would it?"

"Ah," I replied softly.

"You want to fill me in?"

I looked at him. "Are you sure you want to risk that?" I asked. "If this goes south, I could become far more radioactive than I was after the Professional Standards stupidity."

Norm smiled that boyish smile of his. "I wouldn't have said anything if I was the least bit concerned about that," he said. "Now, what's going on?"

I sighed. "I don't want to ruin your career," I protested. "It might be best—"

"Do you have any beer?" he interrupted as he pulled off his sweatshirt to reveal a technical muscle t-shirt that left very little to the imagination. "We have a lot to talk about, and that was before I found out about the shit you stepped into."

I folded my arms against my chest. "You're sure?"

He smiled again as he moved over to the small dining table I had in the kitchen and pulled out a chair. "Yep," he nodded. "Something smells good, by the way."

"I picked up the special from Millie's on my way back from the pool," I said as I walked over to the stove and cracked the door for a moment. "If you're hungry, I'll split it with you."

"I had a protein shake after the gym," he said as he pulled his MacBook from the backpack and logged in. "But I was serious about the beer."

"All I've got is Sam Adams."

"Perfect."

I took a few minutes to get his beer and then serve up my dinner; at length, I found myself sitting across from him, wondering exactly how to explain myself. "I don't quite know how to begin," I said as I took a forkful of the lasagna.

"I think I know that part," Norm smiled slightly. "You were running an off-the-books, unauthorized investigation into your girlfriend's ex-husband."

"Somehow, it sounds a whole lot *worse* hearing it from you," I sighed.

"It's not great," Norm allowed, "but also not entirely unforgivable.

I've heard the scuttlebutt about how you met Suzanne, and why she'd landed in Windeport in the first place. I also know people in love often do things they would otherwise consider unthinkable."

"That we do," I sighed again.

"You also weren't being terribly discreet, either," Norm continued. "I mean, I fucking handed you the file that came in from the Feds, for Christ's sake."

I smiled slightly. "That you did."

"What did you find out?"

"Hardly anything," I replied as I took a bite from the garlic-butter roll. "The financials were pretty straightforward, and the job history matched what Suzanne had told me. Clean motor vehicle report, no outstanding warrants — the guy was a paragon of society. Aside from how he treated Suzanne, there wasn't any *there* there."

"That must have rankled you."

I shrugged. "I thought maybe I'd missed something, so I dug a bit deeper. Tax records, voting registration, any kind of data our various systems gave me access to." I smiled again. "I came up with exactly bupkis. The guy may be a misogynistic pig, but he pays his bills on time."

"How does Bartram come into the picture?"

"Hammersmith was found dead in his home over the weekend," I replied. "Reading between the lines, I think foul play is suspected."

Norm narrowed his eyes. "And that brings you into the picture because...?"

"I was at a swim meet the next town over," I shrugged.

Those same eyes narrowed further. "That's pretty thin."

"Yeah, but the unauthorized investigation doesn't look great piled on top of my proximity."

"This feels backwards." Swigging from the beer, he pondered for a moment before continuing. "I don't think I've ever heard of a case where the current boyfriend offs the last one to get the girl. I mean, you've *already* got the girl! What would you gain from killing him?"

"I dunno," I sighed. "I suppose it reads like some sort of delayed retribution."

Norm nearly snorted his beer. "*You*? Meting out retribution? Evidently Bartram's never read your file."

"I'll try not to take that as an insult," I huffed, but for the first time I felt a slight weight lift. "But yeah, not really my style, is it?"

"Hardly."

I eyed Norm. "When, *exactly*, did you get access to my file?"

There was some slight satisfaction in seeing the flame on his cheeks. "You might not have been the only one using his new position's access for, uh, personal reasons," he said quietly.

I glared at him for a moment. "I'm hardly one to judge," I replied. "Clearly."

"Clearly," he chuckled. "So, what do you want to do?"

"Avoid Bartram for as long as I can, for starters," I said. "I'd like to get this East Newberry thing settled first if I can."

"That might be hard to do," Norm replied.

Arching an eyebrow, I replied. "He's already reached out to obtain the location data on my iPhone," I said.

"He did," Norm nodded. "Via Captain Roberts."

"Well, shit," I breathed. "That complicates matters."

"Not entirely," Norm smiled. "Captain Roberts is currently indisposed working this statewide manhunt and has been, unfortunately, unable to reply as yet to the request. The same one you are also working, it seems, making you unavailable for the interview they also requested."

I frowned. "That came faster than I expected."

"Look on the bright side," Norm chuckled. "Now we have time to strategize and get you out of this mess."

"*We?*" I asked, feeling a rising concern that this little episode of mine might ensnare good people who had no reason to be involved. "Norm—"

"I'm already in," he replied, cutting me off. "And so is Caitlyn. And, frankly, the entire department up and down the roster."

My eyebrows went up again. Pulling off my beanie, I ran a hand through my out-of-control curls. "Shit. I just finished putting all the pieces back together from my *last* little fiasco. This could end really badly for everyone."

"It won't," Norm said. Sitting back, he drained the last of his beer and then smiled slightly. "The way I see it, we just have to solve the murder of Leslie Hammersmith."

"'Just,' he says," I sighed. "Are you sure? All of you?"

Norm nodded. "You've been there for just about all of us at one point or another," he said softly; his eyes began to glisten slightly, the only nod to his current struggle with HIV. "Let us help you this time."

"I can't ask that."

"You don't need to," he replied with a slight smile. "And we know you well enough to understand you likely never would. We've got this."

I felt a slight smile appear. "Some would say this edges close to insubordination."

"Some would," Norm chuckled as he toyed with his beer bottle. "Any chance you've got another one of these?"

"I do," I said, nodding to the fridge. "Help yourself."

"Thanks." He stood and quickly made the round-trip to the fridge and continued the thread as he retrieved a new beer and twisted off the top. "Caitlyn is already running down some leads, and I've requested full access to what Bartram's already got, in the spirit of knowing *why* he wants to investigate my boss."

"He's not likely to give that to you."

"Maybe not," he replied, "but if he proves to be the pain in the ass I think he's gonna be, then we can go to Roberts."

"Political chess," I sighed again. "Life was so much easier when we only had the Windeport Village Council to contend with."

"Was it, really?" Norm laughed.

"No," I said after a moment. "No, it wasn't," I added as I rolled my neck slightly.

Norm frowned when he saw me wince at a twinge in the muscle. "This is really getting to you, isn't it?"

Polishing off the last of my garlic bread, I wiped my fingers and sat back in my chair. "Somewhat, though it could just as easily be a sore muscle that refuses to heal after the meet."

He frowned deeper. "Didn't you say you got a massage while you were on the deck?"

"Suzanne recommended it," I nodded as I rubbed at the knot in my shoulder that had formed. "It felt indulgent at the time, but I'm also relatively certain I wouldn't have made it through the rest of the meet without it."

"Would've come in handy when I was swimming in college," Norm observed.

"No kidding," I smiled as I continued to roll my neck. "Why don't you distract me from my troubles and bring me up to speed on our *actual* investigation."

"I'll start with the bad news first," Norm said. "Our shooter seems to have melted away like an early spring snowfall. Despite expanding the search perimeter twice, we've not turned up anything — Roberts finally gave the order around two to lift the checkpoints but kept the APB out there. Not that it would do much good, either, for we don't have a description of the shooter, nor do we have any leads on what they might have been driving."

"I might have something on the first part," I said. "I take it the ATM across the street from the Pizzeria was less than helpful, then?"

"You could say that," Norm rolled his eyes. "It took a bit to get the warrant for the video as the machine belongs to one of those out-of-state companies that place ATMS in gas stations and casinos — and charge exorbitant service fees to anyone unfortunate enough to use it. Once I served the warrant, though, we discovered they'd removed the camera as a cost savings measure. Seems it was cheaper to have their insurance cover any possible robberies than pay someone to monitor the video."

"Damn."

"Yeah." Norm tapped at his laptop. "What did the victim tell you? I assume he's the one that got a look at our shooter."

"Not much," I said as I stood and took my dishes to the sink. Running some water, I looked over my shoulder. "The owner claimed to have seen the shooter when they entered; the description was pretty generic."

"Let me guess," Norm started. "Average height, wearing dark clothes?"

"Pretty much," I nodded.

"That's even less helpful than the ATM machine, Sean."

"I try," I chuckled. "Still, part of the description I got from the eyewitness bothered me enough that I drove back to the pizzeria. The owner — his full name is Leon Angelina, by the way — claimed the shooter was as tall as the coatrack in the vestibule of the restaurant."

"That seems like a solid observation," Norm frowned.

"It would be, had there been a clear line of sight from the retail counter to that part of the vestibule. The planters hide most of it."

I watched the gears slowly begin to turn behind Norm's eyes. "You think the owner is lying?"

"I do," I replied.

"For what reason?"

"I wish I knew," I sighed as I put the dishes into my dishwasher. "Part of me wants to chalk it up to the trauma of the experience; it wouldn't be the first time a witness thought they saw something in the heat of the moment evidence later proved hadn't been there."

"I feel like there's a 'but' coming."

"Yeah," I smiled as I dried my hands on a dishtowel, then re-hung it on the front of the oven. "I had Heather take the coatrack off the wall; there were two bullet holes hiding behind it."

Norm's eyes widened. "From the—"

"No," I cut him off with a hand wave. "There was evidence they had been there a while; someone had tried to patch the wallboard — not well, I might add — and then hung the rack over them. I think it was designed to mask their presence."

"How old?"

I thought about that for a moment. "The paint on the wall beneath the coatrack looked to be a match for what was in the rest of the space; my initial impression is the Pizzeria hasn't gotten a lot of love since it opened, save for the vestibule. That seemed fairly recent, actually."

Norm tapped at his computer. "I'll see if we can pull any renovation permits," he said. "And then dive through the financials once we get them. Maybe we'll get lucky and find a five-gallon bucket of paint in there somewhere."

"You never know," I smiled. My eyes drifted down to the Sam Adams sitting beside Norm's laptop; it took but a moment for me to decide to join him, despite having planned on a nice glass of red wine to go with my Italian feast. Grabbing what appeared to be the penultimate bottle from my fridge — damn, now I had to squeeze a grocery run in at some point on top of everything else — I popped open my beverage and returned to the table. "I found a second surprise at the pizzeria, by the way."

Norm rolled his eyes. "Of course you did. Someday soon, I hope you teach me this dark magic you use to solve all of your cases."

"It's not magic," I replied a bit defensively. "I just poke at things until they begin to make sense."

"You go right on telling yourself that," he laughed. "The rest of us will continue believing you have some sort of deal with the devil."

"If I did have such a bargain, I wish I'd gotten better terms. Being indirectly accused of murder doesn't sit too well."

"Sounds pretty typical for the devil, actually. He can be pretty squirrelly with those bargains," he smiled. "Lay your surprise on me."

"I sat in on most of the postmortem Lou did on the body that was found in the rear stock room," I said. "The one with cufflinks."

"And the backwards apron?"

"Yeah," I nodded. "Turns out, the victim is some sort of finance guy from Boston."

"That's... weird," Norm frowned. "So, not a cook?"

"Nope. And also not killed on Monday."

Norm's beer was halted halfway to his mouth. "Say *what*?"

"It gets better," I assured him. "We already knew the on-site estimate of TOD was affected by how cold the rear room was; Lou did a bit of newfangled science and came up with a TOD that points to the guy being shot as early as Sunday morning. The test is fairly new and likely not admissible in court, but it does help explain what we found."

"Shit," Norm breathed. "Are you actually thinking someone *placed* him back there to try and make it look like the shooter killed him?"

"Yeah," I nodded. "And I think I found where the body was stored until that point; there's a drawer in the walk-in fridge that's just big enough for the task. I left Heather swabbing for DNA."

"That's... that's just making my brain hurt," Norm said. "I mean, it's either the most unbelievable confluence of circumstances, ever, or—"

"Someone is using a mass shooting as cover for a murder," I finished for him. "Exactly."

Norm ran his hands through his thick hair. "Wouldn't that imply whoever killed cufflink guy knew in advance the shooting was going to happen?" he asked thoughtfully.

"Yes. Brings a whole new meaning to premeditated, doesn't it?"

"No shit." Norm looked at me for a long moment. "You really think we're dealing with a murder on top of a mass shooting?"

"Lou said the bullets that killed our victim are a smaller caliber than what was used in the restaurant proper."

My partner began to massage his forehead. "Yep. I feel a *massive* headache coming on."

"And here you thought coming to Windeport would lead to a nice, quiet career in law enforcement," I smiled.

"Hardly. I'll have the team start to look at that angle in the morning; Lou's results are in the case system, I presume?"

"Probably, but my laptop is DOA so I couldn't tell you." When Norm arched an eyebrow, I shrugged sheepishly. "No, it's really dead. I have an appointment with the Apple Store tomorrow to get it straightened out."

"You must feel like you've lost a body part."

Well aware of my reputation as a Steve Jobs acolyte, I smiled slightly. "Any other updates from the scene?"

"Yeah," Norm nodded. "With help from the Medical Examiner's office, we've got tentative IDs on the majority of the adults; the children will take longer, but we can make some informed guesses in the interim. We'll still need official identifications from next of kin, of course." Tapping at his keyboard, he looked at me over the lid. "I've never had to do so many notifications at once."

"There's a protocol, but it doesn't make it any easier." I paused. "Fortunately, we won't have to do it alone; unlike Windeport, the State has the resources to make sure a grief counselor is present."

"Not sure that makes me feel any better," Norm said.

"Yeah," I replied after a moment.

"Anyway, we seem to have quite the eclectic mix of East Newberry residents," he continued. "At least two families were having what they thought would be a quiet night out, along with a handful of senior citizens; the teens in that one booth were members of the regional high school basketball team." Norm tapped at the laptop again. "Our best guess is that the youngest victim was twelve- to eighteen-months, with the oldest being fairly close to eighty"

"Wow," I breathed as I slowly shook my head in disbelief. "Was there anything in particular connecting the patrons Monday night?"

"Other than it being two-for-one on pizzas?" Norm asked. "Nothing that jumped out at me. Just based on the addresses we were able to run down on the victims, none were clustered; save for our mystery guest in the rear stockroom, everyone — including who we think were the hired help — lived less than five miles from the pizzeria."

"The way you said that makes me think we've not gotten the employment records yet."

"We haven't, no," Norm said. "With the owner still in the ICU, there seems to have been a reluctance to serve the warrant."

My eyebrows went up. "Not by Captain Roberts."

"I got the sense it was further up the food chain," Norm replied.

"Ah," I nodded, thinking I knew who had killed the request. "I guess it could be bad optics to have a uniformed official demanding access from the last remaining eyewitness. Screw it. Track down our contact at the Revenue office and see if you can back into that information from the tax filings for Pizzeria Angelina. I'd like to rule out our stockroom corpse once and for all."

"Can do," Norm said.

"What else can you tell me about the business?"

"I'm still digging through the financials," Norm admitted. "So not much beyond top-level stuff. Leon Angelina is listed as the current owner of the pizzeria; he apparently co-owned the business with his wife until she disappeared in 1988. It's somewhat profitable, which is rather amazing considering the state of East Newberry itself. I also had a look at the employment—"

"Hang on," I interrupted. "His wife *disappeared*?"

Norm nodded. "I did manage to track down the missing persons report Leon filed; East Newberry P.D. handled the initial investigation before passing it on to the State." Norm tapped at his screen for a moment. "Here it is — Leon's statement was that Beryl had gone to visit her kid in Massachusetts and never came back."

"Weird," I murmured. "Leon said he was a widower."

"I suppose in a sense he is," Norm said. "I mean, according to the file, Beryl was declared legally 'dead' in 2008."

"Huh," I said, turning the semantics around in my brain and feeling like something was hiding out on the periphery.

Norm waited patiently for a moment. "That seems to be bothering you for some reason."

"Yeah," I said thoughtfully. "Did they search the river?"

My number two arched an eyebrow at the non sequitur. "If they did, the results are in the case file."

I nodded. "Let's roll the divers, then. Have them do a preliminary search a mile up and two miles downstream."

"What are you expecting them to find?" Norm asked as he tapped away at his keyboard.

"I haven't a clue," I sighed. "Other than a gut instinct that our shooter — or our killer — might have used the convenience of the Penobscot to dispose of something incriminating."

"Sean," Norm began carefully, "I might not be the brightest bulb when it comes to hydrology, but I'm relatively certain the river has something of a current through that part of East Newberry. It's highly unlikely anything dumped behind the pizzeria would still be in the vicinity."

"All true," I replied.

He rolled his eyes. "I'll make some calls, but I really don't think—"

Something Norm said earlier had me putting up a finger. "Did you say it was two-for-one pizzas?"

"Yes," he nodded, nonplussed slightly at my rather disjointed interruption. "At least, according to the small sign in the window."

"I must have missed that. But on a *Monday*?"

Norm shrugged. "Maybe they were trying to drum up business on an otherwise slow day. For what it's worth, there was a deli my ex liked in Portland that always marked down classic Italian sandwiches on Tuesdays."

"To draw in traffic," I said thoughtfully. "I wonder if it was a one-time thing or ongoing."

"Would it make a difference?" Norm asked.

"Quite a bit," I replied. "Ongoing means the shooter might have known it would be busy."

"This just gets better and better," Norm frowned as he tapped away at his computer. "I'll dig through what I can. Maybe I'll get lucky and find something on the internet."

"Pizzeria Angelina feels like a place that might have done more traditional advertising," I observed. "If East Newberry doesn't have a local paper, I'd be willing to bet there's one of those semi-regional shopping rags that might have carried it. I'd bet even *more* that Charlie has a copy of it at the Windeport Public Library."

"Then I'll swing through there first thing in the morning," Norm said. "Unless you want to catch up with your cousin instead."

"I've got to get out early for my trip to Portland, unfortunately. I'm not even going to make swim practice."

Norm's eyebrows went up. "That's not like you."

I shrugged. "I was at the mercy of the Apple Gods," I said, which was mostly true. "Since I'm already halfway to Boston by then, I'll probably head down to see if I can talk to someone at First Beacon about Kirk Nevelson."

"Do you want me to call ahead and set up something?"

"Thanks, but I have a sense I'll get more out of them if they don't know a detective is on the way."

"What if they don't want to talk to you?"

I smiled slightly. "I can be very persuasive when necessary."

"That," Norm said as he closed the lid to his laptop, "is quite true. That's all I've got for now; I'm off to fall into the arms of my boyfriend. I'll touch base with you in the morning."

"Sounds good. Thanks for popping in," I said, then paused for a moment. "Despite the fact I still think you might be throwing your career away to help me, I... well, thank you for offering to help me dig out. It means quite a lot."

"It's the least I can do," he replied with his boyish smile. "Get some rest."

"I could say the same," I said, "though I have a sense your evening might just be getting underway."

The smile went a bit wider. "You could say that."

EIGHT

I'd done the round-trip to Portland so many times over the years that I'd begun to wish the promise of self-driving vehicles had come to pass. The endless miles of pine tree-lined highway had a way of putting you into a catatonic state if you weren't careful, something not terribly conducive to operating a vehicle at speeds over eighty miles per hour. Vasily had used the monotony as an excuse to get me to upgrade the fleet of vehicles in Windeport to include satellite radio; I'd taken the same tact with Roberts when he'd begun the process of requisitioning new SUVs for Major Crimes. There had been some good-natured grumbling that the rank-and-file troopers didn't get such luxuries, but it was also not lost on me that the shiny new vehicle Roberts seemed to have suddenly acquired shortly after my hiring just happened to include the same feature.

That early morning, though, I found myself restlessly cycling through the presets on the radio, unable to commit to one of the many favorites I'd programmed into the device. My tastes generally ran to the jazz end of the spectrum, but even the smooth rhythms from the contemporary jazz station seemed just as flat as the dashed yellow lines running down the center of the pavement. When nothing to suit my fancy had appeared by the time I'd turned onto the southbound inter-state, I gave up entirely and settled in with only the sound of the air whistling around the SUV as my traveling companion.

About forty miles north of Augusta, I found myself truly missing all of the hours I'd spent driving with Vasily; as I figuratively put more distance between the time when he'd been an inseparable part of my life and the new reality I was currently living, those moments we'd had together had become cherished memories — and an unpleasant reminder of just how much had changed since. Not seeing him every day had been, admittedly, something that had taken far too long to adjust to; I was thankful that we still talked regularly in some form, but a quick text message would never be a replacement for catching the sly smile on my best friend's face as he ribbed me about something stupid. I'm not certain I'd understood the full definition of unconditional friendship before Vasily had decamped to California; now that he was gone, I had the full measure of what I had clearly taken for granted. It had also crystallized just how important *all* of my relationships were — and why I'd become far more diligent about being there for the people in my life that I truly cared about.

Thinking about Vasily reminded me that I had a call scheduled with his fiancé, Alejandro Ortega-Cortez, on Thursday; the two of us had been secretly plotting a wedding extravaganza I was far from certain Vasily hadn't already gotten wind of. If he *had*, he'd done a pretty good job of playing along with us, which if true, was totally on brand for my friend. Alex and I had a minor crisis to work through, for the venue we'd originally selected had suddenly become unavailable; considering how close we were to the date, finding a suitable replace-ment was going to be difficult if nearly impossible, so the plan was to sort through our list of Hail Marys and decide which we could live with. (If the decision had been up to me, the duo would have been exchanging their vows on the deck of the pool that had been used for the 1984 Los Angeles Olympics; while I'd pitched it as being appro-priate for two decorated athletes, Alex had tactfully informed me the venue didn't quite exist as it had back in 1984 and shelved the idea. Permanently.)

My introspection wound down as the pine forest finally gave way to farmland; residential neighborhoods quickly sprouted and became ever denser the closer I drew to Portland. When the spires of downtown — such as they were — finally appeared on the horizon, I became mired in the late rush hour traffic that tended to clog the stretch of I-295 that hugged Back Bay. Judging from the exposed mud flats, the tide appeared to be out at the moment, allowing a flock of seagulls unparalleled access to the shellfish hiding just below the muck. The slash of off-white from the birds seemed especially stark against the earth-colored exposed seabed; I spied a batch of runners trying to sneak in a workout prior to reporting to the office making the three-mile circuit around the inner bay and then shifted my gaze briefly to the rearview mirror and very top of the swim backpack sitting behind me. Enormous mountains of guilt always descended upon me when I missed a session at the pool, a call-back perhaps to the nasty consequences wreaked upon us by Coach for failing to report to practice on time. I wasn't sure there would be time for little more than a short run that day, but as the backpack proudly proclaimed, hope sprung eternal.

Per usual, traffic became even more snarled just after the Forest Avenue exit; for such a small city, Portland nonetheless seemed to experience all the worst aspects of being an urban corridor. As I crawled across the bridge over the Fore River, I watched in some amazement as a commercial passenger jet made its final descent into the Jetport; the blues and reds of the Southwest Airlines paint scheme popped against what was turning out to be a thickly overcast morning, overcast in a way that made me concerned I'd not packed a heavier jacket or the thermal gloves Suzanne had given me the prior Christmas. It wasn't unheard of to get a blanket of snow at that part of the season, but a significant part of me simply wasn't ready to transition to the long gray winter we often endured.

Shifting lanes, I managed to get off at the Maine Mall exit without smashing into anyone; coasting down the offramp, my stomach rumbled loudly enough to register on the Richter scale. Eyeing the clock on the dashboard, I confirmed I didn't have as much of a margin as I'd hoped for and was sadly forced to bypass the siren call of the Dunkin Donuts sign in favor of getting to my appointment on time. At that hour of the day, the massive parking lot surrounding the Maine Mall was relatively empty, so locating a spot close to the entrance I needed proved to be fairly easy; grabbing the backpack with the offending laptop out of the rear of the SUV, I locked up and then strode across the pavement to the doors, zipping up my fleece pullover in a futile attempt to keep out the chill of the morning. Despite it being a short jaunt, I was thoroughly chilled by the time the warmth of the interior embraced me, another sign that I had misjudged the weather. In Maine, it was always something of a crapshoot anyway, so I shrugged off the worst of it and headed down the wide corridor to the sleek exterior housing the Apple Store.

Like most malls outside of the ones I'd visited in Southern California, it was hard to ignore the number of store fronts that had been covered over with glossy ads promising a reinvigorated retail experience; at the rate the merchants appeared to be leaving, I had a sense the place was destined to become a mixed-use space. Then again, I had read somewhere that despite the massive shellacking traditional brick-and-mortar stores had taken from online behemoths over the past few decades, people born at the millennium or beyond seemed to be fueling a resurgence of in-person shopping; glancing at the glossy overlay on another empty storefront I was passing, it felt a bit like Maine was once more behind the curve. I wasn't terribly surprised then to find the space extremely quiet save for the silver-haired set getting their steps in before breaking (presumably) for a hand or two of pinochle prior to lunch. A stray custodian popped up here or there, dusting the fake plants or emptying the various trash containers stationed at irregular intervals; completing the atmosphere was an unnaturally upbeat pop soundtrack washing over everything from unseen speakers in the ceiling. I had no idea what artist I was currently being subjected to but had to admit the reverberating baseline wasn't half bad.

Rounding a corner, I worked my way through a garden of vending carts before arriving beneath the tastefully understated sign illuminated with the logo of my favorite computer. I was a little surprised at the paid security guard that nodded at me as I walked inside, and even more shocked to see the place was packed. It took me a moment to locate one of the Apple employees, but when I did, it seemed as though the retail smile being trained on me was somewhat strained.

"Morning," the young man said. He was dressed in the standard black t-shirt and jeans ensemble I assumed was the de facto uniform for the store. "How can I help you?"

"I've got an appointment at the Genius Bar," I replied as I shifted the backpack. "My MacBook seems to have gone into a coma."

"Ah," he said as he looked down at the tablet in his hands. "What's your name?"

"Sean Colbeth."

"Here you are," he nodded. "One second while I check you in…"

"No problem," I said. "Place seems quite busy for a Wednesday."

He looked up and smiled. "Actually, this is pretty normal."

If you want to see *busy*, come the day after we release a new iPhone or computer. That's when this place looks like a mosh pit."

"Wow," was all I could think to say.

"Exactly," he laughed. "Head on back. Philipe will grab you once he's wrapped up his current appointment."

"Thanks."

Readjusting my backpack again, I charted a course through the throngs toward the elevated service desk at the rear of the store; I tried very hard to ignore the long table I passed trumpeting the latest edition of the iPhone despite my inner sixteen-year-old desperately screaming my current trusty device wasn't quite as cool. To my dismay, they were stacked four deep at the genius counter; with no way to know exactly how long I would have to wait, I managed to snag an open chair at a nearby display counter and dropped the back-pack to my feet. With my phone still off and locked in the glovebox of my SUV, I was reduced to people watching and would have quickly lost interest in even *that* had my attention not been attracted to an elderly woman standing just a few feet away. Leaning on the Genius Bar as though she were a regular patron at a local watering hole, the frowning expression on her face as the tattooed twenty-something on the other side tried to explain something to her told me it wasn't going well. Oddly curious about her reason for being there, I surreptitiously slid my chair a bit closer and strained a bit to hear the conversation.

"But the message said I had a virus," she stated flatly.

"And you have a malware software package installed," the employee said. "I've run the scan three times since you arrived and there is actually nothing to be found."

"But—"

"Most pop-ups like that are scams," the clerk said cutting her off but doing it with a smile and just enough gentleness she didn't seem to be taking it as the rebuke it was. "Especially on social media sites."

"But—"

"You did the right thing," he continued as he slowly shut the lid on her laptop. It seemed clear the appointment was winding down, whether the customer realized it or not. "By not clicking on the link, you didn't fall for the scam and pay for a bogus piece of software that would have likely itself been the very malware the message was warning you about. Closing out the browser shut down the JavaScript and solved the problem."

The woman didn't look convinced but seemed unwilling (or unable) to argue the point. "So nothing is wrong?"

"Nothing at all," the clerk smiled again. "If you do run into anything, though, you can come right back and see me again, Mrs. Hamilton."

"I *will* come back if there is."

"I'd expect nothing less," he said, again with a sweetness that belied some definite snark.

"Then until next time, Philipe."

The twenty-something watched with interest as Mrs. Hamilton carefully slid her Mac into a tote bag bearing the logo of the statewide public radio station, then glanced at his tablet before scanning the room. His eyes met mine almost instantly, and at my slight nod, he moved over to stand at the edge of the display table perpendicular to where I was sitting. "You must be Sean Colbeth?" he asked.

"I am," I replied as I reached for his hand and shook it. "I happened to catch the end of your last appointment; I take it she's a frequent flyer?"

Philipe rolled his eyes. "She's in at least twice a month," he sighed. "And, unfortunately, always asks for me."

Hearing something in his tone, I looked at him askance. "Not because she's a fan, I take it."

"No," he smiled before tactfully changing the subject. "What seems to be the problem?"

I pulled out my laptop, set it on the surface of the table and flipped the lid open; in seconds, the same exclamation icon I'd seen earlier popped up. "This," I said simply as I waved at the screen.

Philipe twisted the laptop in his direction and immediately began chewing on his lip. "Oh, shit."

My eyebrows went up. "As technical diagnoses go, that sounds particularly bad."

His eyes went to mine, and a slight shading to his fair complexion appeared; only then did I realize his short-cropped hair had been dyed jet black. "Sorry," he said sheepishly. "It's already been a long morning, and if this is what I think it is, it's likely to get longer. Do you have AppleCare on this?"

"I'm not certain," I frowned. "The office bought this for me back in September—"

"Then it will still be under warranty, at least," the clerk said. "Look, I'll be totally honest here: if you had anything of value on this machine, it's probably toast. At the very least, I'm going to have to rebuild the hard drive, though there is an excellent chance we'll have to send it out for repairs."

"Seriously?" I said, my surprise evident in my voice. "I've used Apple MacBooks for years and never had a problem before."

"It does happen," Philipe allowed without elaborating. "If you want to proceed, I'll get the paperwork ready."

"What are we talking, timewise?"

"Two hours if I can do it here, three days if I have to send it out."

"I don't suppose you have a loaner program?" I asked with a wry smile. "I'm not local, so getting back here could be a problem if it takes longer than a few hours."

"No, we don't," he replied. "But we can ship it to back to you, assuming the address on file for you is accurate."

"It is," I replied. "Let's do it."

"Okay, give me a moment to get the intake work done," he said as he began tapping at his tablet.

"Sure." I glanced toward the entrance and smiled slightly to see that Mrs. Hamilton hadn't made it very far; she seemed to be deep in discussion with one of the salespeople standing beside a massive prop version of an iPad. "I wonder what sort of website she was visiting when that virus warning came up," I murmured thoughtfully.

"Who clicked what?" Philipe asked.

I turned toward him. "Oh, sorry," I smiled. "That was more for me than you."

He looked up and saw Mrs. Hamilton in the distance and then seemed to understand what I'd asked. "My father had a name for someone like Mrs. Hamilton," Philipe said after lowering his voice. "Are you familiar with the term 'tin foil hat?'"

"I am," I smiled. "So she's something of a conspiracy nut?"

"Big time. If the browser history I saw was accurate, she'd been on a blog detailing some sort of cabal being run out of a pizza parlor upstate that specialized in child sex trafficking."

I felt both my brow furrow and my stomach twist simultaneously. "Like that pizza gate thing down in New York?"

"Pretty much," he nodded as he returned to the tablet.

"Upstate, you said?" I asked, feeling like I had stumbled into something important.

"I think so," he replied. "An old mill town along the Penobscot," he added before turning the tablet toward me. "Make sure we have your accurate phone and shipping address, then sign here."

"Sure." I paused for a moment, then pulled my badge out of my pocket. "I hate to ask this, but would you be willing to help me get a look at that site?"

Philipe's eyes went wide at the appearance of my badge. "Am I in some kind of trouble?"

"Far from it," I smiled. "I think you might have just inadvertently given me a break in my case."

NINE

"The woman is truly nuts," I said, "but as you can see, the site is very real."

"Shit," Norm replied.

I was sitting in my SUV, parked in the public lot just in front of DiMillo's floating restaurant. My particular spot happened to be facing in the general direction of the long pier that served as home for the various Casco Bay ferries and the more-than-occasional cruise ship. Based on the direction the various boats moored between myself and the pier were pointed, it looked like the tide had finally turned; glancing toward the restaurant itself, I could see the gangways leading to the ship appeared to be leveling out. Dropping my eyes back to the iPhone in my hands, I replayed the miniature debate I'd had about turning it back on again and wondered if I'd made the right decision. The number of missed calls from a New Hampshire area code had me thinking maybe not.

"Whoever posted that page specifically identified Pizzeria Angelina as the hub of operations for this mythical cabal," I continued. "Despite how ludicrous the notion is, the traffic on this blog post is high enough to make me think it got noticed."

"You think our shooter saw this?"

"I think we need to consider the possibility," I replied. "But I also want to know who posted this in the first place. In the absence of having our suspect in custody, they might be able to answer some motivation questions for us."

Norm paused. "Whomever they are, they had quite the axe to grind. This is nothing but vitriol of the highest order."

"I caught that too," I said. "It's almost *too* over the top, actually."

"Yeah," he said after a moment. "I can run it past our Federal colleagues and see if it tracks with any known hate groups. Maybe we will get lucky."

"Maybe. In the meantime, get the technical service nerds at the crime lab to track down what service is hosting this shit, and who owns it."

"Can do. Are you heading to Boston now?"

"Not immediately. There's a slim chance I might be able to retrieve my MacBook before I head further south, so I'm hanging out until I hear otherwise."

"I can't picture you aimlessly wandering the halls of the Maine Mall," Norm chuckled. "You don't strike me as the type to paw through comic books or feed quarters into the arcade games."

"Maybe I have a hidden thing for kitchen gadgets," I replied as I watched some sort of heron deftly swoop down from nowhere to alight upon a navigation buoy. For whatever reason, I felt uncomfortable revealing I was using the time to meet with my lawyer.

"That will be the day. If you get too late of a start you'll likely not find anyone at First Beacon," Norm observed.

"True," I replied. "Push comes to shove, I'll stay over and hit them in the morning. I'll let you know either way."

"Okay," he replied. "Safe travels."

"Thanks."

Hanging up, I stared at the face of my iPhone for a long moment before sliding the possibly traitorous device into a pocket; grabbing my backpack, I locked up the SUV and then wandered toward the gangway. The lunch hour appeared to be in full swing, though, forcing me to cool my heels for a bit before the hostess finally seated me at a table for two beneath a tall window looking out onto the bay. The amazing vista was quite different than the one from my back porch, for Windeport Harbor had only a handful of islands to block the horizon; Casco Bay, on the other hand, was well-stocked with them, making the otherwise endless expanse of ocean swells seem somehow bounded and cloistered. As overcast as the day had continued to be, the sea had taken on that dark quality that often presaged a nasty winter storm; for the second time that day, I found myself thinking I might well be ankle-deep in the white stuff by the time I'd finished my little foray to Massachusetts.

Turning my attention to the menu, I'd barely gotten through the extensive list of appetizers before movement across the dining room caught my eye; looking up, I saw the familiar form of Arabella Steinman working her way toward me. She was dressed in a pant suit in a dark conservative color, a style I had come to think of as typical lawyer; an overcoat was hanging off one arm, while a massive satchel made from dark leather was on the other. Arabella smiled as she reached our table and paused at the edge to allow the waiter who had materialized out of nowhere to take her jacket.

"Sean," she said as she settled in across from me. "I know better than to ask how you're doing."

"Arabella," I smiled in return. "Astute as usual. How was your seminar?"

"It sucked, frankly," she sighed before waving to the waiter.

"Madam?" he asked once he appeared table side.

"Whisky sour on the rocks," she said before putting a finger to her chin. "Better make it a double," she added before looking at me. "That's the only way I'm going get through the afternoon. What are you drinking?"

"I was thinking of coffee," I replied. "I have to drive to Boston after this."

Frowning, Arabella turned back to the expectant waiter. To my eye, he looked all of twenty, but then again, the older I got, the more *everyone* younger than me seemed like a teenager. "Do you have Samuel Adams on draft?"

"Yes," the waiter nodded.

"Then a beer for my dining companion, please." Arabella looked at me after the waiter departed. "This is on me, by the way; order whatever you like. I can write it off as a business expense."

"And bill it back to me, too," I smiled.

"Indeed," she laughed. "The very definition of a win-win." Arabella leaned over and rummaged around in her satchel for a moment before coming up with a small portfolio bound in a similarly colored leather. "I did some preliminary digging before class this morning," she said as she opened the pad and began scanning the yellow-lined paper. "I don't imagine Bartram told you how Hammersmith died?"

"No," I replied. "I wouldn't typically reveal that to a suspect unless we were in the final stages of the investigation and were using that information as a way to corroborate our evidentiary trail."

"That's what I assumed," she said before squinting at her hand-written notes. "Damn this lighting," she swore before returning to the satchel and retrieving a pair of cheaters; sliding them onto her nose, she squinted again at the page. "The postmortem revealed Hammersmith died from blunt-force trauma to the head."

My eyebrows went up. "How did you—"

"Probably best you don't ask that right now," Arabella interrupted. "The important thing is that there was evidence the trauma wasn't entirely self-inflicted."

"Not *entirely*?"

"The coroner thinks there was a killing blow from behind," she nodded. "The trauma was substantial, though, so they can't rule out a fall, either."

My brain clicked into full investigator mode. "DNA?"

"Yes," she nodded. "Recovered from the scene; presumably from whomever administered the aforementioned killing blow."

I felt my heart begin to race. "I'm not a match," I said.

"No," she said with a slight smile. "As you correctly intuited, they ran the sample through the usual databases when it was collected; I'm assuming at some point, you had to provide an elimination sample for a case you were working, and that was pulled in automatically. The donor at this point remains unknown."

A massive wave of relief washed over me, though I also immediately felt rather silly; the way Bartram had clearly rattled me underscored how easily someone could be coerced into admitting guilt where none existed. Still, I felt myself frowning. "When did the DNA results come in?"

"Well before Bartram called you, if that's what you really want to know," Arabella said. She paused long enough for our waiter to drop off our drinks before continuing. "I'm a little unclear as to his motivation for fingering you based on the thinnest of circumstantial evidence, unless he's actually going after someone else."

It took a full minute for me to digest the meaning behind what Arabella had said. "What did you say the gender of the DNA recovered was?"

"I didn't, but it was biologically female," she replied quietly.

Shit, I thought as my mind began to race. *Shit!*

"Suzanne was with you that entire weekend, right?" Arabella asked.

"Yes," I said after a moment. "But if you are about to ask if I can vouch as her alibi, I spent a healthy amount of time in the water competing. I would be the first to tell you just how much flexibility she had to slip out of the stands while I was occupied."

"Then we have a new problem," she said. "For I think it's far more likely Bartram is going after Suzanne." Glancing at her portfolio, she flipped a page up and scanned the text. "Especially since she stands to inherit a rather sizable fortune from her ex-husband."

"She *what*?"

Arabella looked at me over the top of her half-moon cheaters. "Between the house, life insurance and investments, Hammersmith had a portfolio valued north of six million dollars," she said. "I was able to pull his filing with the probate court to confirm that she's both the executor *and* sole beneficiary."

My eyes went wide. "That's incredible. Suzanne never mentioned he was so wealthy; in fact, the way he treated their finances while they were together made me think he'd been squandering the cash he'd taken from her."

"Quite the opposite, it would seem," Arabella said. "I'd have to get a look at his finances to be sure, but I've seen this sort of thing before in relationships where one partner dominates the other. The income isn't necessarily pooled so much as used to bankroll particular activities. In this case, I'd say Suzanne's ex was using her money as though she were some sort of credit line that he'd never have to pay back."

I felt my heart sink. "And if Suzanne knew what was going on at the time, or found out later what happened, she might have decided killing her ex-husband was almost righteous."

"We have to assume that's the angle from which Bartram is going to attack this," Arabella said softly. "And now we know he has the motive, on top of the means and opportunity."

"Suzanne didn't do this," I said firmly.

"You've told me yourself she was psychologically abused by her partner," Arabella reminded me. "If this gets to a court, and the DNA is hers, there's not much any defense attorney could do other than try to plead out for a lesser sentence."

"It won't belong to Suzanne. It wasn't her."

"Unless you can provide me with another suspect to point Bartram toward, it doesn't look good."

"I'm already working on that," I replied. "I might have something before too long."

"I suspected as much," she smiled.

I looked at her. "Can I assume from the way you are talking you've already decided to take Suzanne on as client?"

"I have," she said as she closed the portfolio. "Assuming she wants me."

"I don't think that will be an issue," I replied. "I'll call her tonight and—*oh, fuck*," I breathed as I closed my eyes in agony. "Suzanne went to New Hampshire to deal with the estate."

Arabella closed the portfolio and took her cheaters off. "That complicates matters a bit," she said as she threw both into her satchel and then waved for the waiter. "Bartram is likely to arrest her on the spot. I'll leave now and see how much damage has been done."

"I'll go with you—"

"No, you won't," Arabella said firmly. "I don't need a love-blinded law enforcement official under foot while I try to sort this thing out."

I felt an eyebrow arch. "Are you saying I'm not capable of handling this in an unemotional way?"

"Most definitely," she smiled. "And why would you be expected to? This one cuts a bit too close to home for you, I think."

"Yeah," I nodded slowly after a moment. "Yeah, I suppose it does. I can't guarantee I won't show up anyway."

"Sean," Arabella started, her eyes locked onto mine. "You need to do this my way."

While my heart was saying something else, I slowly nodded again and tried to hide how my fingers were crossed under the table. *Not that I'm fooling her in the least,* I thought as I watched a knowing smile appear on her face. "All right," I said as the waiter finally materialized. "No lunch then, I take it?"

Downing the rest of her whisky sour, Arabella shook her head. "No. I've got to head back to the law school and arrange coverage so I can get to New Hampshire."

Arabella paid the tab and then vanished in a flurry of fabric and leather, leaving me alone with my whirling thoughts. After reviewing the menu two more times, I realized I wasn't all that hungry myself.

Downing the last of my beer, I left a few bucks on the table as my tip contribution and then exited back out into the bracingly cold afternoon air. Standing in the parking lot, I pulled out my iPhone and then tried to call Suzanne; unsurprisingly, it went straight to voicemail. I hesitated for a moment before sending her a quick text message; when no reply seemed forthcoming, I feared the worst and popped over to the Find My function. Sure enough, her phone appeared to be switched off; while it was possible she'd done that as a result of our earlier conversation about tracking, it seemed like far more likely something else was going on.

Still, it felt best to play my cards close to my vest and proceed as though I knew none of what had transpired; besides, Arabella was in a far better position to untangle everything than me. While patience was a strong suit of mine, knowing someone I loved was in trouble was making me eager to jump into the fight — a move my investigator brain reminded me would probably hurt her more than anything at that particular junction. Shaking my head, I walked back to my SUV and got in; after doing a quick check to ensure I'd not gotten a call back from the Apple Store, I bowed to the inevitable, started up the SUV and then pulled out of my spot. Boston now had to be my priority, for better or worse.

I'd barely paid the eye-popping parking fee and pulled out onto Commercial Street before my phone went off; triggering the Bluetooth function, I smiled slightly when I saw the number. "Detective Sergeant."

The laugh of my former ace admin and now lead detective on many a case filled the cabin. "Hey boss," Caitlyn Romero said. "Norm said you weren't using your phone."

"Fuck that," I replied.

"Tell me how you *really* feel," she laughed again. "Got a moment?"

"I do," I answered. "I'm on my way to Boston and have plenty of time to kill. What's up?"

"Norm passed to me that awful blog post you discovered this morning," she replied. "Oddly, it had also surfaced in some background work I'd done on the pizzeria."

My eyebrows went up. "How so?"

"How much do you know about trolls on the internet?" she asked.

"Only what I've read in the research from the Feds," I replied.

"Then I will spare you the basics and move on to the good stuff," she continued. "I was originally digging into the strange pizza deal you focused in on; as it turns out, you were correct in assuming ads were placed in a small shopping newspaper. Charlie had copies in Windeport."

"I figured she would."

"Here's the odd part: she has two years of papers, and the deal only began to appear six weeks ago. I had to go online to the State Library in Augusta to confirm my instinct that Pizzeria Angelina had never advertised before that point."

"Ever?"

"Not in print," she confirmed. "I went through back issues of the *Bangor Daily*, *Lewiston Journal* and *Portland Press Herald.* Aside from occasional articles written about the place — did you know President Bush swung through back in 1989? — there is absolutely nothing, advertising or otherwise."

"Until six weeks ago?"

"Yep."

I tapped at my steering wheel. "That was, what, September?"

"Just after Labor Day, yes. And then weekly through this week. I've got a call into the publisher of this rag — it's the *Casco Current*, if you truly want to know — to see if there is a reservation beyond that, but haven't heard back yet. I think they are a small mom-and-pop operation."

"Likely. But where's the overlap with the blog post?"

"That's where this gets interesting," Caitlyn replied. "When I did a web search for Pizzeria Angelina and the special Monday deal, I hit on the online version of the ad; unfortunately, the software the *Casco*

Current uses is pretty generic newspaper stuff, allowing comments to every article or ad. And that's where I saw the first angry post about the pizzeria being a front for child sex trafficking."

"One comment?" I asked as I merged onto I-295 and began heading south.

"Hardly. There are *pages* of this stuff for *every* appearance of the ad. It's clear that someone was targeting the pizzeria; quite a number of the comments included a link that matched the one you sent Norm." She paused. "I think the person behind the blog post was stirring up trouble, though I'm not entirely certain why."

"My thoughts exactly," I said. "Any frequent flyers on the comments? Either on the ads or the blog?"

"I've not fully read everything," Caitlyn said. "I'm going to pull in some help to get through them. You would not believe how many we have to dig through."

"I might," I sighed. "Good work and let me know if you see a pattern."

"I will. I've also got a call into the hosting firm for the blog; technical services were able to do a reverse lookup on the site and it's being run on servers managed by a company in Bangor."

"We'll need a warrant—"

"Already in progress," she said. "Judge promised to have it to me by this evening."

"Well done," I smiled. "Call me once you have a name."

"Will do. And good luck in Boston."

"Thanks," I said. "Hopefully it will unravel something."

"You wouldn't be headed down there if you didn't think it would," Caitlyn observed.

I smiled. "True, that. Talk to you later."

TEN

The thought of the meal I'd been denied at DiMillo's weighed on me enough that I decided I needed an emergency seafood fix shortly after crossing over into New Hampshire. Years earlier I'd stumbled upon a hole-in-the-wall clam shack while working a case in Portsmouth, one that catered to the round-the-clock shift workers from the sprawling naval shipyard that was the heart of the community. Truth be told, I had a terrible weakness for anything deep fried; to my everlasting delight, the shack offered a wide variety of seafood covered in the delectable breading that was only found in New England. The investigation had been a gruesome one, made tolerable only in the knowledge a healthy portion of freshly cooked shrimp piled high on hand-cut French fries awaited me at the end of each long day.

My order of fried scallops with a side of freshly baked rolls wasn't nearly as refined as what I'd thought I'd be having for lunch that day, but the spectacular view of the Atlantic from where I parked the SUV along the shore while I ate was, arguably, far better than the marina I'd been facing at the restaurant. Snarfing down the meal before the scent of grease could completely fill the cabin, I took a little more care with the rolls — but not much. Less than ten minutes after pulling off of I-95, I was back on the highway headed toward Boston once more. I made reasonably good time right up until I took the exit for Route One just north of Danvers; by then, the first indications that my timing was truly lousy had begun to appear in the form of clogged lanes and slow-moving traffic. Rush hour was never fun anywhere, but in the Greater Boston area, it took on a meaning wholly its own; even as many times as I'd driven in Los Angeles, I still felt like the manic atmosphere on the West coast was pedestrianly sedate compared to the no holds barred, bare-knuckled fight mentality endemic on any Massachusetts highway.

Whatever hope I'd had of reaching the offices of First Beacon before closing for the day had dimmed entirely by the time I reached the Tobin bridge on the stroke of five o'clock. Thankfully, I'd had a backup plan and shifted lanes with a passion so I could take the proper offramp for the Ritz Carlton downtown. It took another twenty minutes to work my way down to Tremont Street, then another ten to get around a semi-truck double parked on Avery. My blood pressure only began to fade back into the normal range after I handed the keys to the smiling valet; grabbing my gear from the rear seat, I made for the relative sanctuary of the lobby and checked in for the evening. As I tossed my bags onto the king bed in my room a few minutes later, it occurred to me I'd not been at the Ritz since that fateful trip with Vasily years earlier; pulling back the curtains, I looked out across the skyline but only had eyes for that singular moment in time, one where the comfortable lies I'd been telling myself about those I had cared the most for had been shattered completely. By the end of that weekend, I'd lost my fiancé *and* my best friend, seriously challenging my preconceived notions of what it meant to love and *be* loved. I let the smooth fabric of the curtain slip from my fingers, obscuring my view of the sparkling early evening lights, an appropriate metaphor perhaps for just how blinded I had been.

Feeling melancholy, I opted for a room service Caesar salad and turned in early.

Sleep, however, didn't come easily. I tossed and turned on the normally extremely comfortable bed, worried about Suzanne; I'd tried to call her again after my erstwhile dinner, but it had once more gone to voicemail. Concerning me more were the unanswered text messages I'd sent to Arabella; snapping off the light left me staring at the ceiling in the darkness, hoping that the lack of a response meant the situation was in hand (and not, in fact, the worst-case scenario). By four-thirty, I gave up completely and threw off the bedding, pulled on my workout gear and found my way to the fitness center. Thirty minutes of running to nowhere was about all I could take, though; I managed to force myself to complete a full circuit on the various pieces of weight training equipment before literally throwing in the towel and returning to the room for my normal morning ablutions.

Breakfast at the hotel restaurant held little appeal, but my rumbling stomach insisted that I give it a try; the western omelet I ordered was reasonably good, but the home fries had been over salted and left to wilt under a heat lamp in the bowels of the kitchen, a shocking act for such an upscale spot. About the only redeeming quality of the meal was the rich flavor of the imported coffee — and the waiter's unexpected offer of hunting down a takeaway mug so I could face the day properly braced. I may or may not have overtipped him as a result.

According to the map on my iPhone, First Beacon was just a short walk from the Ritz Carlton; having been mired in thoughts of what once was, the delicious irony that the insurer's offices were in the building that also housed the scientific journal Vasily and I had visited during the Pelletier investigation wasn't lost on me. I half expected to see snow flurries as I pushed through the glass doors to the street in front of the hotel; while none were to be found, it was bitterly cold in the way unique to cities with tall skyscrapers. Wrapping my fleece a bit tighter and once more wishing I'd dressed more appropriately, I started up the street at a pace to try and get my blood pumping enough to generate some warmth; by the time I reached the classic Art Deco entrance of the structure, I realized I'd made very little progress in that area when the warm gust of air from the lobby felt far more welcome than it should have.

I took a moment to frown slightly at the space on the wall where a wonderful mural had once hung; some idiot in their zeal to renovate the building into modern blandness had removed the work created by Dean Cornwell specifically for the then-tenant, New England Telephone, when the tower was built back in the late 1940s. Featuring that classic heroic style emblematic of the Public Works Administration era, it had been hard not to marvel at how it had depicted the history of telecommunications with a panache clearly lacking in what passed for public artwork currently. When the mural had still been present, there had never been a shortage of people milling about in the lobby reviewing it with a quiet reverence for the masterpiece it was; the now-empty curved wall painted in an unassuming light color seemed only to attract an occasional glance as people sought out the small digital directory quietly standing in a corner.

Sighing at what had been lost, I turned toward the elevators and worked my way into the flow of worker bees queuing up to access the upper floors. It took a few cycles for me to step into a carriage, flanked by nearly a dozen new friends; I had to reach around one rather portly businessman to touch the indicator for the fifteenth floor, then groaned inwardly when I realized multiple floors below that one had already been selected. After enduring the elevator equivalent of stop-and-go traffic, it was something of a relief when the golden doors finally opened for my floor.

Like most skyscrapers, the elevator lobby I found myself in was more-or-less in the center of the tower; it took a moment for me to find the discrete signage directing me toward the offices of First Beacon. The marble floor of the lobby gave way to muted industrial carpet that was, frankly, in need of a good cleansing; slowing down as I approached the glass doors for First Beacon, it occurred to me that whatever monies had been expended on the lobby down below had not been extended to other parts of the building. While the paint wasn't exactly peeling, the scheme felt like something out of the late 1970s, with a palette heavy on harvest orange and olive green; that seemed at odds with the still-resident Art Deco wall sconces in gold and white.

I pulled open one of the glass doors and found myself experiencing whiplash; the reception area I'd entered was extremely well appointed and humming with activity. A long counter in dark wood ran along the far end of the space, acting as a sort of bulwark against all trespassers; two receptionists wearing wireless headsets were working unseen phone lines, while one was speaking with a tall woman dressed in a fairly conservative power suit. Both turned toward me as I walked in their direction, and only then did I catch that the woman had an ID badge hanging from a lanyard around her neck.

"Hi," I smiled as I reached them. "Judging from that massive logo hanging on the wall back there, I take it I've finally located First Beacon Insurance?"

"That you have," the older gentlemen behind the counter replied. "Do you have an appointment?"

"I don't, actually," I replied. "My name is Commander Sean Colbeth, and I run the Major Crimes unit for the Maine State Police. I'm hoping I can talk to someone about an employee connected to a case I'm working on."

"Maine State Police?" The woman asked as a frown created a furrow on her face. A quick glance at her badge told me her first name was Nila. "Aren't you a bit outside of your jurisdiction?"

"Quite," I answered amicably.

"I'm sure Human Resources would be able to help you," the man behind the counter said as he reached for something under the desk. "Let me see if I can get someone to come down for you."

"I appreciate that," I said. "I'd also like to talk to their supervisor, too, if that's possible."

Now it was the man's turn to frown. "I'll have to clear that with HR," he replied after a quick glance at Nila. "Who is the employee?"

"Kirk Nevelson." From the corner of my eye, I caught the slight tensing from Nila at the mention of my victim; turning, I took a longer look at her badge. "Though I suspect you might be the person I'm looking for."

"I am," she replied. "I'm the Chief Investment Officer; Kirk runs one of our teams and reports directly to me."

"Is there a place where we can talk?" I asked.

Nila considered me for a moment. "Did you seriously drive all the way from Maine? Without calling ahead?"

"Yes," I replied honestly.

"Well, shit," she said with a slight smile. "Then I think I can spare ten minutes for someone so bold."

"Thanks."

"Rog, tell Clementine I'll be up later to talk about the quarterly results."

"Got it, Ms. Silone."

Nila looked at me again. "This way, Commander."

I followed Nila down one of the two hallways leading away from the reception area; the one she chose quickly opened into a large cubicle farm fully populated by a small army of employees in business formal attire. Having pretty much lived my entire professional career in polos and khakis (and the occasional pair of sweatpants), I never understood the attraction managers had to forcing their people to dress like they were members of the board despite the fact they were likely spending ten hours a day staring at a computer monitor. Nila skirted one edge of the farm with a deftness that spoke to her longevity as a leader; without missing a beat, she greeted several employees by name while never actually stopping long enough to speak to anyone. Turning a corner, I found myself surprised to see a rather ornamental staircase leading up to the next floor; despite her heels, Nila took the treads two at a time, forcing me to do the same just to keep up.

The next floor up was clearly executive territory, populated by offices along the edge of the tower that provided (I assumed) stunning views of the Boston skyline. Small, half-height cubicles stood guard just in front of each door, housing (I assumed) the administrative assistant assigned to do the bidding of the occupant within. Two decades and change into the new millennium, I was finding it hard to wrap my brain around the fact that there were still organizations out there staffing in such a manner; what seemed worse was the subtle bowing of the heads of the ones we passed as though they were not worthy to meet the eyes of either Nila or the guest she had in tow. I'd only been at First Beacon for a few minutes and already had a decent idea of how the place appeared to be run.

Despite how friendly Nila had appeared in the far larger cubicle farm behind us, she pretty much ignored all the admins we strode by; as the number of possible offices to enter dwindled to the single digits, I began to wonder if this was some sort of elaborate stalling technique intended to waylay me until building security arrived. When it became apparent that Nila was in the corner office at the end of the hallway, I revised upward the importance of the executive I appeared to have accidentally buttonholed. Nila nodded slightly at the older woman sorting paperwork into various manilla folders as we passed her; I couldn't help but notice the completely out of place IBM Selectric typewriter huddled on one end of the crowded desk.

Pushing open the door of lightly colored faux wood, Nila inclined her head toward the space within. "Home sweet home," she said with a retail smile that seemed anything but genuine.

Thus warned, I smiled myself and stepped into the large space. Tall windows on two walls did indeed command an interesting view of Boston, though not as magnificent as I had expected. The completely overcast day may have had a bit to do with that, especially in the way the lack of sunshine had drained away any and all color from the city. Aside from the view, the rest of the office was pretty much decorated in a standard Corporate theme: an imposing glass-topped desk sat at an angle between the windows, facing two comfortable looking guest chairs. At the other end of the space was a six-person conference table in light wood just beneath a fancy wall-mounted smart board currently displaying several stock tickers. Nila predictably moved behind her desk and magnanimously waved toward the guest chairs. Not usually one to indulge in power plays, I instead smiled and continued to wander her office.

"This is quite a space," I said as I ran a finger along a shelf of books.

"Yes," she replied simply. "Are you normally in the habit of just dropping in unannounced?"

"I am," I replied as I turned to face her. "Mostly because in my line of work I never really know what direction I might be going in on any given day."

Nila eyed me thoughtfully for a moment before pulling out a chair that had to cost more than my annual salary and taking a seat. "I can believe that, actually. But why drive all the way here? You could have just called to confirm his employment with us."

I shrugged with my Maine *aw shucks* smile. "I guess I'm a bit old school when it comes to investigations," I said. "There's only so much you can do over the phone."

"Do you do that for all of your cases?"

"Yes," I nodded.

"Interesting," she nodded. "What can I tell you about Kirk? Beyond the fact that he worked for us, which you clearly already know."

I smiled again while also wondering why she'd not asked about the *reason* I had landed in her office. "You mentioned earlier that he worked for you directly."

"Yes," she replied. "He leads one of the three investment teams managing our assets."

"Three?"

"Three," she nodded. "One for each of the major exchanges we work on: New York, London and Shanghai."

"Sounds like you have quite the diversified portfolio."

The slight look of surprise on Nila's face was hard to ignore. "I wouldn't have expected a cop to understand the world of high finance."

"I've read my share of balance sheets over the years," I smiled slightly as finally claimed one of the guest chairs, then casually crossed my legs. "As they say, the secrets are usually buried in the footnotes."

Nila appeared to adjust her estimation of me. "That they are; it's one of many reasons why our investment team is so large. Especially when dealing with overseas organizations."

"Which group was Kirk leading?"

"Our London desk, actually," she replied. "He landed a spot over there with Goldman Sachs right out of college and built an impressive track record working the European market. I don't think there's an investment banker anywhere with a finer understanding of the FTSE 100."

I nodded sagely as though I knew what that was. "When did he join First Beacon?"

Nila pursed her lips. "After that damn Brexit vote, I think? So, late-2016 or early 2017, I guess. Once those idiots cleaved themselves from Europe, most people with Kirk's background escaped the industry while they could. We had a senior vice-president role open at the time, so I snapped him up pretty quickly."

"Vice-president? Isn't he unusually young to hold such a position?" I asked.

Nila shook her head. "With his experience? Hardly. Within six months of his arrival, he'd made enough to cover the losses on the insurance side of the business from the past eight years." She smiled slightly. "I'm not a fool — and I've done this job long enough to recognize we'd made a solid investment. Kirk's acumen is a critical part of our strategic plan, now; if we can keep him happy, I fully expect the board will plunk him into this chair in less than a decade."

"That's high praise, but it sounds like you think he's not happy here...?" I asked, careful to keep my tense appropriate as I tugged at an ephemeral thread I thought I saw.

"It's just a sense I have," Nila said. She eyed me for a moment before continuing. "Why are you here, exactly?"

I shrugged. "Like I said out in your reception area, Kirk appears to be connected to a case I am working at the moment. I'm just getting some background so I can understand the exact nature of the connection."

"What case?"

"Would it be possible for me to talk to Kirk?" I countered, knowing the answer but wanting to gauge her reaction to the question. "I promise not to keep him from his duties for any longer than is absolutely necessary."

"He's not in today," Nila replied. Her eyes narrowed. "*What* case?"

"Does he normally miss work?"

"Kirk is taking a few days off," she replied. Her eyes narrowed even more. "I'm not answering anything else until you tell me *exactly* why you are here."

I wasn't entirely surprised at her question; in all honestly, I'd gotten far more out of her than I'd expected to get before she became wary. Nodding my head, I tried to answer her while skirting around any major details. "It's an open investigation, so I can't really say much about it at this stage."

Nila frowned. "That doesn't explain why you are so interested in my employee."

"I know, and I'm sorry," I replied, then smiled sheepishly. "It's the curse of the investigator: we're forced to ask a bunch of seemingly random questions without revealing the proper context to understand them."

"Sounds like a shitty job," Nila said. "Or at the very least, frustrating."

"There are days," I nodded. "Let me ask you this: would Kirk have any reason to be in Maine this weekend?"

"Maybe," she replied after considering me for a long moment. "He's been dealing with a family issue; I don't have all the details other than knowing at the core it's some sort of dispute."

"Over what?"

"Property, I think."

"What kind of property?"

"I have no idea," Nila said. "Kirk didn't really talk about it."

"And yet," I smiled slightly, "you seem to know something about that. Did he confide in you?"

Nila blinked, having been caught slightly. "He might have mentioned it in passing, I guess," she allowed. "Something about his maternal grandparents owning a business that they were reluctant to sell."

"What kind of business?"

"I honestly don't know," Nila replied. "Our conversation, such as it was, revolved around ways to finance a sale of such a business."

"So you gave him advice, then?"

"Of a sort," she said grudgingly. "It's not really an area of expertise for me, so I recommended that he talk to someone at an actual bank."

"Do you know if he followed your advice?"

"I don't," she replied.

"How long ago did you have that conversation?"

"Last week. Tuesday, if you must know an exact day."

"That helps, actually," I nodded.

Nila glanced at her watch, a classic move that was immediately followed by an expected declaration. "I've got a meeting that can't be missed. Is there anything else I can answer for you?"

"No," I said as I took the not-so-gentle hint and stood. "I appreciate the time."

"Of course," Nila replied. It wasn't lost on me that she remained seated. "You can find your way out?"

"I think so," I answered. "Thanks again."

Reaching for her desk phone, she simply nodded as she picked up the handset and began to dial a number. I smiled again and then exited, carefully closing the door behind me. Turning, I caught the furtive glance in my direction from the admin working outside of Nila's office and was struck by a thought; I decided to lean into my instinct and paused at the opening to the cubicle. The older woman worked away at something on her desk, but I could tell from how she had tensed up that she was aware of my presence. Eyeing the ancient typewriter on the desk beside her, I decided I had the perfect angle to strike up a conversation.

"I haven't seen one of those since my dad closed his pharmacy," I said.

The admin paused and looked up at me. "Excuse me?"

"Your Selectric typewriter," I continued with a nod in the direction of the antique. "It looks to be in pristine condition."

A slight smile tinged with pride appeared. "I treat it with respect," she said, "and as a result, it has never failed me."

Sensing there was a double meaning in her response, I nodded again. "Respect often has to be earned," I observed.

"That is quite true." She eyed me. "You said your father ran a pharmacy?"

"Yes. The business had been in our family for generations."

Her eyes dropped to the badge clipped at my waist. "You don't seem to have followed in his footsteps."

"Much to my father's everlasting regret," I said. "This firm seems to embrace the latest technology; why do you still have a typewriter?"

"I don't use it as much as I once did," the woman allowed, her voice touched with wistfulness. "Every now and then I still need to do an old-fashioned three-part form, and that beauty is still the most efficient way to fill them out."

"Wild," I replied. "Have you been Ms. Silone's admin for some time?"

"I've been the executive assistant to one of the vice presidents for the past twenty-six years," the woman answered. "I was assigned to Ms. Silone when she took over from Mr. Nevelson last year."

I felt myself start. "Was it a smooth transition?" I asked, wondering why Nila had essentially misrepresented Kirk's history with the firm.

"More or less," she shrugged. "Mr. Nevelson needed time to deal with family issues; setting aside the Chief Investment Officer duties allowed him the flexibility to do so."

"Health issues?" I asked.

"From what I understand," the admin nodded. "I don't know all of it — Mr. Nevelson was pretty private about his personal affairs, but I gathered there was an issue with the family business."

"What sort of business do they have?" I asked, thinking I might already know the answer.

"Restaurant, I think," she replied.

Before I could ask a follow-up question, the door to Nila's office suddenly opened. "Georgette, pull the report for the last three quarters of—" she began to order before her eyes connected with mine. "Commander, I thought you had left."

"I was just being a bit social," I smiled.

"That's not a quality I would associate with a police officer."

"Sometimes it can't be helped," I continued to smile. "Your executive assistant happens to have a pristine version of a typewriter my father once—"

"My staff are extremely busy," Nila interrupted. "And you've already gotten what you came here for."

I slowly nodded. "I have indeed," I replied. "You've been most helpful."

"Good. Now if you need help getting back to the elevators, I'd be happy to have Georgette call security to escort you out."

"No need," I replied. "I can see myself out."

Nila glared at me for a moment; I nodded at Georgette and then turned to walk down the hallway, acutely aware that two sets of eyes were boring into my back. As I turned a corner, I chanced a glance behind me and saw Nila's stone-faced expression; it was clear she'd be interrogating her admin as to what our discussion had been about. Unsure if I wanted to still be in the area after that happened, I picked up the pace so as to get to the relative safety of the street far, far below — all the while wondering how many other lies First Beacon might be hiding.

Eleven

I'd gotten the impression Norm was on the move when I touched base with him as I left Boston later that morning; while I hadn't thought too much about it, I was also not all that surprised to find him waiting for me in the parking lot for the rather dowdy Glenn Hills police station just ahead of noon. Leaning against the hood of his unmarked SUV, arms folded against a hooded sweatshirt bearing a logo I didn't recognize, he smiled slightly at my single arched eyebrow as I slipped from behind the wheel of my SUV and wandered toward him. The overcast skies had lingered, making it feel far later than it actually was; the crisp chill in the air made me think once more that snowflakes were highly likely before the end of the day. Pulling the light jacket closer — and wishing for the millionth time I'd paid closer attention to the weather forecast — I tried to ignore the way the light breeze was slicing through my attire as I took in our surroundings.

The small lot for the station had slots for maybe a dozen vehicles, if that; more than half were filled, including two that held tired looking Ford Interceptors in police livery that hadn't been standard issue for at least a decade. A small driveway at the far end of the lot appeared to loop around the rear of the squat concrete building, presumably for deliveries and, if I had to guess, any holding cells the department might have. Flowerbeds that had gone dormant ringed two flagpoles nestled into a grassy verge between the lot and the state route it huddled against; I wasn't sure, but the American flag appeared to be slightly tattered, a commentary perhaps on the fiscal state of the community it flew over. On a pole slightly shorter, the colors for the state of New Hampshire fluttered anemically every few heartbeats. Two doors at the center of the building appeared to be the only public entrance, enhanced slightly by the embossed sign mounted above it that said in bold letters, *Police*.

Norm caught me sizing up the competition. "Not much to look at, is it?"

"No," I nodded. "Though neither is our quaint little spot in Windeport, either."

"Never judge a book by its cover, eh?"

"Something like that," I smiled slightly. "You didn't have to come down here."

"And you weren't supposed to come at all," he reminded me.

I glanced at the extremely ugly building. "I'm not sure I had a choice, really."

"I suppose not." Norm nodded in the direction of the ugly building. "How do you want to play this?"

"I'm going to make Bartram an offer he can't refuse," I replied.

An eyebrow arched on Norm's youthful face. "You might not want to play the angry boyfriend card, Sean," he replied. "That won't help either of you."

The sudden throbbing at my temple presaged a headache I'd known was coming; rubbing at the pain, I let out a long breath. "Yeah, probably not the best angle to start from. I must be more tired than I thought."

I looked at the gravel beneath my boots for a long moment, waiting for a plan to magically materialize; as I stood there, I was forced to face the truth that I'd been so intent on *getting* to Suzanne, I'd not actually considered how I was planning to approach the situation. About the only thing I'd done was attempt to get through to Arabella, but those calls had gone unanswered, ratcheting up my anxiety accordingly. It wasn't like me to be off the cuff, but it appeared it just might be my only option. I turned my eyes back to Norm, a wry smile on my face.

"I guess we're going to have to go with the flow on this one," I said.

Norm's eyes widened. "That'll be a first."

"Don't remind me," I laughed ruefully.

Eyeing Norm, I considered for a moment how much the two of us had been through over the course of his first year by my side. He'd quickly grown into his new role as my number two, and while he'd never be a replacement for Vasily, I'd come to rely on his steady presence beside me. Having him there while I faced down whatever awaited me inside the station went a long way toward reeling in my emotions — emotions that had up to that point distracted me far more than normal from the main tasks at hand. Reaching out, I placed a hand on his shoulder and smiled slightly at the inquisitive rise of his eyebrows in response.

"I appreciate you being here," I said. "I don't think I realized until just now how much your moral support means to me."

He smiled himself. "Isn't that the role of the second-in-command?" he asked lightly before looking meaningfully toward the doors. "Shall we?"

I nodded, and we started toward the entrance. "I truly don't know how they will react to my appearance . I called the lawyer representing Suzanne a number of times on my way up to get a sense of where things stood, but it went straight to voicemail."

"That could be good or bad," Norm replied. "Maybe they were just busy extricating Suzanne and didn't have time to talk."

"Yeah," I said, a one-syllable response that didn't begin to convey the depth of my concern.

Pulling at the handle to one of the doors, I felt a bit like I'd suddenly been plunged into a dark comedy when I found it to be locked; trying the other side, I frowned at nothing in particular when it easily turned at my touch. The doors opened into a small vestibule with an extremely stereotypical raised intake desk against the far wall; more flags were present, flanking the mounted logo for the Town of Glenn Hills and looking slightly better than their peers outside. Several rows of empty bench seating were arrayed in front of the desk, all presently empty but hinting that there had once been a time when the station did a brisk business; a massive poster from the Feds with information about stopping human trafficking hung on a wall beside a large window. Two other doors on opposite ends of the room led further inside the station, both sporting RFID readers currently illuminated in red; a flat-screen television was hanging from a mount in the ceiling, tuned to the all-news station out of Boston.

Aside from Norm and me, the space was completely empty.

Walking up to the intake desk, I discovered a small doorbell had been glued to the front of the faux wood finish; two slashes of blue were beside it. Leaning forward, I realized they were loops of painter's tape, clearly pressed into service to hang a sign that was now just as clearly missing. Casting a glance at Norm, I shrugged and then pressed the button; somewhere deep inside, the slightly off-key chimes that may or may not have been of the Westminster variety were barely audible.

"Service doesn't appear to be high on their list," Norm remarked dryly when our wait continued unabated.

"Apparently not," I sighed.

Pressing the button again, the chiming echoed a second time but didn't bring forth anyone; hesitant to annoy whoever *might* ultimately appear, I debated about pressing the doorbell a third time. My angst over the action was short lived, for at length one of the two doors suddenly opened to reveal a short, balding man wearing a standard police uniform with Sergeant strips along the sleeves; his eyes were magnified behind horn-rimmed glasses, eyes that immediately sized us up in the short time it took to make his way behind the counter.

"Yes?" was the only thing he said as he sat down behind the intake desk.

"I'd like to speak with Chief Bartram, please."

"About?"

It seemed that efficiency was the order of the day for this particular intake officer. "The Hammersmith case," I replied simply.

The Sergeant's eyes widened for a moment before his face settled back into something inscrutable. "The Chief is currently not available."

"Tell him Commander Colbeth, Maine State Police, is here," I smiled. "I think he'll want to talk to me."

Those eyes widened again. "Wait here."

We watched as he slid off whatever stool he'd been using behind the desk and then trundled back through the door he'd entered; I'd expected our wait would be brief and was rewarded when the door opened again nearly immediately to reveal a tall, athletic looking man. Also attired in a standard police uniform, his had the standard pips-and-slashes denoting his status as Chief; eyeing me carefully as he entered the waiting room, I took the opportunity to return the favor, holding his light blue eyes nearly to the point of discomfort. It felt like a small victory when he was the first to look away, if only to appraise my number two as he stood beside me. Bartram had sandy hair, close cropped, with a beard to match, and carried himself with the air of a man accustomed to using his physical bulk to lend weight to his words. I wasn't entirely sure such a tactic would work on me, given how I seemed to easily have a foot on him in height; still, it felt like the right play to resist the very real urge to display my own physicality by standing just a bit taller.

I reached a hand out to him as he approached and kept my expression pleasantly neutral. "Chief Bartram? Sean Colbeth, Major Crimes. Nice to finally meet you in person."

Bartram looked at me for a moment, clearly trying to determine if there was any sarcasm in my voice. "I guess I'm not surprised Captain Roberts sent *you* to pick up everything, as inappropriate as that might be. Regardless, your timing is excellent. We've finished uploading everything to the master case file and have the evidence boxes ready to go; you'll just need to sign for them and then you can be on your way and out of my hair."

For the first time in a long time, I felt completely caught off guard. "I'm glad you agreed to allow us to assist in this case," I said, my brain furiously working overtime to connect some dots. "Though I wasn't aware that Captain Roberts had already made the arrangements. I've been tied up tracing leads from another case I'm working and haven't touched base with him in a bit."

"Roberts alluded to that," Bartram replied. "I want to reiterate just how extraordinary it is for us to be outsourcing this case to not just another jurisdiction, but one that is *outside* of New Hampshire."

I shook my head. "It's actually far more common than you think these days," I said. "I've consulted on hundreds of cases throughout the country over the years, always working hand-in-hand with the originating agency at every step." I paused, watching the thinly veiled anger play just beneath the surface of Bartram's otherwise placid expression. "We'll do the same with this case, as I'm sure Captain Roberts already assured you."

"He said as much, yes," Bartram allowed. "The proof, as they say, is in the pudding."

"I've never understood that expression," Norm said. "But if you're worried about us keeping you in the loop, I can assure you that won't be an issue." Looking at me briefly, he continued. "I'm not sure what your staffing situation is like here, but I have to imagine having the full resources of the State in play will help greatly—"

"I don't need them to solve this case," Bartram interrupted tightly. "Either from Maine *or* New Hampshire. This is a blatant attempt to bury a politically thorny incident, nothing more."

My eyebrows went up. "I'm sorry you see it that way," I said. "That's truly not the intention here."

"It is what it is," Bartram replied, then paused. "If you aren't here for the case files, why did you come? Not to accept my invitation for an interview, I assume."

"No," I answered. "Not for an interview, especially since you've already determined I'm not a viable suspect."

The slight flicker of astonishment on his face was enough of a validation I'd read the situation correctly. "Well, if you were intending to break your girlfriend out of my holding cell, I'm afraid she was never there; her lawyer made it abundantly clear that Dr. Kellerman wouldn't be answering any questions."

I had a mental image of Arabella standing toe-to-toe with this guy and honestly found myself wishing I'd been a fly on the wall when it happened. "My main interest in diverting here was to gauge what sort of investigative progress you'd made," I replied. "And to offer my services to assist; given how slowly the wheels of our mutual bureaucracies grind, I thought it prudent to visit personally while Captain Robert's request was pending so we could informally get started."

Bartram eyed me again, an affectation that was truly beginning to grate on my nerves. "Bullshit."

"Believe what you want," I replied easily. "How about we get those boxes loaded?"

Bartram continued to glare at me but still nodded. "Wait here."

The Chief disappeared through the opposite door he'd entered from and mere moments later returned pushing a small hand truck loaded with standard-issue evidence containers. All were clearly sealed with tape bearing what I assumed was the logo for the department; once he'd come to a rest beside me, I took a moment to examine each one of the containers to ensure the tape was still intact before accepting the clipboard he handed me. I took another moment to scan the standard chain-of-custody paperwork, then flipped it up to reveal the formal MOU creating the consulting agreement between Glenn Hills and Major Crimes. Flipping back to the first document, I scribbled my signature in the appropriate spot and handed the clipboard back to Bartram.

"I'd like to visit the scene," I said. "Can I presume your techs are through with it at this point?"

"They are," Bartram nodded. "I don't know what you expect to find, though. The State Crime Lab is pretty thorough."

"I'm sure," I replied. "I just want to get a sense of the space. It often helps me understand the case better, if not the overall circumstances."

"Whatever. Knock yourself out."

As it was clear our presence was infuriating to no end for Bartram, I smiled slightly and shook his hand once more. "Then we will be off — and we'll be in touch."

The grasp was more perfunctory the second time around. "I'll be waiting."

I'm sure, I thought as Norm grabbed the hand truck and we headed for the exit.

Out in the parking lot, I popped open the hatch for Norm's SUV and began loading the boxes into the space; considering there were only four boxes in total, we made quick work of the task. While Norm ran the hand truck back to the station, I ran a finger along the labels of the containers, taking something of an informal inventory. The exterior labels by design didn't do much other than denote what case the evidence belonged to; still, the fact that there were so many made me wonder about what had caught the crime scene nerds' curiosity. My own would have to wait to be satiated until we returned to Windeport. Turning to my number two, I nodded slightly at the boxes.

"I'm going to run over to Hammersmith's house before heading back to Windeport," I said. "You are welcome to join me unless you have other pressing matters to attend to."

"I don't," Norm replied. "And it goes without saying I had no idea Roberts had stepped in. Had you asked him to?"

"No. And that troubles me a bit."

"Why?" Norm asked with a hint of a smile. "I'd think it indicates just how well he knows you."

I found myself nodding slowly. "Yeah," I agreed. "I suppose it does."

At that particular moment, my phone buzzed in my pocket; retrieving it, I smiled slightly before answering it. "Arabella, I was beginning to think you'd forsaken me."

"Hardly," she laughed. "The cell coverage in this part of New

Hampshire is for shit. Please tell me you're not actually at the Glenn Hills police station?"

"Guilty as charged," I replied. "I had to come."

"I figured as much. I'm heading back to Portland, but Suzanne is obviously in the clear at the moment. I left her sorting through the knick-knacks at her ex-husband's home."

"Obviously?"

"Yeah," Arabella said. "Didn't Bartram tell you? There's social media video of the two of you at the swim meet — looked like you got in one hell of a nice massage, by the way — as well as security footage of the parking lot. Both prove neither of you left the meet during the period when they think Hammersmith was killed. That, and like I said, cell coverage is for shit; location data from Suzanne's phone shows it didn't move more than a few feet at the pool during the same time frame — which is the same story for your phone."

"Bartram didn't say much of anything," I replied as I realized Arabella had told me more about the case in under two minutes than anyone else. I found myself very curious what other little nuggets might be in the files Bartram was sharing with me. "Other than to express his displeasure that I'm now consulting on the case."

There was a moment of silence. "I won't ask how that happened, but I do wonder if that is wise."

"Time will tell," I sighed.

TWELVE

Pulling up the long driveway to Leslie Hammersmith's home, I began to understand why my calls to Arabella and Suzanne had gone to voicemail. Nestled into the eponymous hills of the small town, it was a solid fifteen miles of narrow, winding roads from the police station that had to have been hell to navigate during the winter. That portion of New Hampshire wasn't exactly part of the better-known White Mountains, but the peaks rising away behind the rambling split level ranch were significant all the same. As my SUV rumbled over the loose gravel toward the spot where Suzanne's Forester was parked, I took in more details of the place; overall, the house itself seemed to be in excellent shape, sheathed in cedar shakes that appeared to have been recently stained a relatively innocuous shade of brown. A small aerial antenna was fastened to the brick chimney that served as a sort of bookend, hinting perhaps at a classic fireplace anchoring the large room just visible through the tall bow windows. The far end of the driveway swooped around to an even larger barn-like structure with two tall garage doors; one of them was open, exposing the grill of a GMC Yukon model that hadn't been made in years. Pulling to a stop, I wondered how long it had taken to hack the several acres of now-lawn from the thick forest surrounding the home; in another indicator that not all was as it should be, the grass appeared to be slightly more than ankle height and was waving in an unseen breeze.

Shutting off the engine to my SUV, I smiled when I saw the familiar form of my girlfriend suddenly duck out from the barn; her raven black hair had been put up in a casual ponytail, a style she rarely used save for when she was puttering around her apartment or my bungalow and had nowhere else to be. The deep red vest she was wearing was a nice contrast to the vibrant blue of her jeans, and I could see as I slid out from behind the wheel she was holding a pair of thick work gloves in one hand; with the other, she reached up and tucked a strand of that luxurious hair behind an ear. Suzanne had a natural beauty that always took my breath away, even in dust-covered casual clothing; as I wandered toward her, I caught that knowing look in her eyes and the slight smile that appeared along with it.

"Hey, stranger," she said as she pulled me into a hug. "Am I glad to see you."

I leaned in for a kiss. "Same," I replied warmly as I pulled back. "How are you holding up?"

She shrugged. "As well as can be expected," she answered before looking at me. "I thought you weren't going to come to New Hampshire?"

"I was on my way back from Boston," I replied. "It was on the way."

One of her sculpted eyebrows arched. "Hardly," she smiled. "For the record, Arabella figured you'd ignore her."

"I tried to call," I continued as she interlaced her hand in mine.

"After being here for a few hours, I'm convinced the nearest cell tower is in Bangor," she laughed. "Pretty sure that's why Leslie has (had) an old-fashioned land line inside the house."

"The joys and perils of living in the boondocks."

"Exactly." Suzanne reached her other hand to my face. "I really am glad you are here, Sean."

"There wasn't any way I was going to let you go through this alone,"

I said softly as I leaned into her warm touch. "Not after everything you've been through."

Suzanne smiled at that. "Has anyone ever told you how endearing that stubborn streak of yours is?"

I blinked. "Is that some sort of backhanded compliment?"

"Just an observation," she laughed.

Feeling a little nonplussed, I decided it might be best to shift the subject. "How far have you gotten?" I asked before nodding to the house. "I don't want to interrupt if you're in the zone, but I do want to take a look at scene."

"I've barely scratched the surface, honestly," Suzanne replied. "I did a quick once-over of the house and then moved out here to the barn. Leslie was nothing if not organized, so I think I have a good sense of what I'm dealing with." She sighed as she looked over toward the house. "I don't think there's much that I'm going to want to keep, so I'll probably cheat a bit and use one of those estate sale organizations to clear out everything."

"What about the acreage?"

"That's a bit tougher," Suzanne replied. "Part of me wants to dump it at cost and be done with that part of my life for good."

"I hear a 'but' in there."

She looked at me. "This is an amazingly peaceful place," she continued. "And exactly the kind of spot Leslie and I had long talked about retiring to. It's frustrating as fuck that he managed to pull it off without me; having said that, I'm more than a little ambivalent about selling."

Something in my heart fluttered with uncertainty. "Your life is in Windeport now," I said, then saw a flicker of emotion cross her face. That flutter in my heart turned into a bona fide skipped beat. "Isn't it?"

"Yeah," she replied after a moment. "The temptation to escape from it is real, though."

I felt my eyes widen. "You're not happy in Windeport?" I asked, before adding mentally, *with me?*

Perhaps sensing my discomfort at the turn the conversation had made, Suzanne looked me in the eye and took my hand into hers. "More than I have any right to be," she replied with a warmth to her expression that softened my anxiety slightly. "It's taken me a long time to accept that, but a certain handsome former Olympic swimmer with green eyes that I constantly get lost in has convinced me I can." Suzanne paused for another moment, allowing a gleeful glint to appear in her deep blue eyes. "He also happens to look damn sexy in a Speedo."

"Does he?" I chuckled as I pulled her into a hug again. "Good to know."

"C'mon, Kitty," Suzanne said as she started toward the house. "I'm done out here, let me give you the nickel tour."

Taking her hand into mine once more, we walked hand-in-hand toward the house; as we neared, the rumble of another vehicle coming up the long dirt driveway had both of us turning to watch Norm pull up beside my SUV. Pushing out of the driver's side of his vehicle, he took a moment to zip up his fleece before joining us at the bottom of the short steps to the porch hugging the front door. Nodding in the general direction of the house, he smiled slightly before speaking.

"I assumed you'd be done by now."

"I've not been here long," I replied. "I wasn't all that far ahead of you."

"Far enough," he laughed. "I forget how slow dump trucks can be on roads like these. There were points when I thought I could walk faster than I was driving."

"Amen to that."

Norm produced a tablet that he'd apparently been carrying and quickly consulted it. "I suspected cellular data would be hard to get out here, so I downloaded the case files before we left the station," he said as he flicked through something on the screen. "I'm pulling up the report from the techs now." His eyes glanced to Suzanne. "I know this is no longer a crime scene—"

"Don't worry, boys," Suzanne said as she went up the steps and crossed to the front door. "Knowing either of you were bound to find a way here, I made a point of not touching anything. The scene is exactly as the techs left it." Holding the door open for us, she smiled at me. "Call it a hazard of dating a police officer."

"Indeed," I smiled as we passed through the door.

I'd been in my share of homes over the years, enough to know that there seemed to be a finite set of patterns used by builders. Judging from the slight landing we were standing in, Hammersmith's split-level seemed pretty typical; to the left, a short set of steps descended into the daylight basement, and to the right, the same number of steps rose into the long living room that had been presaged by the bow window, with the fireplace about where I'd suspected it would be. Suzanne guided us upwards, and we paused at the head of the steps for a moment; directly in front of us was an arched doorway to a pretty standard kitchen, with windows looking into the backyard. Ducking my head inside for a moment, it appeared to have been recently modernized with the requisite stainless-steel appliances enhanced by subtle canned lights in the textured ceiling. Dishes were partially hidden behind frosted cabinet doors, and a small table for two was pressed into a corner, stacked with what appeared to be a few days of mail. Another doorway revealed the edge of a long table, hinting at a more formal dining room — an artifact of a time when families regularly gathered around such things.

Ducking back out, I spared a second for my eyes to sweep the living room. The space was comfortably furnished with couches and a few armchairs, all oriented toward a sizable flat screen television mounted over the red brick of the fireplace. Wider than normal hardwood flooring appeared to have been well maintained, showing a slight sheen of reflection even in the darkened light from the overcast day. Several oil paintings in a style reminiscent of those I'd seen Bob Ross whip up hung along the wall between the living room and kitchen, breaking up an otherwise wide expanse of emptiness. Suzanne had turned slightly, her eyes focused on a small banquet table nestled into the bow windows. To my surprise, a rather well-crafted model of a tall ship had pride of place on top of the table; the scale-sized sails had been unfurled and angled such that the entire tableau felt as though it were moving, despite being completely stationary. I watched my girlfriend for a moment, surprised at the look of nostalgia that crossed her face.

"Leslie had quite a knack for building wooden ships," Suzanne said. "I used to joke with him that he loved his boats more than me."

I thought perhaps there was quite a bit of truth in that observation but was saved from saying something appropriate by Norm. "It's a work of art."

"It is," she nodded. "They found the body over here in the den."

Turning, Suzanne had us follow her down a short hallway that ran away from the living room and bisected the other half of the house. About the only thing not standard in this particular floorplan was the set of six-panel wooden doors guarding the entrance to the den; one of the doors was already open, and Suzanne stepped back against it to allow us to enter ahead of her. The slightly stale odor of processing chemicals mixed with biological fluids hit my nose a fraction of a second before I saw the remnants of dura matter against a bookcase hugging a wall perpendicular to the entrance; years of experience had me immediately tracing a path across the top of a fairly typical executive chair and land on the jumbled surface of a very large desk that made the one in my office back in Windeport look petite. A dried pool of blood had gathered to one side of the surface, encircling a stack of open books and tinting several piles of paperwork a deep crimson; a canister holding pens and pencils had been knocked asunder, splaying its contents across the front edge of the surface. Globs of dura matter hung on almost everything; taken along with the telltale blood spatters accompanying it, the violence of what happened to Hammersmith was brutally clear.

A small metal box of tools appropriate for doing finely detailed woodworking was open on the other side of the desk, sitting beside what appeared to be the inner skeleton for another small sailing ship. Three tiers of small glass containers of paint were housed in a plastic caddy just next to the hull, helping to keep flat a large blueprint of the ship being built. The size of the desk started to make sense, for the context seemed to indicate that it was essentially a workbench for whatever project was currently being undertaken. Helping underscore that was the gangly work light clamped on one edge, focused down on the work-in-progress.

Stepping further into the room, I noted an oval woven rug with a unique pattern of shapes and colors was on the hardwood in front of the desk, and appeared to be slightly misaligned, almost as if someone had pushed something heavy across the surface and snagged it in the process. Several smaller pools of dried blood dotted the carpet just in front of the desk, though with all of the clutter it was hard to tell how it had dribbled off the surface. Tall windows looked out toward the rear of the parcel, framing the stately pine trees at the edge of the green lawn; the slight rise of the ridge behind the home was just visible through the thick expanse of needles. Two more oil paintings done in a similar style to what I'd seen in the living room had me thinking Hammersmith might have been an amateur artist; another, smaller wooden ship sat on a shelf, this one appearing to be a work in progress — one that would now ultimately never be completed. Crouching slightly to get a better look at the detailed model, I felt a momentary wave of sadness over that, despite my feelings about the modeler himself.

Turning around, I folded my arms against my chest and examined the desk from afar. While I was a little surprised that the den hadn't been professionally cleaned after the crime scene techs had completed their work, it actually allowed me to more-or-less see the space pretty much as they had found it, save of course for the dead body. From that vantage point, it was fairly easy to make out where Hammersmith's head had likely been on the desk, though I frowned a bit at why the blood had pooled where it had. My working assumption from the splatter behind the desk had been a gunshot wound to the head, but the angles seemed off somehow.

"What does the report say?" I asked Norm, frowning as I did so.

"About what you might expect," he replied, "given this mess they don't seem to have bothered to clean up. Blunt force trauma to the head, specifically around the left temple. Coroner thought it was something made from wood based on slivers removed from the head wound, though there was too much damage to assess a shape or size to the weapon."

My eyes widened. "*Left* temple?" I asked as I moved back toward the desk. Glancing between that and the doorway, I let a note of surprise creep into my voice. "He would have to have been facing the doorway when the first blow was delivered, then."

"That supports the positioning of the body as they found it," Norm replied.

He turned his tablet toward me to display a photo from the scene; it clearly showed what was left of Hammersmith lying on his left cheek, up against the stack of books and the paper. His left arm was thrown across the surface, apparently the primary reason the pencil canister had been knocked over. Staring at the photo, I felt my frown deepen.

"He was facing the doorway," I said again, my eyes moving from the photo back to the desk. "Looking at, what? Exactly?"

"It wouldn't have been the killer," Norm said, clearly on the same page as I was. "If the blow came from here..." Norm took up position in front of the desk and angled a finger as though it was the barrel from his Glock, then continued. "...that would mean there were multiple people in the room, right?"

"Or he was trying to escape," I countered. "From the killer."

Norm looked at his photo. "That might work. The chair is angled a bit in that direction," he said, drawing my eyes back to the screen.

"So it is. Did they lift any prints from the scene?"

Norm nodded. "They printed just about the entire house if I'm reading this right," he said. "Which is something of a challenge. Unlike Heather's team, these techs are anything but loquacious."

"I think Heather might take that as a compliment," I smiled, thinking of the senior crime scene tech we often worked with back in Maine. "Maybe. What did they find?"

"The majority came back to the victim, though there was a partial on the kitchen door; not enough there for anything to match, apparently."

"That's it?" I asked.

"Pretty much. The only other highlight is that the toxicology screen came back clean, save for some hits on likely prescribed regimen drugs — Atorvastatin for cholesterol and Montelukast for allergies." Norm looked up with a slight smirk. "Last meal was apparently coffee."

"Sounds about right," Suzanne laughed quietly. "When he was in one of his modeling moods, he pretty much subsisted on caffeine and not much else." I caught the slight twinkle in her eye before she added: "A bit like someone else I know."

That's where the comparisons end, I think, I thought to myself before being struck by something Norm had read. "Norm, did you say the partial was on the kitchen door?"

"Yes," he replied.

I looked at Suzanne. "I don't suppose you've moved anything since you've been here?"

"I've barely had time to walk the entire property," she replied, arching an eyebrow as a reminder she'd already said something like that earlier. "Why?"

"It feels like there should be visitor chairs here," I said, gesturing toward the space in front of the desk.

She shrugged. "I can't speak to *this* house, but in the one I shared with him while we were married, he converted that den into his workshop — mostly because we could never keep the basement completely dry. Depending on what he was doing, he'd either work behind the desk in his chair or perched on a wooden stool he'd bought at a flea market years ago."

"Any reason he would have changed the pattern?" I asked, my eyes dropping to the shifted rug on the floor.

"Doubt it," she replied before smiling slightly at a memory. "Whenever he was doing something particularly messy — painting, gluing or something like that — he'd use the stool. It's pretty much why he got it."

"Then where is it?" I asked of no one in particular.

Norm crouched. "This carpet looks like it's been shifted," he said, echoing my thoughts from earlier. "Something was dragged across it."

"Yes," I murmured. *Kitchen door? Why the kitchen door and no other surfaces? Why take the time to be gloved while inside the house only to leave a smudge —*

Digging into the pocket of my pants, I retrieved a pair of standard latex exam gloves that I usually carried with me at all times. Holding them up to the light, the first part of an answer started to crystallize.

Because they snagged. Snagged and tore and they didn't have a spare.

I looked back at the shifted rug, then the desk.

Snagged on a piece of the weapon? When it fractured...? Which it likely did given the violence I'm seeing here... I'll bet it fractured into multiple pieces, all of which were carefully removed. But to where...?

Hang on.

Moving to the tall windows on the exterior wall, I looked out into the backyard. "I imagine they don't have trash service this far out from the center of Glenn Hills. Is there a transfer station?"

I heard tapping behind me. "Yeah," Norm answered. "Map has it on the other side of Glenn Hills, about twenty miles from here."

"That's a bit of a hike," I murmured as my eyes finally found what I was looking for.

Norm came over to stand beside me. "You think the stool was the weapon?"

"I do," I nodded. "Or some part of it."

"The murderer wouldn't hike it all the way to the transfer station just to get rid of it," he countered. "It would be far easier to dump it in the woods somewhere."

"Only to have us find it?" I asked as I turned and started out of the room.

"Good point," Norm replied as he and Suzanne followed me. "Where are we going?"

"There was a time," I began as we went back down the hallway and I turned into the kitchen. The door to the rear deck was actually a glass slider, wide enough to allow sunshine on a brilliant day to cascade into the space; given how overcast it continued to be, it felt less spectacular. Pulling at the handle, I quickly slid the door open and stepped onto the deck. "A time when there wasn't such a thing as a transfer station, a time when people were forced to dispose of their waste on their own."

Crossing the deck with me, Suzanne surprised me by swearing. "Holy *shit*. The burn pit," she added when Norm and I turned in unison to look at her. "It's just at the edge of the backyard. You think they dragged the stool over there and set it on fire?"

"Yep," I replied as we trundled down the steps and into the overgrown backyard. "I saw it from the window in the den. If the stool was pretty standard, it wouldn't be hard to carry." I paused for a moment. "Especially if it was in pieces."

It took but a moment to cross to the far side of the yard; there, we found a shallow pit that had been dug into the ground, full of ash in various shades of gray. There was a small metal storage cabinet beside the pit with a shovel and rake leaning on one edge; pulling on the gloves I'd been carrying, I gently twisted the handle to the door to reveal several boxes of matches and more than a few bottles of charcoal lighter fluid. Closing the door, I reached for a rake and gently began pulling it through the ash; almost immediately, I came up with the sort of screws often used to connect various pieces of furniture together, along with several irregular shapes of thin, discolored plastic. Digging around more, I came up with charred fabric that could have come from nearly anything, though the color seemed familiar. Leaning against the rake, I knew what I was looking at wasn't entirely definitive — at least, not without the sort of high-priced laboratory tests the nerds in Augusta tended to favor. I presumed — or hoped, rather — the New Hampshire equivalent could do the same. Moving back to the cabinet, I knelt in the high grass and peered at the set of handles. I couldn't be sure without better equipment but thought I could see some smudges about where someone would grasp it. Slowly, I started to smile and turned to look at Norm.

"Prints?" he asked with a smile that matched mine.

"Quite possibly," I replied. "We're going to need the crime scene nerds again."

"Bartram's not going to like that," Norm replied.

"I don't give a fuck," I answered.

THIRTEEN

"How long has this been a *Sheraton*?" I asked incredulously.

"Long enough that I thought it wise to finally correct you," Suzanne laughed from where her head was lying against my bare chest. "Since you're such a regular, the clerks at the front desk have been humoring you."

I brushed a strand of dark hair away from her forehead, smiling a bit at how it was still glistening from our recent extracurriculars. Shifting the pillow slightly so I could get a better angle on the beautiful woman draped across my rather sweaty torso, I thanked my lucky stars for the millionth time that we'd managed to find our way back to a relationship that meant more to me than life itself. Hugging her a bit closer, I sighed contentedly while trying to ignore the inquisitive finger that was currently working its way down my stomach and toward a decidedly sensitive portion of my body that was rather surprisingly already responding to her touch. Shifting again, I tried to refocus on the conversation and not the electric feel of her skin against mine.

"That explains why you gave me that look when I suggested we stop overnight at the Marriott," I said.

"It does," Suzanne replied.

Predictably, Bartram had been extremely unhappy when we'd reached out to have him dispatch the crime scene techs for a second round of evidence gathering; I was sure he'd assumed my request was an implied rebuke of his skills. I didn't truly care, but if he had, I can't deny I might have taken a small measure of satisfaction from his barely controlled irritation. That was short lived, of course, for the retribution — punitive as it might have been — was a lengthy wait for the team to arrive from Concord. Once they had done a second, and by my estimation, far more thorough canvassing of the home and surrounding grounds, it was close to seven and I found myself facing the prospect of a long drive back to Windeport. While she'd originally planned on continuing to go through the estate of her ex-husband, Suzanne seemed to sense the dark clouds that had begun to once again circle me and made the decision to postpone her efforts, instead suggesting that we overnight at my favorite hotel in South Portland. The impish twinkle in her eyes as she got into her Forester to follow me back to Maine told me everything I needed to know about *how* the rest of the evening would go, and I wasn't disappointed. Mere minutes after closing the door to our room at the Marriott, we'd managed to find our way beneath the sheets, passionately making up for the stress of the past few days. We'd not come up for air until well past one, pleasantly exhausted yet keyed up sufficiently that sleep wasn't in the offing.

So, we'd begun chatting, ostensibly to catch up from having been apart for a few days but in reality, allowing our bodies a few moments to recharge. Not wanting to talk about *why* we were in a hotel room together past the witching hour, though, had the effect of directing the conversation into strange areas, including, apparently, my continued ability to not see something that was directly in front of me. In this case, it was the fact that my beloved Sable Oaks Marriott had become a Sheraton; I'd apparently been striding right past the new logo for more than a year only to have Suzanne finally point it out to me when we'd checked in. Thankfully, it was still a part of the wider Marriott family, and for my purposes, still kept to the same high level of customer service I'd come to appreciate.

Feeling Suzanne's tentative touch at my growing arousal drove home the point that rest wasn't what my girlfriend was after; having dated a doctor for some time now, I knew her views on the healing power of sex and bowed to the inevitable. As I carefully rolled her onto her back and gently began kissing my way down her damp neck, I figured it wouldn't be the first time I'd needed a near-constant cup of coffee in order to get through the day. Nibbling at the intersection of her neck and shoulder generated a slight gasp and had her arching into me; the slight shock that she'd used the movement to guide me back into her was the last thing my logical brain noted before more carnal impulses took over.

While I'd intended to get up early enough to arrive back in Windeport to start the day in my office, I knew as soon as I smelled the savory scent of bacon that I was already well-off schedule. Blinking my eyes open — and realizing I'd pulled a Vasily and slept in my contacts — the view of my breathtakingly beautiful girlfriend arranging the room service dishes on the small side table confirmed my suspicion. Wrapped in one of the terry cloth robes bearing the logo for the hotel, Suzanne turned and smiled; my eyes, true to form, immediately fell to the tasteful expanse of breast peeking out from the fold of the fabric.

Laughing slightly, she came over to sit beside me on the king bed. "I know what that look means, but I suspect you're going to want to somehow table your libido so we can hit the road."

I glanced at my phone on the nightstand and immediately grimaced. "I overslept."

"We both did," she nodded. "I ordered breakfast — come grab a bite and then we can cycle through the shower."

I started to smile wolfishly. "Cycle?"

"*Cycle,*" she emphasized before putting a finger on my nose. "Or we will be even *later.*"

"I'm a Commander now," I reminded her as I slipped from beneath the sheet and fished my boxer briefs from the pile of clothing beside the bed. "I can come and go when I wish."

"Best perhaps not to push it, kitty," she said as I pulled the briefs on. "You've not spoken to Captain Roberts since he found out about your off-the-books investigation into Leslie."

I felt myself flush slightly as I followed her to the table. "True."

"Will he be upset?"

"Probably," I sighed as I sat down across from her and then picked up a fork.

A comfortable silence embraced us for a few minutes while we dug into the mountain of food Suzanne had ordered; halfway through my excellent scrambled eggs it occurred to me I'd not eaten since having breakfast at the Ritz yesterday morning. It wasn't much of a surprise, honestly, given how wound up I'd been over not knowing how things were going for Suzanne in New Hampshire; now that we were on a more even keel, my appetite had rebounded with a vengeance. Grabbing a third piece of bacon while eyeing a second English muffin, I felt that momentary pang of guilt that I'd be unable to get in a workout until much later. Knowing a few extra carbs wouldn't kill me, I reached for the muffin and was rewarded with a chuckle from the other side of the table.

Looking up, I saw Suzanne smiling. "Considering how many calories you burn in a typical day, I think you can ease up on yourself just this once."

I felt myself flushing slightly. "Was it that obvious?"

"Only to me," she nodded.

As I separated the muffin, I watched Suzanne's expression become pensive. "Something's troubling you," I observed as I snagged a small container of orange marmalade from the pile of jelly tubs off to one side of the spread. I'd never had the stuff before I'd begun traveling as a competitive swimmer, and once I'd discovered it, could never get enough. Oddly, I never had any back at my bungalow.

"Yeah," she replied.

Pulling the top off the tub of marmalade, I smiled slightly. "Let me guess: my investigation into your ex-husband?"

"Yeah," she nodded. "What were you thinking?"

I knew I'd skirted around the core of the situation when I'd come clean with her the day Bartram had called me, fully aware Suzanne wouldn't likely leave it there. "Answering that with the sincerity you deserve," I replied as I put the tub back down, "is likely going to make me look like a petty teenager with a score to settle and not the pulled together, totally professional police officer you've fallen in love with."

Suzanne put down her fork and reached across to take my hand into hers. "You want to know a little secret?"

"Sure."

"I've never had someone like you in my life before," she said softly. "Someone willing to immediately defend my virtue without so much as a second thought." Suzanne paused, then squeezed my hand. "Someone who loves me for the woman I am, not the one they want me to be." She smiled that brilliantly beautiful smile for a moment, the one that always made my innards go all mushy. "Warts and all."

"I've never seen any warts," I replied. "Ever."

"That's your heart speaking, methinks."

"Maybe," I smiled wryly. "All the same, I should never have let my emotions run wild like that. Using department resources to gather intel on your ex wasn't exactly a best practice."

"I suppose not. You've not answered my question, though."

"No," I sighed. Picking up what was left of my bacon, I tore off a piece, stared at it for a moment and then, suddenly finding myself no longer hungry, dropped all of it back onto the plate. "I guess the truth isn't too far off from what I told you before: I wanted to know more about the asshole."

Suzanne waited patiently, using my patented witness interviewing technique against me.

"And... maybe I kind of wanted to see if I could nail him on something," I finally admitted. Guilt had me glance toward the window of the room. "Anything. After what he did to you, I... I felt he needed to pay."

Hearing myself say that out loud was something of a shock for both of us, which lead to a sudden and very heavy silence. I continued to watch the leaves on the trees out in the parking lot of the hotel as they waved in the unseen breeze, finally realizing just how far over the line I had gone — and the full measure of the trouble I *could* have gotten into had I pursued it much further. The irony that Hammersmith's untimely death might have saved my ass wasn't lost on me.

"An eye for an eye?" Suzanne asked. The slight trace of humor to her voice had me turning back to her. "I never figured you as an Old Testament kind of guy."

"There are days," I replied. "How could there not be, given the kind of work I do? But no, my ideas of justice are, shall we say, somewhat more progressive."

"Well, if it helps what I can clearly see from your face is an extremely guilty conscience, Leslie did wind up paying — after a fashion."

My eyebrows went up. "Really? I didn't see anything in the files I pulled together."

Suzanne shook her head. "Nothing like that," she replied. "You already know that our divorce was, to put it mildly, a flaming mess. I pretty much had to start over from scratch, both financially and psychologically; I had a decent lawyer who managed to claw back most of what Leslie took from me while we were married, plus half of the proceeds from the sale of the house we'd lived in."

"That let you buy the practice in Windeport?"

"And begin a new life," she nodded before smiling. "You want to know the best part? Leslie being such an asshole is, at the end of the day, what led to my being at the Halloween party." Suzanne squeezed my hand again. "I love what you were trying to do for me, but you have to see that I stopped giving a fuck about Leslie around the time you became the most important thing in my life."

My heart nearly stopped. "Are you saying what I think you are saying?"

Suzanne replied without hesitation. "I love you with every fiber of my being, Sean Colbeth. I have for some time; Leslie's parting gift to me — the fear that I might be taken advantage of again — was one that nearly saw me toss it all away this summer. Thankfully," she smiled warmly, "a certain green-eyed swimmer against all odds reminded me I could be loved. And that it was safe *to* love."

"And always *will* be loved," I replied softly. "So long as I live." Ginning mischievously, I nodded toward the bed. "If it helps, I'm quite happy to clear up any lingering misgivings you might have."

"How very chivalrous of you, Kitty," she smiled, "but I believe the two of us still need to hit the road. I've got to deal with some stuff at the practice so I can head back to Glenn Hills on Sunday to finish dealing with the mess Leslie left me."

"Party pooper," I pouted.

"*That* is so not a good look for you," Suzanne laughed as she stood. "Do you mind if I borrow your UEM sweatshirt? I seem to have misplaced my sweater — I thought it was in the backseat of my car, but I must have left it at the swim meet."

"Of course," I replied before. "The purple one? Wasn't that the one I gave you for Christmas?"

"One and the same," she replied. "Which is why I hope I've not lost it."

"Damn. You can call the pool and see if it's in lost and found."

"That's the plan, provided it hasn't already been donated to Goodwill," Suzanne sighed. "I'm going to dash through the shower—"

My iPhone took that moment to sing out unexpectedly from where it was sitting on the nightstand. Frowning slightly, I stood and quickly retrieved it; the number on the display had me frowning deeper. "Captain," I answered. "This can't be good."

"It depends on your perspective, I guess," Roberts said. His voice was thick with fatigue; my eyes guiltily darted to the messed-up sheets on the bed, a visible recrimination that I had been making rather merry while my superior burned the candle at both ends. "We located the shooter."

I felt myself stand a bit straighter. "Really? Where?"

"Brewer," he replied. "I'll text you the address, how quickly can you get there?"

"I'm in South Portland now," I answered. "Two hours, maybe less if I push it."

"South *Portland*?"

"I was following up on a lead that took me to Boston yesterday," I replied defensively, having caught the subtle rebuke. "My return was late enough that it was just easier to overnight here instead of driving straight through to Windeport."

"Ah," Roberts said, though I could also hear the gears turning in his brain. "What lead was that, exactly? The body in the rear storeroom?"

"Yes," I replied. "Lou was able to identify our bonus victim as Kirk Nevelson, a financial guru for a Boston-based insurer. I was trying to pin down a reason for why someone with a home address in Concord, Mass-achusetts happened to be at Pizzeria Angelina on the night of the shooting."

"That's one hell of a commute," Roberts observed. "What's the connection to East Newberry?"

"I'm not sure," I replied.

"But you have an idea?"

I smiled slightly. "I do, yes, though confirming my suspicion is going to require another visit with the owner."

"Good," Roberts said. "Because I'm already getting grief that my star investigator appears to be MIA in the middle of a statewide manhunt." He paused for a moment. "I wouldn't run interference for anyone else, Sean, but even I can only do so much. Get your ass to Brewer as fucking fast as your SUV can go."

"Message received," I replied. "I didn't intend to put you in such a bind; I should have crosschecked with you before I left. With this thing in New Hampshire, I'm afraid I'm a bit off my game."

"Which is why I called in a favor from my peer over there," Roberts said. "I figured you'd stick your nose in that one even if I told you not to, state lines be damned."

That made me laugh. "Indeed. I'm leaving now."

"Good. Put in an appearance for the cameras and look a bit like you're engaged; that might get the brass off my back for a bit — and maybe give you some wiggle room to continue investigating this other angle." Roberts paused. "If I recall my geography correctly, Brewer just *happens* to be across the river from Bangor."

"Really? I had no idea," I deadpanned.

"Right," Roberts laughed before the line went dead.

I sighed a bit as I tossed my phone back down on the nightstand, but not before belatedly seeing I had multiple unopened voicemails. Not wanting to deal with any of that, I instead turned and caught Suzanne's look of concern. "I'm okay," I replied, answering her unspoken question. "Jimmy knew what he was getting when he hired me, though I think the reality of how I work is just now starting to sink in."

"Good," she said. "I think."

"I probably should grab the first shower, though," I continued as I retrieved my overnight back and started to fish through it for a clean set of clothes. I frowned slightly when I realized all I had left was a polo with the old Windeport P.D. logo on it. *Jimmy won't be very happy when he sees this on the evening news tonight*, I thought. *I hope this isn't a harbinger for the kind of day this is going to be.*

"No worries," Suzanne replied. "Are you going to be home for dinner?"

I looked at her for a moment, for it had literally been *months* since she had called either my place or hers that. "Yes," I replied foolishly, knowing that I might well be lying; then again, the insane excitement I was suddenly feeling inside that we might — maybe — have turned the final corner in our relationship seemed worth the effort required to make good on my promise. "You want me to pick up something?"

"No," she said. "I was thinking of making Alejandro's enchiladas, assuming you are game and don't mind me making a mess of your kitchen."

Our kitchen, I mentally corrected as I felt an eyebrow arch. "You know he stole that recipe from someone else, right?"

"Did he?" she smiled. "I had no idea."

FOURTEEN

I rarely drove the Maine Turnpike with my lights and sirens going, mostly because the number of emergencies requiring such extreme measures had been few and far between; that, and dodging other drivers on the highway at high speeds tended to be a perilous adventure that I wanted no part of unless it was absolutely necessary. Despite Captain Roberts' insistence my immediate presence in Brewer mandated such measures, I nonetheless felt no small amount of anxiety when I flipped the appropriate switches on the SUV's dashboard and then began weaving back and forth across the striped lanes at upwards of ninety miles per hour. Training and years of experience as a police officer dictated that my full attention be focused on not plowing into that one sedan or semi-truck that failed to yield as I came upon them; for that reason, I reluctantly tabled my musings on the case until I'd gotten through the morning's obligations.

The tension that had begun to accumulate in my shoulder blades began to dissipate as I slowed down for the I-395 cloverleaf just south of Bangor. A quick glance at the clock on the dashboard told me I'd made good time; Roberts had texted me both the address and the media schedule, and it appeared I'd be arriving with about twenty minutes to spare. Keeping one ear on Siri's directions, I worked my way through the mid-morning traffic; with my lights still on, the pathway cleared as though I were a modern Moses, a metaphor that became all the more apt as the deluge that had been threatening my entire drive suddenly dropped from the heavens. I'd not thought to lookup the weather forecast before leaving South Portland but figured having gone as many overcast days as we had without seeing anything meant we were due — though getting it all at once hadn't been my expectation.

Rain pelted my windshield with a vengeance as I turned off I-395 and headed southeasterly on Route 15; while I was a frequent visitor to Bangor, I'd never worked a case in Brewer, so I was unfamiliar with the area. The tree-lined road appeared worn out and tired, countless winters having taken their toll; one- and two-story residential homes gradually gave way to a densely wooded forest broken only occasionally by the odd farm. Slowing as Siri warned I was nearing my destination, the glow of flashing lights from the assembled emergency vehicles was a far better indicator I had arrived. Pulling off the pavement, I parked behind the recognizable van from the Medical Examiner's office; the rear doors were open, providing an unobstructed view of a black body bag atop a gurney.

One question answered, I thought as I turned off my SUV. *So much for questioning the suspect; hopefully Lou will be able to provide answers.*

Pulling out my woefully inadequate UEM-logoed windbreaker, I shrugged into it and then exited into the cold embrace of the day. Within moments, I was thoroughly drenched from the downpour and feared for ever, *ever*, feeling warm and comfortable ever again. Sloshing through the ice cold puddles, I followed the trail of personnel as they walked up and down the long dirt driveway for the farm we were all parked in front of; if the rain continued for another hour or two, I could easily see the dirt turning to mud, which may well have been why most of the larger State vehicles were parked out on the main drag. Nodding at a random member of the force I didn't know who recognized me, I looked up at the stately three-story farmhouse off to one side of the driveway; based on the construction angles I pegged it to be something from the late nineteenth century, a hypothesis partially confirmed by the date hanging over the front door. The obligatory sagging barn was across the dooryard, clad in the same weathered white clapboard as the house; one of the two doors had been pushed open, revealing a length of crime scene tape flapping in the breeze. I appeared to have found the entrance to our scene.

Pulling the windbreaker tighter against the wind, I strode across the viscous surface of the dooryard and was in the process of fishing out my badge for the officer checking people in when I heard my name being called. Looking up, I smiled when I saw Heather Graham standing just inside the barn door, holding the tape up. "Hey stranger," I replied as the young officer scanned my ID and tapped at his tablet. "Fancy meeting you here."

"Glad you could grace us with your presence," she replied icily as I ducked under the tape.

My smile faltered slightly, for Heather was normally rather upbeat. "How much trouble am I in?"

Stepping back from the doorway, she folded her arms against what looked like a far warmer jacket than anything I had in my inventory and frowned, an expression I hardly ever saw. "Enough that you'll be shipping me lobster from your aunt's restaurant for the next few months."

"Shit," I breathed, my eyes widening. "I'm truly sorry — I got here as fast as I could, but I was returning from checking on a lead in Boston. It wasn't my intent to make you wait."

"Captain Roberts filled me in," she replied. "It's not just the waiting, but you've also been ghosting me all week. I've left multiple voicemails regarding this case, and you've not answered a single one." Heather's eyes narrowed. "It's not like you waste my time."

"No, it's not," I replied. "I've had a hard time balancing the demands on my time. Clearly."

"You wanted to sit at the big boy's table," she reminded me. "This is what that means. Now tell me what the fuck was more important than giving me the courtesy of a response."

"Suzanne's ex-husband was murdered," I answered simply. "And for a brief period both she and I were being considered as prime suspects."

Heather's face went from anger to shock to something a bit softer. "Oh, holy *hell*," she said. "Seriously?"

"Seriously. We cleared it up yesterday, but not before I took over *that* case, too." I smiled wryly. "Why work one murder when I can do *three* for the same cost?"

"There is not enough of you to go around," Heather observed. "Damn."

"In my defense, the cell coverage was for shit in New Hampshire," I added. "We couldn't have called in a pizza order, let alone..."

My train of thought suddenly swerved. *Who found Hammersmith? I found myself asking. And how did they call it in? It couldn't have been by cellphone. I need to get my hands on the landline records — there might be something there—*

I felt myself suddenly standing in that den back in New Hampshire, oblivious to the crime scene I'd barely entered. In front of me was the desk, piled high with clutter. Focusing for a moment, I tried to recall whether I'd seen evidence of a phone and realized I hadn't, either there or in the kitchen or, frankly, in any other room we'd walked through that day.

Shit.

"Sean?"

I blinked. "Sorry, was I saying something?"

"Yes." Heather's mouth quirked. "And then you got that faraway look you always have when a piece of the puzzle drops into place."

"Ah," I coughed. "Apologies — again — at suddenly ignoring you." I nodded toward the interior of the barn. "What do we have here?"

Eyeing me for a moment, Heather decided to let it pass and then began to lead me further into the barn. "The main point of interest is over here, stashed in what had once been hay storage. I hope you've taken your allergy meds today, because it's kind of intense."

"Sadly, I didn't."

"I've got plenty of Kleenex for you, then," she chuckled. "I suppose it's appropriate penance."

I decided not to push my luck and simply nodded as I fell into step beside her. The barn did indeed have the overwhelming odor of ancient hay, mixed in with a healthy dose of manure and just a touch of decay. While it was clear the space had not been in use as an active farm for some time, it nevertheless seemed to be in far better shape than the slightly leaning exterior had belied. It was also extremely empty, save for the equipment the technicians had brought in to light and then catalogue every square inch of the barn. The hay storage area had been walled off to the left of the major portion of the space and tucked just inside was an astonishingly modern fishing boat on a metal trailer. By my eye, it looked to be a little under twenty feet in length, with a rather aggressive looking outboard motor perched on the rear. On the wooden floor of the barn were arrayed various parts of the boat, including the seats, an anchor, several life vests and multiple tackle boxes; a handful of fishing rods were carefully laid out nearby, tagged (as with everything else) by a small, numbered evidence placard. There was a temporary staircase erected at the front of the boat, and Heather waited for a tech to climb down before leading me upwards.

"We found the body here," she said as we paused on the top step.

"I can see that," I replied as my eyes went to the blood and other biological matter against the far edge of the interior. "Gunshot wound?"

"More like *wounds*," she answered. Her tone made me look at her sharply. "Anonymous tipster called the hotline stating they thought someone was in the barn," Heather continued as she pointed to the bullet holes in the side of the boat that I had initially overlooked. "Naturally, we dispatched a reaction team."

It didn't take much imagination to see how the rest of the situation went down. "How many rounds?"

"Too many," Heather replied quietly. "Lou will have the final details. She's doing the PM this afternoon."

I groaned inwardly; so much for my promise of being back to Windeport in time for dinner. "That is a bit more expedited than normal."

"There are a lot of eyes watching this case now," Heather said softly. "Something you might want to keep in mind from this point forward."

"Ayuh," I breathed. "There goes my evening."

Heather smiled slightly and then carefully stepped into the boat; I waited on the small landing of the staircase and watched as she knelt. "My read is the victim likely took a fatal shot while crouched down about here," she continued. "No way to know which one of the hundreds of rounds it might have been unless Lou has a particular brand of magic I am unaware of." Standing, she put a gloved hand on her hip. "I'm not looking forward to having to do the ballistics testing."

"Nor the paperwork."

"*Especially* the paperwork," she sighed. Then looked back at the spot where the gunman had died. "He was found with a semiautomatic and one extra clip; just eyeballing it, I feel like it could be a match for what was used at the pizzeria, but of course we'll need to run ballistics on *that*, too."

"No rest for the wicked."

"There are days when I think I'm paying penance for a past life's transgressions," Heather continued as she stood and stepped back over the transom. For the first time in all of the years I had known her, she looked truly world weary. "This is one of them."

"You know as well as I do the deities that control law enforcement love to watch us sort through shit like this," I reminded her. "Or did you not read the fine print on your contract?"

"Was that in there?" Heather smiled slightly, a welcome touch of humor lightening her mood. "I must have missed that."

"Everyone does," I nodded solemnly as we traipsed down the steps.

Back down on the floor of the barn, Heather led me over to a cluster of stacked crates bearing the logo for the department that had been pressed into service as a field desk. One stack unsurprisingly held several of the clear plastic evidence containers the lab favored, though considering the size of the crime scene, the paltry number was concerning. The next stack over held a laptop and a digital camera, both of which appeared to be idle. Tapping at the keyboard with a gloved finger, Heather's eyes narrowed for a moment at the screen before she turned back to me.

"We were able to get prints before the body was carried away — the hands were about the only part of the cadaver that hadn't become Swiss cheese — and I had them scanned in so the computers could chunk through the matches while we sifted through the scene." Pointing to the digital ten print card showing on the screen, she continued. "The supercomputer down in August almost immediately came back with a hit to partials we found at the pizzeria."

"How partial were the partials?"

"Enough that the match was in the ninetieth percentile." She smiled grimly. "If you were still going to court with this, it would hold up."

"I may yet," I murmured. "Where were the partials?"

"The front door, around the planter in the lobby and the cash counter at the rear."

My eyebrows went up. "Anywhere else?"

"No." Heather looked at me for a moment. "I can see from your expression that was unexpected."

"More like confirmation," I replied thoughtfully. "In any event, it's hardly conclusive in terms of the shooter's movements within the pizzeria."

"True."

"Can we identify the body?"

Heather shook her head. "No — well, at least not yet. Nothing came back on the prints, so the lab will try for a match with the DNA. Nothing was on the victim to give us a hint of who he was; no wallet, no phone, no name sewn into the neckline of the shirt."

"I don't think people do that any longer," I said before adding with a slight smile: "At least, not anyone over the age of ten."

"I wish more people would," she sighed. "It would make my life a lot easier."

"No kidding."

Heather glanced over her shoulder at the boat, and for a moment I had a sense she was picturing the body as she had found it up there. "Along those lines, our shooter didn't seem to be wearing the same outfit as described by the eyewitness."

"Oh?"

Her eyes came back to mine. "Yeah," she nodded before looking down at her tablet. Tapping at the screen, she turned it toward me so I could see the crime scene photo with the body *in sito*.

I had seen a lot of dead bodies in my career, so it was rare for me to blanch; still, it took quite a bit of effort not to be overwhelmingly appalled at the violence that had been wreaked against this particular suspect — no matter what he had been credibly accused of doing. Trying to look past the bloody mess, I focused on the tattered clothing hugging what was left of the body and found myself a bit chagrined I'd not picked up on that fact. "Military-style fatigues," I observed. "Hard to miss, even under stressful circumstances." I glanced at Heather. "I presume there was no bag — no change of clothes?"

"There was a bag, actually," Heather confirmed. "Containing a few days' worth of food and water, plus the extra clip I mentioned. No change of clothes, though."

"I can't discount the possibility our shooter stopped somewhere and cleaned up, but it seems extremely unlikely."

"I agree." She paused. "We've also not come up with the weapon that would match the bullets in the clips," she added. "Not in the barn, and not on the surrounding grounds. I'm beginning to suspect it might have been dumped somewhere else."

"Lovely," I sighed. Turning away from the makeshift table, I took in the empty interior of the barn again. "How did he get here?" I asked.

"Other than our vehicles out there, I don't recall seeing anything else —unless the geeks towed something back to the lab already."

I heard Heather chuckle and turned back toward her in time to see the remnants of a smile. "Nothing gets past you, does it?"

"I wish that were true," I smiled wryly.

"In this case, it is," she continued. "When the team arrived, they discovered the owner had already decamped to Florida for the winter; the yard was completely empty."

"That's... convenient," I said. Thinking about that for a moment, I glanced back toward the boat. "How close are we to the river?"

The smile returned to Heather's face. "Close enough that we considered that option as well," she replied as she pointed to the rear of the barn. "The Penobscot is about quarter of a mile in that direction, mostly downhill. One of my techs found evidence of recent passage through the undergrowth, including fabric snagged on a raspberry bush. The lab will have to match the swatch with what was on the victim; while not entirely conclusive, it seems like our shooter arrived via water."

"Let's take a look," I said.

Heather eyed my boots. "At least you're dressed for the walk," she observed as we threaded our way through the techs that were clearly starting to pack up. "I lost a sneaker making the trek earlier."

"Put it on my tab," I laughed.

"Already did," she smiled.

The rear doors to the barn were nearly a mirror of the front, save for the strange architectural decision to have them arch upward in the center; I suspected since Maine farmers were a pragmatic bunch, it had been a prudent choice to accommodate some sort of now long-gone equipment in use at the time. Heather tugged at the right side of the portal, and after creaking in protest, it slowly began to slide open; a slight gust of the chilly November air whistled through, bringing with it the first indications that the rain had finally started to turn over to snow. I let Heather take the lead and fell into step behind her as we walked across the frozen surface of the field. Less than twenty yards from the rear of the barn, the edge of the forest surrounding the farm loomed large; pausing for a moment, my guide gently pushed aside some low-hanging branches and ducked into the thick undergrowth. Following her, I quickly spied the tufts of yellow crime scene tape that had been tied every few feet along a surprisingly visible pathway, one that quickly began to tilt downward.

"This looks like it has gotten some use over the years," I remarked as I carefully ducked around a large branch from a fur tree.

"I think that's why our victim used it," Heather replied, her voice muffled slightly by forest. "There is also some evidence of a dock along the shoreline. We've not had a chance to interview the owner, but it's not much of a stretch to assume supplies might have once been delivered by boat."

"That was pretty common in the eighteenth and nineteenth centuries along the Penobscot," I said. "A highway before there were highways."

"Or rail," she added. "I imagine that became far more practical once the station was built in Bangor; its former location is about six miles away."

"Good point."

We lapsed into a short silence at that point, for the trail — such as it was — had suddenly become incredibly steep; by the time a small clearing appeared at the edge of the river, I'd begun to feel for anyone who had lugged massive bags of supplies up to the farm. The space we arrived in wasn't more than a few feet square, though; massive overgrowth had reclaimed what might have once been a far larger landing area. What was left, though, appeared to have gotten a fair amount of use recently as evidenced by the number of footprints in what looked more like a partially melted chocolate milkshake than semi-frozen mud. Squatting slightly where the edge rolled down into the dark surface of the Penobscot — all the while wary of losing my balance and toppling in — I took a moment to examine a single deep groove in the mud that had been partially filled in with water from the river. While not someone who typically spent much time on a boat, having worked the majority of my career in a state well known for its outdoor traditions meant I could easily recognize the signs of a small watercraft being dragged ashore.

I glanced at Heather, who was standing just to my side. "Canoe?" I asked.

"Or kayak," she nodded before smiling wryly. "Neither of which is obviously present."

Looking out across the deceptively placid surface of the river, I frowned. "It's hard to tell from this vantage point, but I'd have to assume the current is pretty strong even here; if whatever had been used wasn't anchored properly, I'd imagine it's far, far downstream by now."

"That's the angle we're taking," Heather said. "I called in a favor with the Fish and Wildlife Service; two of their wardens are working the river, coming at this location from both ends."

Arching an eyebrow, I smiled slightly. "It's not likely to have headed *toward* Bangor."

"Just trying to be thorough," she replied. "On the chance it had an engine and took off on its own."

"Uh huh," I chuckled. "If they don't find anything, we may have to dredge the river."

Heather rolled her eyes. "Lovely. And before you ask, yes, we took impressions of what we could; I'm not sure how much good that will do us, though, as the mud was pretty soft. But you never know."

"Your lab down in Portland could be handy," I said. "It came through for us on the Donohue case."

"That they did. But these are in pretty sad shape. It would take a miracle to get an actual shoe print from them."

Leaning back on my haunches, I managed to continue keeping my balance by placing my hands on my thighs. "How far upstream are we from East Newberry?"

"As the river flows?" Heather sighed. "I don't know without using some sort of GIS software, but if I had to guess, maybe ten miles? Fifteen at the outside."

I nodded slowly. "Maybe your theory about an engine is right," I said. "Unless you see our victim as one who paddled his way up the river."

"I'll let Lou be the final judge on that," Heather replied, "but from what little I saw, I'd not have said he was all that athletic."

Standing up, I looked downriver. "A canoe, then. One with a small outboard — enough to make headway against the current."

"And not much more," Heather nodded. "The only problem in your theory is that we didn't find any evidence that the shooter took off via the river."

I smiled slightly. "We have no evidence of how he took off, *period*," I reminded her. "All options are open still, including a helicopter."

Heather looked at me askance. "Someone would have noticed that."

"Okay," I smiled wider. "Maybe not a helicopter then. Good to rule *something* out at this point." I pointed at a small stub of wood peeking just above the surface of the river. "Is that the dock you mentioned?"

"What's left of it," she nodded. "I don't think it was very big originally."

"Or if it was, years of ice ramming up against it ripped it apart."

"True." She paused for a moment. "That's about it. Ready to head back?"

"Yeah."

Heather again took the lead, guiding me back toward the barn; the return trip seemed shorter, though that may have also had more to do with my attention being focused on sorting through what I had learned. I was so engrossed in my thoughts that it took a moment for me to realize Heather had been speaking. "I'm sorry," I interrupted. "What was that about dredging?"

She glanced over her shoulder at me. "I was just saying it would be totally on brand for you to be two-for-two if we had to search the river back there."

I came up short. "What did the divers find behind the pizzeria?" I asked, suddenly oblivious to the cold rain that seemed to have gotten more intense.

"You haven't read the file yet, have you?" Heather accused, eyeing me critically. "You really *are* being stretched a bit too thin."

"No argument there." I paused. "What did they find?"

"The answer to a thirty-five-year-old missing person's case," she smiled enigmatically.

Fifteen

The press conference was predictably awful; I'd never been a fan of the feint-and-parry tactics beat reporters tended to use when they sniffed a bigger story below the just-the-facts recitation I tended to drop into at such things under the best of circumstances, and standing there in the pouring rain had been anything but. Still, I managed to smile and nod and generally finesse my way through ninety minutes of poking and prodding without revealing much more than I'd done at the very top of the conference; by the time I was back behind the wheel of my SUV, I was chilled to the bone and just as thoroughly soaked. Cranking the heat as high as it would go, I did a quick U-turn on Route 15 and sped off into the gathering dusk, intent on thawing out as much as I could before arriving in Augusta for what now appeared to be a marathon autopsy session. Bowing to the inevitable, I'd texted Suzanne that our plans for the evening were definitively dashed; still, her response had contained enough implied sizzle for what might *still* happen once I arrived at the bungalow that I'd privately vowed to set a land-speed record for my return to Windeport.

Unfortunately, the storm that had been threatening for days had finally been unleashed by Mother Nature; shortly after turning south on I-95, the rain shifted over to sleet, and then in quick order became snow thick enough I could barely see beyond my headlights. I'd not needed the blinking reminder from the Turnpike Authority that the speed had been temporarily reduced, for the icy surface made anything faster than what a Galapagos tortoise could manage downright dangerous. Adding insult to injury, the temperature had dropped so low so fast it was impossible for my defroster to keep up; before too long, frost had formed on the *interior* of my windshield, framing the view with a quaint holiday feel I could have done well enough without. The normally hour-long drive between Bangor and Augusta stretched into more than two, and demanded my entire attention; save for a brief contemplation of the whatever it was Heather's team had apparently dragged from the Penobscot, all thoughts about any of the cases I was currently working were set aside in the pursuit of making it to the morgue in one piece. I lost another thirty minutes slipping and sliding across the city before finally pulling into the lot behind the facility just a hair shy of seven. Though the lot had clearly been plowed at least once, snow was falling fast enough it was nearly above my ankles as I trudged across to the entrance; my frozen hands fumbled with my ID at the badge reader, and I nearly recoiled at how icy cold the handle was when I was able to finally pull the door open.

Considering I felt a bit like a popsicle, I took the unusual step of showering before changing into a set of scrubs for the postmortem; despite the anemic pressure, for the first time the relative warmth of the water was a blessing I appreciated immensely. Toweling off, I stuffed my out-of-control curls into a cap, tugged on the paper-thin scrubs and then set off in search of Dr. Hamilton. Unlike my last quest, I quickly found her in Exam Seventeen, one of the few rooms that had been refreshed with Federal money the State had received as part of the current fiscal year's appropriations. Our senior Senator had campaigned for re-election on the promise not to defund the police, a sketchy position given that no one had actually been calling to do so in the first place. Nevertheless, they'd surprisingly made good on their promise by funneling a rather large amount of cash to the state — though, predictably, hardly any of it had trickled down to those of us who might actually have had a use for it. As the impressively automatic silver doors parted at my presence to allow me into the exam room, I wondered a bit at whether that was how Captain Roberts had magically obtained his new unmarked and then decided it might be best to never know the answer to that particular mystery.

Lou turned at the sound of the doors sighing open. "There you are."

I smiled despite knowing she couldn't see it beneath my face mask. "People keep saying that to me this week. I'm starting to get a bit paranoid."

"Only if it's warranted," she laughed. "How's the driving?"

"Awful," I replied as I approached her. "I fear I might have to spend the night in Augusta."

"There could be worse things."

"No offense against this fair city, but I'd prefer to be in my girl-friend's arms tonight."

"None taken," she laughed again.

I wasn't surprised to see a cadaver already in progress on the stain-less-steel exam table in the center of the room; what got my eyebrows arching upwards were the two *additional* gurneys parked beside it, each bearing their own body. "I know you well enough not to ask if these are all related," I said as I took up position beside the main table.

Lou laughed slightly. "Indeed. Well, you're partially right — two of them are," she said, then waved at the main exam table with a gloved hand before I had a chance to ask for clarification. "This is the body Heather's team pulled from the river in East Newberry. As I think she already told you, its presence on my table answers a three-decade-old question."

"Heather was a bit coy on the details, actually," I replied, frowning beneath my mask. "I don't think she wanted to spoil your moment, although I might have already guessed some of it."

"That doesn't surprise me in the least," Lou sighed. "Lay it on me, then."

I turned fully toward the body that had pride of place beneath the exam lights. Considering it had been pulled out of the river, it was in remarkably good condition; aside from the normal lividity associated with the deceased, the former Mrs. Angelina looked like she'd passed away just a few days ago — not three decades earlier. By my reckoning she was slightly over five feet tall; the smooth features of the face made her seem youthful, but the telltale marks of a Cesarean still visible despite Lou having already opened up the upper chest told me she'd been a mother. A subtle but beautiful wedding band encircled the ring finger on her left hand, and the nails appeared to have been recently done. One ear still had a simple diamond stud; the mate seemed to be missing. Long hair in silvery gray still had a few accents of the dark brown it had once been; I wasn't sure if the slight sheen to it was due to having been underwater or some sort of hair product. Her eyes were closed, sparing me the strange sightless gaze of the dead; remnants of eyeshadow hinted at an unusual color that probably would have looked better were the skin not that strange sallow hue all cadavers ultimately get.

"It's only conjecture at this point," I started cautiously as I looked back at my friend of many years, "but based on what I know so far, this is the late Beryl Angelina."

Lou's eyes narrowed. "Heather *did* spoil it, didn't she?"

"No," I answered, shaking my head. "However, it fits a theory I'd been contemplating since finding the bullets in the wall at the pizzeria."

The Chief Medical Examiner narrowed her eyes further. "How long have you been sitting on that one?" she asked. "There's nothing in the file to indicate you had a side investigation going on into the owner's wife."

"Too long, perhaps," I answered honestly. "My interview with Leon

— that's the owner — was somewhat curtailed given I had to conduct it in his intensive care suite at Bangor General. One thing he did mention, though, was becoming a widower in 1988; I didn't think too much of it until Norm told me later how Beryl had essentially disappeared into thin air. In retrospect, it feels like a strange way to characterize his loss — and it's been bothering me ever since."

"Widower?" Lou asked. "I guess that's true now that we've found Beryl but would have hardly been the case back in '88."

"Exactly," I nodded as my eyes moved down to the body on the table. "Assuming this is her, she's in remarkably good shape considering she died thirty-five years ago."

"Being tightly wrapped in plastic will do that to you," Lou replied. "I won't recount how long it took me and two of my geeks to carefully cut away the duct tape and what appeared to be cling wrap." She tapped at her computer for a moment. "All of it is being processed now for trace, but we already know the tape is pretty standard stuff, available at any hardware or box store. The plastic wrap, though, was commercial food grade, common in just about any restaurant."

"Like our pizzeria?"

"Most definitely," Lou nodded as she stepped back toward the table. "I don't think I'll be able to get you an exact manufacturer given how old the sample is, but if I had to guess, it's not the kind of thing that changes much over the decades."

"Norm's already looking over the business records," I said thoughtfully. "Maybe we'll locate an unusually large purchase of cling wrap back in 1988."

"I can send what we have to the Feds, too," Lou offered. "They have better industrial databases and might be able to narrow it down a bit for you."

"I'll take any help I can get."

Lou eyed me over the rim of her mask. "I won't ask if you think she was murdered — the wounds I'm about to walk you through more or less underscore that. But you think she was killed at the pizzeria?"

I nodded. "Something you might be able to confirm for me if you came up with a bullet."

From the way Lou's eyes crinkled, I knew she was smiling. "We'll get to that, too."

"Good," I chuckled. "The plastic wrap really preserved her, didn't it?" I remarked again.

"That," Lou said, "along with the insulated — and airtight — container she'd been stuffed into."

I nodded again. "Weighed down as well, I take it?"

"Yes," Lou replied. "Photos of everything are in the case file for you to peruse, though like I said, my minions are still swabbing everything for trace and further testing."

"I trust them," I laughed. "So, Doctor, what can you tell me about Beryl Angelina?"

"Enough to fill several notebooks," she replied.

"Just give me the précis."

"Don't I always?" Lou chuckled. "We were able to make a preliminary identification using the photo we had on file with the Department of Motor Vehicles; if you can track down next of kin, we'll do something more definitive with DNA." Leaning toward her computer, she tapped at the keyboard for a moment. "Height, weight and other characteristics matched what was on the license, though, so I'm reasonably certain I've got Beryl Angelina on my table."

My eyes went back to the body on the table, still amazed at the condition it was in. I'd already seen that Lou had opened the chest for inspection; I knew the small plastic containers holding the key major organs were already off to the lab for analysis but frowned a bit when I saw a segment of the rib cage had been specifically exposed. That usually meant my friend had located something intriguing, but I also knew better than to spoil her presentation by asking about it. I was struck again by what looked like freshly painted nails; glancing to the discolored feet, my eyebrows went up when I saw those nails had been professionally done as well.

"What was she wearing?" I asked as I bent down to take a closer look at the nails. "And do these look like they were recently done?"

"They do," Lou replied, answering the questions in reverse order. "As far as clothing goes, nothing out of the ordinary for a middle-aged woman. Typical undergarments found at any moderate department store, and then a standard Maine ensemble of a turtleneck, polyester sweater and jeans, all from L.L. Bean." Lou paused. "While she was wearing sox, no footwear was recovered."

I crossed my arms against the thin fabric of the scrubs. Despite the shower, the normally cold temperature Lou kept the exam room at had begun to seep into my bones. "That might confirm when she went missing," I mused. "Assuming she disappeared between November and April. I'll have to check the police report."

Lou nodded and then continued her tour. Moving around to the far side of the table, she began pointing out things on the body as though they were landmarks for a cross-country trip. "Indications of a Cesarean, though a hysterectomy was also performed."

"Is that usual for someone of her age?" I asked, frowning.

"No, but if what I found in the major organs is any indication, I think it was just the tip of the iceberg." Tapping a gloved finger against a small wound that had been sutured up just beneath a breast, she sighed. "The most telltale evidence was a mass I removed from the left breast; I've seen enough over the years to recognize metastasized cancer."

"Oh... wow," I said, leaning back on my heels. "So if she hadn't been killed...?"

"Five months," Lou replied. "Maybe six. I'm running some other tests that will tell me if she was on any sort of therapy, but from what I'm seeing, I'd guess whatever she was on wasn't working."

"Shit."

"That was what I thought *before* I found enough plaque build-up in one of the major arteries to have landed her in a cardiologist's office. I'm having a standard panel run with the bloodwork, but I doubt it will tell me much at this point." Lou sighed again. "This woman was a mess."

I looked at her fingers again. "And yet she had her nails done."

"People often focus on the small things they can control in situations like this," Lou replied. "I worked one case years ago where a ninety-nine-year-old woman landed on my table hours after getting her hair permed."

"Huh."

"Yeah." Leaning over the body, she folded back the flap of skin that she'd lifted to perform her interior inspection then pointed a gloved finger at an obvious gunshot wound nearly exactly between the breasts; it had a companion wound just below the right breast. "Evidence of at least two gunshot wounds, one here — which went through the lower part of the heart — and this one over here." Picking up the portion of the rib cage she'd removed, she indicated a spot between two of the bones. "Fortunately for you, one of the bullets came in at such an odd angle, it got lodged here. I was able to pull it out mostly intact, and the lab ran it against everything in the database." Lou paused. "You'll never guess the hit we got."

"It came from the same gun that killed Kirk Nevelson?"

Lou smiled. "Yep. Same gun."

"That's a relatively welcome piece of good news."

"I thought you might appreciate that."

I leaned down again. "If it got lodged in there, the shot had to be from some distance away, right?"

"I'd have to run the numbers, but yeah. And down low, almost as if the shooter were on their knees."

"Both shots?"

"Yes."

"And the one to the heart killed her?"

"No question."

"And there would have been a lot of blood, too," I mused. "Something else to check."

"Probably, though if you found anything after all this time, we'd not be able to do much with it at this point."

"Other than verify a series of events," I murmured before looking to the second body. "This is our shooter?"

"Yes," Lou replied as we both moved over to the gurney. "This story is less clear, aside from the fact he died from multiple gunshot wounds. No identification of any kind was on the body; we're rushing a DNA test as we speak, and prints have been sent to anyone and everyone that has a database. Nothing's come back yet."

The body was in partial shadow given the spotlights were trained on the main exam table; that made the gruesome mess that was left of a human being slightly easier to take. Bullet holes riddled nearly every square inch of the cadaver, quietly testifying to just how much force had been brought to bear on whatever soul had once been inside. "Heather did say the prints matched some from the pizzeria."

"Yes," Lou nodded. "And that's about all I have on our shooter."

"If he *is* the shooter," I replied.

An eyebrow went up on Lou's face. "You don't think he's the shooter?"

"All I know for certain at this point is that this poor guy was hiding out in a barn outside of Bangor — and that he had visited Pizzeria Angelina somewhat recently. There are a number of possible explanations for that, *including* being the shooter."

"Don't go telling the Captain that," Lou replied.

"I don't plan to," I said. "And the third body?"

"Ah," Lou said before gesturing at the second gurney. "Meet Leslie Hammersmith."

I felt my eyes widen. "How on earth—?"

"Captain Roberts," she said by way of explanation. "The body arrived about an hour ahead of the shooter, along with the results of the postmortem my compatriot in Concord ran."

"Wow," I said for what seemed like the millionth time.

Lou leaned a little closer to me. "I've known you a long time, Sean, so I don't say this lightly. Whether you intended to or not, you've called in quite a few chips on this one. Yours were earned multiple times over, but still, I hope it was worth what comes next."

"I'm not sure I like the sound of that," I replied. "What, exactly, comes next?"

"Whispers, mostly," she replied. "The accusations of favoritism will come later, usually when they can be used to further certain political ends." Lou paused. "You don't run a small police department any longer, Sean — you're not answering to a bunch of village novices. Our actions, big or small, can cause ripple effects across the entire organization — especially when they attract the unwanted attention of those who are campaigning for reining in law enforcement."

I felt my face flame slightly. "How bad is it?"

"Bad enough that you'd better solve these cases in a hurry so everyone is distracted by your brilliance once again," she replied. "To that end, I've pretty much confirmed the results of the prior exam: Mr. Hammersmith died from blunt force trauma to the temple, from something round and made from wood. Probably oak, maybe birch; it was hard to tell based on the few slivers removed from the wound."

"Time of death?"

"I see no reason to dispute the original window, which was last Sunday, between noon and midnight."

My mind was still turning over the not-so-subtle warning from Lou, enough that it took a long moment for my eyes to focus on the body in front of us. I'd not had the privilege of meeting Suzanne's ex-husband; given how he had treated her, that was probably wise for if my off-the-books investigation had proven anything, it was how clearly emotionally compromised I was when it came to Leslie. I 'm not sure I would have trusted myself to be alone with him, which was a strange realization given my normally unflappable equanimity. The body below me was that of a very average middle-aged man, one who seemed to enjoy his food if the slightly bulging stomach meant anything. If it weren't for the smashed-in section of his skull, I could've been forgiven for thinking he was just taking a quick nap.

"Defensive wounds?" I asked, deciding to try and short circuit the presentation Lou was clearly gearing up to give.

"No, none," she answered.

I thought about the den in the New Hampshire house. "If he was facing his killer, he would have seen it coming," I said thoughtfully. "Unless he was slightly angled away from the coming attack."

"Or looking down," Lou offered. Pointing to the fracture, she drew a circle in the air as she continued. "This could be evidence of a direct hit, or a glancing hit; either way, it was more than enough to kill him."

"Could it have come from behind?" I asked. "Like if he'd been turned away, and then rotated into the blow?"

Lou narrowed her eyes. "Perhaps. I can run some numbers and see what the computer says. Is it important?"

"Possibly," I smiled slightly.

"Then I'll get on it."

"Thanks," I said. "Anything else?"

"That about does it." She stepped around the gurney and unexpectedly put her gloved hands to each arm. "Look, I feel badly about what I said earlier—"

I smiled despite knowing she couldn't see it. "Hey, someone needed to talk sense into me — and I can't think of a better person to deliver the message, frankly." I reached up and squeezed her gloved hand. "You weren't wrong. I've spent my entire career running things my way; you would have thought I'd have learned my lesson, considering it's why I work for the State now." I paused for a moment, letting a jolt of insight wash over me. "I think I am just now realizing how difficult a transition it's been for me."

"You're a good man, Sean," Lou said softly, "and an even better investigator. Don't let the crazy political intrigue that comes with working for the State destroy everything you've achieved."

"I won't," I replied firmly.

"Good."

"Jimmy did promise me a job that would be different than my old one," I added as I headed for the door. "Seems he wasn't wrong."

"The Captain is a smart man," Lou laughed. "Everything will be in the case system tonight, so go work your magic."

"Don't I always?" I smiled as I pushed through the door.

SIXTEEN

Against my better judgement — or at least, the conventional wisdom of the meteorologists charting the storm that had dropped multiple inches of snow across the entire state — I topped off the SUV's gas tank and literally plowed my way back to Windeport, intent on spending the evening in my own bed. Predictably, it was an incredibly difficult drive; by the time I pulled into the driveway of my bungalow a hair past midnight, I could feel the accumulated tension across my shoulders and longed for a few minutes in the hot tub to relieve some of the muscle strain. Seeing Suzanne's Forester parked beneath the carport chased away some of the malaise; the rest disappeared when she greeted me at the door wearing little more than one of my old UEM swimming t-shirts and a smile that I'd not seen since before the quasi-breakup we'd experienced back in August. I'd barely crossed the threshold before she pulled me toward her and gently pressed her lips to mine; while outwardly a simple, subtle gesture, the smoldering heat behind it had me dropping my gear and kicking the door shut behind me with a heel of my boot.

I left a trail of clothing behind me as we worked our way through my house and toward the master bedroom; her hands seemed to be everywhere at once, perhaps seeking physical reassurance I'd indeed made it home in one piece. By the time we reached the bed, I was down to just my boxer briefs and was breathing as hard as if I'd just come out of the pool after barely out touching a competitor for the win. Somewhat surprised I was on such a hair trigger, I knew I needed to slow things down just a bit or risk having the evening end rather abruptly. Despite how hard my heart was beating — and how desperately certain parts of me were aching for release — I carefully reached down and began to slowly roll the t-shirt up Suzanne's torso; pausing at her belly button, I leaned down and gently kissed the smooth skin just above it, then crept ever higher with my lips as I continued to push the t-shirt upward. Suzanne shuddered slightly when I reached the deep valley between her breasts, which was my cue to push her backwards and onto the comforter of the bed.

Sensing what I was about, Suzanne pulled off the t-shirt before leaning against the piled-up pillows, then put her hands to either side of my face, strategically guiding me upwards as I planted light kisses on her now flushed skin. I was in the process of paying extremely close attention to one of her breasts when I felt her hand snake down between us; smiling slightly, I shifted to the other breast but not before adjusting my position just enough to allow her to tug my boxer briefs down. Based on how she was reacting to my touch, I wasn't surprised when I felt both of her hands appear on my rear and then gently — but firmly — begin to press me into her. I shifted slightly at her touch and nearly lost it when I felt myself glide into her; nibbling at the intersection of her neck and shoulder for a moment allowed me to regain some control, but I knew it wouldn't be for long. Fortunately, the hazy way her hooded eyes were regarding me told me I'd done my part, so I bent down and kissed her with a fierceness that tried to wipe away the months of guardedness that had developed between us. Raw, feral instinct took over at that point; almost as though someone else were pulling my strings, I felt my body arch and twist and shudder with release. Beneath me, Suzanne was just a heartbeat behind; as the wave began to crest, she came up from the surface of the bed and pressed her white-hot skin against mine. The effect was so electric that I actually felt myself begin to climb toward another crescendo, one that culminated when Suzanne went over the edge and arched herself into my chest one final time.

When my world reformed itself, I found I was lying against her chest, deliciously spent and feeling more alive than I had in weeks. The *thumpa-thumpa-thumpa* of Suzanne's heartbeat made me smile; I smiled wider when I felt her fingers along the edge of my exposed ear, brushing back one of my unruly curls with a touch so tender, I instinctively leaned into it and nearly began to purr as though I were a feline. Snuggled into her as I was, I thought perhaps it wasn't an inaccurate analogy, especially given how I now seemed to rather adroitly play the part as Chat Noir. Twisting my head slightly so I could see Suzanne's face, I reached up and drew her lips back to mine for a brief taste of what had recently transpired; letting her go, I searched her eyes for a moment before deciding to risk destroying the moment.

"Are we back?" I asked so tentatively I wasn't sure she had heard me.

Suzanne ran her fingers along the side of my face again before answering, simply, "Yes."

The rush of emotion that filled my soul at her answer was so intense, I thought I might burst; Suzanne seemed to be able to hear how my heart had begun to race and glanced meaningfully at the rather physical manifestation I had also developed. Donning a knowing smile, she deftly flipped me over onto my back and then shifted so she could straddle my thighs. "You need to get some sleep, kitty," she observed, though it wasn't lost on me how she had carefully begun to run her fingers along my pectorals.

"Someone once told me about the healing powers of sex," I said, trying hard not to gasp as Suzanne gently guided me back into her for the second time. "Someone — oh, *shit* — far wiser than me."

"A bit sensitive, are we?" she laughed quietly as she leaned down to brush another kiss across my lips.

"More than I realized," I said, acutely aware of every minute movement Suzanne was making. I began to wonder if I'd let my libido lead me places my body wasn't quite ready to handle and saw the answer in a rather mischievous look in Suzanne's eyes.

"Be careful what you ask for, my love."

Very little sleep was to be had, in fact; perhaps owing to the stress of the multiple cases I was currently working, I easily lost myself in the expert ministrations of my girlfriend and lost all track of time. Only the blaring reminder from my iPhone for swim practice was I ultimately able to break the enchantment Suzanne had cast over me; reluctantly, I pulled myself out from beneath her embrace so I could track down a swimsuit and warmups from the master closet. The snow had apparently stopped falling sometime after I'd returned to Windeport, but it still took me a few minutes to clear enough of a path to back the SUV out of my driveway; the rest of the roads in the Village had been plowed down to the pavement, so getting out to the UEM pool was relatively easy compared to the nasty drive I'd had from Augusta. The parking lot at the Aquatics Center was unusually empty when I pulled in a few minutes before five; aside from our Coach, the pool deck was deserted, and only two of the lanes appeared to have any swimmers.

I decided to eschew the locker room and simply shucked out of my sweats standing at the edge of the bleachers; digging my goggles and swim cap out of my bag, I tugged them both on as I wandered toward the lane I usually claimed. Glancing at the small whiteboard Coach had leaning against the wall, I smiled slightly to see the workout had been partitioned as always: the normal workout for the team was on the right, while the so-called Olympian set of tasks were on the left. I never failed to be impressed at how deviously long my task list always seemed to be, but then again, I'd also never stopped working out as though I were headed to another Games, either.

Stepping up to the starting block, I shook out my muscles slightly before lacing my hands together and diving into the cool water of the pool; kicking underwater, I came up at the fifteen-yard mark and allowed my brain to begin to get into the workout. I had long used my routine in the water as a way to decompress and, occasionally, ponder cases I was currently working on; the secret to doing so, though, often required me to give myself over to the process and allow my subconscious to begin to connect the dots. As of late, I'd had a great deal of trouble getting to the Zen-like state that had served me so well in the past; I was sure quite of bit of that had to do with my preoccupation with where things stood between Suzanne and myself, though I was also well aware that my misgivings about my new gig with the State seemed to always be there in the background. Hitting the wall at the end of my first twenty-five yards, I did a smooth flip turn and began to head to the other side, wondering once more why I felt so unsettled as Commander, Major Crimes.

Whether she'd intended to or not, Lou's gentle warning had crystallized alarm bells that had been going off in the back of my head for some time now; after being, essentially, my own boss for nearly a decade, subsuming my decisions in favor of the bureaucratic process the State observed had been very difficult to adjust to. Hell, if I were being honest with myself, I'd never actually *tried* to adjust to it; in fact, in my three months running the department, I'd managed to figure out ways to circumvent or even ignore workflows that I'd felt were contrary to getting to the truth. Hitting the second wall, I felt myself smile slightly as I flipped underwater; it was a delicious irony that the former police chief who had held himself and his staff to such high procedural standards now felt no compunction about selectively keeping to an even *higher* one.

Maybe I wasn't as good a law enforcement officer as I thought I was.

I suppose the real question I'm avoiding is what to do about it, I mused as I headed toward the far end of the pool again. *It's an open question whether I accepted Jimmy's offer too hastily; no, no it's not. I did accept the offer too quickly — I was hurting, adrift and grasped at the first thing that looked like a modicum of normalcy.*

So... what do I do about it?

I took a moment to listen to the water as it flowed past my body, saddened slightly that no answers were being whispered to me from within the gurgling. My faith was also sketchy enough at that point in my life that I figured God probably wouldn't provide any insight, either, so I simply put my head down and focused on the workout. Slowly, the world began to recede until the only thing I was aware of was the line of tile at the bottom of the pool; then, even that faded into the background, the first sign that I had, finally, reached that strange mental space where my neurons began to do their thing.

Thoughts began to swirl around me much like the bubbles I generated each time I did a flip turn; at first, they seemed disjointed, but slowly I began to find myself tracing through the steps that had led me being at that barn in Brewer the prior afternoon. For whatever reason, I seemed to be stubbornly refusing to accept that the body we'd recovered had been that of the shooter; while the evidence *seemed* to point to that conclusion, something seemed wrong though I was hard pressed to say what, *exactly*, was bothering me about it. Did it seem awfully convenient that we found someone vaguely matching the description I'd been given just a few miles upstream from the pizzeria? Yes, it did. Did it seem even *more* convenient that whatever water vessel had gotten them to the farm had conveniently disappeared? More so, perhaps, than where we'd found the body.

Coming up facing the ceiling on my next lap, I slowly began to get into the rhythm of my backstroke as I realized part of what seemed off. *Heather's team will find me a boat if there is a boat to be found*, I thought. *And yet, I don't think there will be anything at all. So, if the shooter didn't get there by boat, how on earth did he get to the farm? There was no vehicle located in the search. It's almost like someone dropped him off—*

I suddenly came out of my stroke and bobbed at the halfway point of the lane.

Someone dropped him off. Holy shit.

Treading water, I wondered about that for a moment. *Someone dropped him off with enough supplies to lay low for a few days. And then what? Quietly move on? Or wait for a pickup? The latter seems more likely, especially if I assume the point was to keep our shooter out of sight—*

The second epiphany hit me with such force that I stopped treading water long enough to sink below the surface for a moment. Kicking back to the surface, I slowly began to stroke toward the far wall, wondering all the while how I had missed something so blindingly obvious. Clearly, I hadn't been firing on all cylinders.

Stay out of sight until they needed to appear, I thought as I hit the wall and then reached up to grasp a handhold along the edge of the gutter. *Only to conveniently reappear when a tip is called in — an anonymous tip. I hope to God the State can backtrace the call, though I think I already know where it came from.*

Shit.

Looking up at the clock mounted to the wall of the facility, I knew it was far too early to begin rallying the troops; as much as I wanted to pull myself out of the water and gather together the disparate threads into a nice bow, I instead let go of the edge and kicked into a set of butterfly, momentarily setting aside my ruminating to focus on getting the flow just right. Two lengths of the pool later, though, my brain shifted into yet another gear, teasing out tidbits from my visit to the farm in Glenn Hills. While Leslie Hammersmith's death was in no way related to the events in East Newberry, I felt a little bit like I'd not brought my full faculties to bear on it, either. Having been tangentially accused of murder hadn't helped, of course; nor, I supposed, had my feelings for Suzanne — or, rather, my antipathy toward her ex-husband. I allowed anger at my actions to infuse an insanely fast set of butterfly, relishing for a few minutes the grueling burn as my muscles began to scream for relief. Hitting the final wall in a wave of water, I recognized and then forgave myself for the many mistakes I had made over the past week; as I bobbed under the starting block, gasping for air, I felt the final pieces of the man I had always been finally reassert themselves for the first time since being fired from my job in Windeport.

Damn, I thought as a wry smile appeared on my face. *Between passionate sex and vigorous workout, nothing feels impossible, does it? I wonder now if that's why Coach never fully discouraged us from hooking up; if nothing else, it finally explains the free condoms that were always available in his office...*

Pulling myself smoothly out of the water, I wandered back toward my gear and fished my towel out of my backpack. Only then did I realize in my haste to make practice, I'd not packed a change of clothes; while technically it was Saturday, I *had* planned on going to my office to pour through every last piece of information I had on the cases I was working. Unlike Vasily, I wasn't one to find excuses to dodge my standard Business Casual polo-and-khakis, but neither did I want to make a side trip back to the bungalow to change.

Fuck it, I thought as I toweled down. *Wouldn't be the first time I'd been forced to dash straight from swim practice to something else. Maybe Vasily knows something I don't,* I smiled to myself as I pulled my sweatpants over my swimsuit. *Seems as good a day as any testing theories, doesn't it?*

SEVENTEEN

The knock at the door to my office wasn't quite enough warning to whip the cheater glasses from the bridge of my nose, so instead I glared over the half-moon lenses at the figure of my number two. "I've been going through the financials of the pizzeria like you asked," he said by way of introduction. "I might have found the connection you were looking for."

"Which one?" I asked as I pulled the glasses off and rubbed my eyes. Their scratchiness was an annoying reminder that I'd had them in since leaving the Marriott Friday morning. "I've been looking through the latest results from the crime lab geeks and have, quite frankly, lost track of *any* of the connections I thought I had."

Norm pushed the door open further and strode across to my battleship-sized desk, then tactfully slid some papers to the side so he could place his MacBook on the surface. "The cling wrap?" he offered.

"Right," I said as I pushed back from my desk. Grabbing my empty coffee mug, I wandered over to my Keurig. Shoving the mug under the spigot, I turned and smiled wryly. "I'm not going to be surprised if you tell me it was something they bought regularly."

"Nor would I," Norm chuckled. "Like you suspected, though, the quantity purchased was pretty consistent, save for one month in 1988." Tapping at his keyboard, he turned the screen toward me. "The order in December of that year was triple their normal amount."

"How does that align with Beryl's disappearance?" I asked as I plunked a K-cup into the machine. I decided it would be best not to tell Suzanne that evening I'd lost count of how many I'd had that day; considering it was barely noon, I was on a pace to break my personal record.

"It depends," Norm replied. "I had Lydia track down the missing persons report Leon Angelina filed; East Newberry took the initial call the second week of November 1988 but passed it up to the State a few days later. If we assume her death occurred prior to the report being made, the cling wrap order would support your theory she was killed in the pizzeria and then dumped into the river."

I folded my hands against my chest and leaned on the counter as the Keurig huffed away. "The ballistics haven't come back on the bullet Lou pulled from the wife, but I'm willing to move forward assuming it will match the one Heather pulled from the wall. Did you find—"

"Paint and wall repair items?" Norm smiled. "As a matter of fact, yes. But not on the financials from the pizzeria. Those were purchased by Leon on his personal credit card, one that was closed in 2007."

"When?"

"Three days before the missing persons report was filed."

"There it is," I smiled.

"There's what?" Norm frowned.

"The connection. As well as evidence of a coverup."

"All we've got is Leon buying paint," Norm frowned deeper. "Paint purchased three decades ago. I'm not sure a jury will give us that much leeway."

"They won't," I agreed, "but it *does* give us a nice timeline now."

Norm thought about that for a moment; as his eyes lost their focus for a moment, I noticed he looked as tired as I felt, a sense accentuated by several days' worth of stubble. When combined with his much longer hairstyle and burly form, he looked a bit like a backwoods lumberjack. "So, you're thinking that Leon shot his wife sometime in early November 1988, dumped her in the Penobscot and then filed a missing persons report a few days later?" he asked. "Why draw attention to her disappearance?"

"For legal reasons," I replied thoughtfully. "If they owned the Pizzeria jointly, he wouldn't be able to do anything with it until she'd been declared legally dead."

Norm nodded. "And the first step in that direction would be making a formal report." He turned the computer back toward him. "Looks like the formal filing to declare Beryl dead was in April 1989." Norm paused and then swore. "Hot damn."

"What?"

He looked up at me. "I missed the connection earlier, but in August of 1989, Leon took out an equity line of credit on the business. The records indicate it was for renovation work."

I nodded. "That's when the forward portion of the restaurant got its makeover. I'll bet we'll find records of the coat rack being purchased during that period."

"I'll dig through it. I'm not sure what to make of the fact that they tried to sell the business a few times between 1985 and 1989; obviously, there were no takers, but also no further attempts beyond that."

"Not surprising, considering the situation in East Newberry."

"That tells me what you're thinking about Beryl's death," Norm said, eying me. "How does that tie into the shooting? And the bonus body in the back room?"

Pulling my almost-forgotten mug from beneath the Keurig, I took a sip of the toasty brew before answering. "Are you certain the pizzeria wasn't still for sale?"

"I'm not sure anyone would want to at this point," he replied. "It's barely broken even over the last decade; in fact, the negative cash flow from the past couple of years was hidden with infusions from personal savings and loans." Norm looked thoughtful for a moment. "If it was for sale, Leon definitely wasn't working through anything mainstream —" Norm suddenly broke off. "Private sale? Connected to the other victim?"

"That's my guess," I replied. "Kirk Nevelson certainly had financial acumen, though I don't know whether he had access to any resources."

Norm narrowed his eyes at me. "Why would a guy from Massachusetts want to buy—" he started before cutting himself off again. Dropping his eyes to the laptop, he swore again. "The DNA results that came back this morning had something important in them, didn't they?"

"That they did," I smiled as I pulled out my chair and sat down again.

"Shit," Norm breathed.

I sipped at my coffee while I watched Norm's eyes dart back and forth as he rapidly accessed information in the case files; I knew he'd found what I'd read when those same eyes snapped back up to mine. "Found it, I take it."

"*Fuck*," he breathed. "How did we miss *that*?"

"I made the cardinal mistake of not asking the right questions," I sighed. "But in the end, we got there."

"Kirk Nevelson is related to Leon Angelina," Norm breathed. "Not his son, though?"

"Grandson," I replied. "Which also explains why he was frequently going to Maine for 'family reasons.'" I grabbed my cheaters and slid them back on to read the report Caitlyn had printed out for me. Without my trusty MacBook, police work was feeling decidedly old school. "His mother lives on the Cape, at the very same address Leon put down on the missing persons report as Beryl's destination."

Norm glared at me. "I missed that, too."

I shrugged as I pulled the cheaters off. "So did I; then again, I only found it when I was searching for next-of-kin so we could do the notification. In fairness, we might have uncovered it faster had I been more persuasive with Nevelson's boss at First Beacon."

"Good to know there are limits to your superpowers," Norm chuckled. "I presume we want to visit his mother?"

"I've made arrangements for us to interview Norina Nevelson this afternoon," I nodded. "Assuming you are up for road trip to the Cape."

"I hear it's beautiful this time of year," he deadpanned. "Raphael had to head to D.C. last night, so I'm flying solo anyway."

"Uh oh. Business?"

"Sort of," Norm replied. "He got pulled into something."

"Since your boyfriend is a well-respected investigator for the National Park Service Police," I began, "I'm going to assume whatever went down is significant."

"Yeah," Norm nodded. "They found a dead body in the Washington Monument."

"In?" My eyebrows went up. "He's going to be there for a bit."

"Probably," Norm sighed. "The cottage is going to feel kinda empty."

"If you get too lonely, feel free to crash at my place," I offered. "I've got a spare room."

"I'll be fine, but thanks for the offer."

"Well, if you change your mind, just text me."

Norm smiled and tactfully returned to the subject at hand. "Kirk Nevelson, the grandson, is killed at the pizzeria," he said. "You really think he was trying to buy it from Leon?"

"Or get him to close it," I shrugged. "I doubt Leon was open to either idea."

"Based on what?"

"A hunch," I replied.

"A *hunch*," Norm repeated, somewhat incredulously. "Seriously?"

"Supported, in part, by Beryl's death."

Norm slowly nodded. "That... that could explain why the pizzeria wasn't put on the block after 1989. Like I said, though, there's nothing in the information I've scrounged up so far for *either* theory."

"Maybe Nevelson's mother will shed some light on it," I suggested. "But keep digging anyway."

"Okay, can do." Norm smiled crookedly. "This family seems like it has a few secrets, doesn't it?"

"More than a few," I agreed. "Especially one about a shooting back in 1988."

Norm nodded. "I've been thinking along the same lines ever since we identified — kind of — Beryl. Going back through the police records in East Newberry didn't net me any sort of incident report; broadening it to the State also came up empty. If we'd not found the bullet holes in the wall, I'm not certain there would have been any evidence something happened."

"Or the body," I added.

"Or the body. Still, Pizzeria Angelina isn't exactly located in a backwater of the city. Someone had to have seen or heard something, right?"

"I agree, but it was more than thirty years ago. At this point, it's highly unlikely we'd be able to track down anyone who happened to be in the area on a random night in November."

My number two looked thoughtful. "Unless there was a reason to be downtown," he said.

I rolled my eyes. "You've seen what passes for downtown," I began. "I don't think much has changed over the last thirty years."

"True," Norm replied.

Something in the way he was smiling had me raising my eyebrows; they went up a bit further when it hit me what he was obliquely saying. "Holy shit. *Nothing* has changed, including the diner across the street from the pizzeria."

"Exactly," he replied.

My eyes dropped to the spot where my trusty MacBook would normally be, and I frowned slightly when I realized I'd not been notified it was ready to be retrieved. *One more item to add to the task list,* I thought morosely. "Did anyone get the contact information for that business?"

"No, but it should be fairly easy to retrieve."

I waved him off. "You know what? Don't bother; we can swing by East Newberry on our way to the Cape. I wanted to try the coffee, anyway."

"Sounds good," he replied. Closing the lid on his laptop, he stood. "When do you want to go?"

"As soon as you are ready."

"Give me fifteen, then." Norm smiled again. "I've finally learned to keep a packed bag in my SUV for such occasions."

"Good man. I'll meet you out front."

As Norm slipped out of my office, I had a momentary flashback to the hundreds of times his predecessor had made much the same move, and for a moment, felt a touch of melancholy. The third anniversary of Vasily departing for California had recently passed, and despite my best efforts, not a day went by that I didn't find myself seriously missing his presence by my side. We talked all the time, of course, and texted constantly, but it really wasn't the same as seeing him sit across from me, smiling that delightfully sly smile as we closed on our latest suspect; glancing at the clock on the wall just above my gold medals from the Olympics, I did the math and realized my friend was probably still in the pool doing his extended weekend workout — assuming, of course, that he'd not landed himself in the middle of a case and was similarly working gobs of unpaid overtime.

Thinking about Vasily gave me a sudden start; I'd been so wrapped up in taking care of Suzanne on Thursday that I'd completely spaced about the call I was supposed to have had with Alejandro to iron out the final details of the wedding. I dug my iPhone out of my pocket and quickly scrolled through my contacts, then tapped the listing for Alex; he picked up after just two rings.

"*Hola*, Sean," he said brightly. "You caught me finishing up at the pool."

"That's on me entirely," I sighed. "I should have called two days ago, but this case I'm working has taken over my life. I didn't even realize it was Saturday until I got a funny look from the intake receptionist when I came to the office this morning."

"No need to apologize," Alex replied with a soft chuckle. "I'm in love with a police officer, remember?"

"That you are," I laughed. "Still, I feel terrible for blowing you off."

"Don't worry about it," he replied. "I will confess to having Vas ping your phone, though. When you didn't reach out, I assumed something had come up; seeing your dot in Boston and then New Hampshire pretty much told me everything I needed to know."

"I'm sure it did," I said. "I had no idea Vas was stalking me."

"You shouldn't have shared your location with him, then," Alex teased. "Given your history."

"Indeed. Is this a bad time?"

"Not at all," Alex said. "The only thing you're interrupting is me re-wrapping my wrist."

"Wait — what?" I asked. "Did you injure it *again*?"

"I'm not sure it ever really healed," he admitted. "Vas has been after me to dial it back, but with regionals coming up, I just can't." There was a brief moment of wry laughter. "I'm not entirely sure I like growing older."

"It happens to the best of us," I observed sagely. "And aren't you, like, barely thirty?"

"That's the nicest thing anyone has said to me today," he laughed. "Anyway, I'm sure you're calling about the wedding."

"I am," I replied. "You mentioned there was a problem booking that wedding pavilion with the stunning view of Cinderella's Castle. Did someone book your date?"

"You could say that," Alex laughed.

"Damn," I sighed. "I know how much you were hoping to surprise Vasily with a Disney wedding."

"Apparently, so was Vas," Alex said.

It was hard not for me to smile, considering how Suzanne and I had conspired to ensure that very outcome. I wasn't looking forward to the inevitable call from Vasily when it became clear we'd been unable to keep the secret wedding planning a secret from each other; then again, what did the pair expect? The fact that Vas had been working with Suzanne and Alex, me, had been bound for trouble from the beginning.

"No *shit*," I breathed, trying to sound genuinely surprised. "Seriously?"

"Right down to the music selections," Alex confirmed with a chuckle. "Unbeknownst to me, the coordinator from Disney that was working with Vasily stumbled onto the double-booking and called *him* first to see what he wanted to do; since I'd already paid the deposit, apparently my reservation was the winner."

"Yay, I guess...?" I said. "Save for the fact that our super-secret plan is now not so secret."

"Exactly. Which, honestly, is probably for the best. I was having a hard time keeping it from Vasily. With the date locked in for sure, we need to talk logistics; I'm thinking a big FaceTime call might be in order. Will you and Suzanne be around on Sunday? Vas and I have a thing in the morning, but we could do something around two our time."

I did the math in my head and nodded. "That's about five for us; unless something goes sideways with this case I'm working, I think we can do that."

"Just text me if something comes up," Alex replied. "By the way, how do you feel about wearing mouse ears?"

"I'm not sure I've much thought about it. Why?" I asked cautiously.

"No reason."

"I know better than that," I sighed. "What am I going to have to wear?"

"I'll show you during the call," Alex chuckled. "All the more reason to make sure you'll be there."

"Now I'm seriously worried."

"As well you should be," Alex laughed. "I've got to run. Vas and I are meeting Rosie for brunch this morning."

"Say hello to her for me, would you?"

"Will do. See you tomorrow."

I found myself smiling as I hung up with Alex; as I'd gotten to know the diver-turned-career counselor better, the more convinced I'd become that he was the perfect match for my best friend. Sliding the iPhone back into my sweatpants, I took a look at the paperwork piled in various stacks on my desk and wondered for the millionth time how my law enforcement predecessors had managed to stay even remotely organized without a computer. My MacBook had only been MIA for less than a week and I was already beginning to feel like I'd become swamped, a feeling compounded by the fact that I'd stubbornly refused to requisition a temporary replacement from central I.T.

They'd probably send me a frigging Windows tablet, too, I snorted as I finished off the last of my coffee and stood to go wash it out in the sink of our break room. *Give them a foothold and they'll think they have license to replace everything else, too.*

Wandering down one of the side pathways carved out of the cubicles for the squad room, I mused a bit on what Vasily had often called my Apple obsession. I could never be entirely sure where along the line I'd become a Steve Jobs acolyte but was reasonably certain I'd picked it up from my mother. She'd been the one to introduce me to technology in the first place, and since she'd pretty much run our family pharmacy business off of one of those boxy Macs from the late 1990s, I'd been exposed to them from an extremely early age. As I pushed open the door to the break room, I thought a bit about how far the tech had come; the laptop I'd had at UEM had been a million times more powerful than the system my mom had used, though the battery life had left quite a bit to be desired.

Hell, I thought as I squirted some dish soap into my mug, *I think my iPhone is another magnitude more powerful as that laptop, not to mention having some cool features that we'd never have dreamed of back in the day—*

I was suddenly struck by a thought as I rinsed the soap from my mug.

Vasily pinged my location.

Holy shit — I am so fucking completely *off my game this week.*

Yanking at the paper towel dispenser, I quickly dried off the mug and then hurried back out into the bullpen. As it happened, I caught Norm as he was exiting his office at the far end and waved at him to wait; he was wearing an expectant expression when I drew up in front of him. "Which judge is on duty this weekend?" I asked.

"Judge Rayo," he replied, completely unfazed by the odd question. "Why?"

"We need a new warrant," I replied as I nodded at his laptop backpack hanging from one hand.

"For?" Norm asked.

"Phone tracking data," I said. "How long will it take for you to type it up?"

Norm narrowed his eyes at me. "You solved it, didn't you?"

"Get me that phone data," I smiled, "and I'll let you know."

EIGHTEEN

Driving in Maine after a massive storm could often be something of an adventure but occasionally became something extraordinary. We'd gotten enough snow that everything — and I mean *everything* — had a significant coating of the white stuff, from homes to barns to the stately tall pine trees that guarded the edge of the road. With the sun no longer obscured by the thick clouds that had dogged us for days, the brilliance reflecting off of every surface was a little hard to take, almost as if I were a vampire suddenly exposed to daylight for the first time in a millennium; fortunately, my Oakley sunglasses were up to the task. The roads were clear down to the black of the pavement, and with the sun now out in force, there was some evidence that the snow was melting; we were still early enough in the season that the snow was unlikely to survive until Thanksgiving, but stranger things had happened.

Conversation between Norm and I had been unusually subdued as I navigated the SUV toward East Newberry; while my partner wasn't nearly as loquacious as Vasily on the best of days, that morning he'd opted to use the time to review the tranche of personal finance data we'd received on Kirk Nevelson. Warrants for anything related to out-of-state residents tended to be tricky, but we'd lucked out and had no pushback on our request; still, I was used to the back-and-forth I'd often had with Vas when he dug into something, so the silence had made me feel somewhat left out of the party. That feeling was exacerbated when I pulled the SUV into the small parking lot beside the boat landing, turned it off and then realized Norm had no clue we'd reached East Newberry. I'd had to tap his shoulder to return his attention back to the here-and-now; he'd sheepishly closed up his laptop and then joined me out in the brilliantly cold day.

Snow squeaked beneath my Bean Boots as we headed down the carefully shoveled sidewalk; for a downtown area I had written off as completely lifeless, there were a surprising number of pedestrians out and about. Considering it seemed as though the diner and pharmacy comprised the entirety of the retail opportunities currently available, I assumed it was more likely the residents were simply taking their morning constitutionals; all things being equal, and despite a murder having occurred, it was actually a rather pleasant walk there along the Penobscot.

As we passed the pizzeria, my curiosity over what Norm had been reviewing finally spurred me to speak. My breath wafted out in front of me as I turned toward Norm. "I take it you found something interesting in the financials?"

"I'm not sure," he replied after a moment. "I wasn't expecting to get quite as much as I did; it seems Nevelson was a very, *very* active investor, so there is a ton to go through."

"I hear a 'but' in there."

Norm smiled. "A few things stood out almost immediately," he said. "Among them, a regular payment of around two grand that looks a bit like rent to me. I was trying to track down the org listed in the records when we pulled up."

"Rent?" I frowned. "I would have expected someone like Nevelson to *own* a home, but then again with recent tax law changes it might not be as beneficial."

"Exactly — which is where it gets interesting. He does also have a regular EFT to Chase for about four grand; that account I was able to trace, which led me to the tax records showing Nevelson owns a smart three-bedroom townhouse just off the Green Line in Cambridge."

I felt myself frown. "Cambridge? Why not Beacon Hill."

"I hear that's a nice starter community," Norm chuckled.

"Indeed. What else caught your attention?"

"Among other things, multiple six-figure payments to a law firm in Boston. They aren't as regular as the other payments, so my read on them is it might be something contractual." He smiled slightly. "I'm not sure exactly how it fits in with everything, but the firm in question specializes in franchising."

My eyebrows went up. "Really? As in *purchasing* a franchise?"

"Or creating one," Norm replied.

I paused and looked back up the street at the now-closed pizzeria. "That *is* interesting, and now I think we have an excellent reason to stay overnight in Boston."

"I thought you might say that," he smiled. "I've got the number for the firm."

"Good. After we're done here, let's see if we can get an appointment with them in the morning."

"Got it."

I started back toward the diner and then paused to let a small Subaru caked in salt residue drive past us before crossing the road; through the wide glass window, I could tell business was brisk, an observation that was validated once I stepped inside and experienced the cacophony firsthand. There didn't appear to be any sort of host stand, so I scanned the room and located an open booth at the far end of the massive window. Norm trailed me as I worked through the surprisingly robust crowd; the smell of short order food hung thickly in the air, and despite my normal reticence to eat anything that didn't directly benefit my exercise regime, I suddenly found myself very much wanting to sample some of the scrambled eggs and hash browns I was seeing on more than a few tables. The diner itself appeared to be a retro throwback to the streamlined era of late 1950s, though on second glance, it dawned on me there wasn't anything retro about it — that, in fact, I was seeing original furniture and equipment kept so pristine that it looked almost new. Sliding onto the plastic cushion of the bench for our booth, I marveled a bit at the period-perfect ketchup and mustard bottles, as well as the squat glass container of sugar; somehow, it seemed entirely appropriate that there was no evidence sugar-substitutes even existed.

My eyes met Norm's as he shrugged out of his jacket. "I feel like we've stepped through some sort of time portal," I said.

He nodded and then looked around for a moment. "Hard to believe this community is dying, isn't it?"

"Totally," I agreed.

Within moments, a comfortably plump woman wearing a brown serving uniform appeared carrying a similarly colored carafe and two of the white mugs I'd seen early. "Coffee, hon?"

"Absolutely," I breathed.

She put the mugs down and then, to my surprise, began to pour the coffee from a height of about three feet into one of them. Completely unconcerned — and not spilling anything — she turned to Norm. "How about you, hon?"

"Yes, thanks."

Repeating the maneuver, she turned her smile back on me. "Special today is eggs any way you like, side of hash browns, sourdough toast and choice of ham or sausage. Rest of the menu is posted over the bar."

Despite it being nearly lunchtime, I'd pretty much already sold my soul for the eggs. "I'll take the special," I said, "scrambled, and with ham, please."

She nodded, and as she did so, I finally saw the name badge pinned to her white apron. Adele seemed like an entirely appropriate moniker, given how her hair seemed to have been teased into the 1960s bouffant the singer had once sported. Turning back toward Norm, she smiled again. "And you?"

"What is the Farm Press?" he asked after looking at the menu.

Adele thought for a moment. "That's a new one; Cookie has been experimenting with a sandwich press. I *think* it's a breaded chicken breast with mozzarella slices between two pieces of Texas toast. Comes with house-made chips, coleslaw or fruit."

"I'd like that, then."

"Gotcha. Anything else?"

"Yes," I said, then smiled myself. "Information, actually. I'm investigating—"

The waitress cut me off. "I thought I recognized you — you're that young guy with the State Police that was on the news last night."

"That's me," I nodded.

Adele frowned. "It sounded like you got the shooter. Can't be much more to investigate at this point."

I smiled slightly. "Just tying up some loose ends," I replied. "There was an older gentleman working here the night of the shooting. Any chance he's working today?"

"That would be Carmine," Adele answered. "The owner. And yes, he's here today. You wanna talk to him?"

"If he's free."

"I'll let him know." She glanced over me and through the window in the general direction of the pizzeria. "Terrible thing, that," she said softly. "I hope they can reopen."

I just nodded and then watched her go; looking over at Norm, I could see a slight smile. "What?"

"I dunno," he said, smiling wider. "I've never had breakfast with a celebrity before."

I rolled my eyes. "You need to get out more, dude."

"Maybe. Can I get a selfie with you?" he asked sweetly.

"Fuck off," I smiled.

As befitting a diner, our food arrived nearly instantly; however, instead of Adele, the older gentleman I'd seen in the window a few nights early had brought the order, which he carefully placed in front of us. "Adele said you wanted to talk to me."

"Carmine?" I asked before reaching over to shake his hand. "Commander Sean Colbeth, Major Crimes. Do you have a minute to join us? It seems kind of busy this morning."

"I can spare a few," he replied. Norm slid over, allowing Carmine to settle on the edge; wiping his hands on the somewhat stained apron, he eyed both of us. "We're always busy on the weekend."

The smell of the eggs and potatoes wafting up from my plate had me nodding. "Good food always attracts patrons," I said. "Do you mind if I eat while we chat?"

"Not at all."

I took a forkful of eggs and was rewarded with the rich taste of an old-fashioned recipe that appeared to use cream in the mix. "How long have you owned the diner?"

"Second generation," Carmine replied. "My dad opened the place in '56. It's been mine since '74."

"That's pretty close to when Leon Angelina took over across the street," Norm observed.

"Ayuh," Carmine replied.

"If you don't mind me saying this, the diner seems to be in excellent shape."

"Dad believed in running a tight ship," he said. "Got that from his time in the Navy during WWII." Carmine shrugged. "I guess I picked it up myself."

"Clearly," I nodded. "Is the pool hall next door part of your business?"

"Originally," he replied. "Wasn't much point in keeping it running once the mill finally closed, so I shuttered it back in '93." Carmine looked out the window. "Used to be a real slice of life here; now, not so much."

"There seem to be a lot of ghosts in this town," Norm said.

"Ayuh," Carmine said.

"How well do you know Leon Angelina?" I asked.

"Well enough. Knew his wife better."

"Oh?"

Carmine nodded. "She was on the council for a bit, helped me get some funding to repair my roof after we had a freak hailstorm in 1982; weren't many like her."

I glanced at Norm. "I understand Beryl disappeared in 1988."

"Yeah. I remember that; I think she was going to visit her daughter and never arrived."

I nodded. "Did she have any reason to want to leave East Newberry?"

Carmine looked at me. "*Everyone* wants to get away from East Newberry," he replied as if the answer should have been obvious. "She'd tried to get Leon to sell the pizzeria so they could go south and be closer to their kid."

"I take it he wasn't interested, then?" Norm asked.

"Hardly," Carmine shook his head. "Leon will only leave East Newberry when they carry his casket out."

My eyebrows went up. "I've known a few people like that," I said. "How did Leon take the disappearance of his wife?"

He shrugged. "Not well. Who would?"

To my surprise, I'd managed to eat almost all of my hash browns while we'd been chatting; for some reason, that made me a bit sad. As I played with a small piece of grilled onion, I considered how to phrase my next question. "East Newberry must have been a bit different back in '88."

"Somewhat," he replied. His quick glance to the kitchen told me I was running out of time.

"Different enough to invest in your business?" I asked. "More than usual?"

Carmine looked at me, startled. "I'd forgotten about that," he replied. "Beryl had gotten some sort of Federal grant to update the sidewalks and lighting; it was an in-kind grant, so the businesses along the street had to show some good faith matching investments to qualify."

"What did you do?"

Carmine nodded at the big window. "Changed out all of the glass to be that super-efficient kind," he replied, "and updated the HVAC. A couple of us did that."

"Including the pizzeria?"

"Leon put in a new fridge, I think," Carmine replied. "That's when he redid the front, too. I always thought the rest of the place was going to get done, but once Beryl disappeared the work kind of stopped. Which is too bad; Beryl had some big plans."

"Such as?"

Carmine shrugged again. "There had been talk of opening a new location, possibly Bangor. I think Beryl had hoped to keep the pizzeria alive long after East Newberry folded."

"Leon wanted that, too?"

Carmine shook his head again. "Hardly. Like I said, he had no interest in leaving East Newberry."

Norm frowned. "If I understood you correctly, it was more like the *business* might be leaving."

"I think the two were one and the same," Carmine smiled slightly. Glancing at the kitchen, he slid out of the booth. "I've got to get back to it. Enjoy your meals."

"Thank you," I said.

Norm watched the owner go before speaking, his voice low. "What do you think?"

"I think," I replied as I downed the last of my eggs and waved to the waitress for our check, "we might have the first inklings that not all was copasetic between Beryl and Leon."

My partner frowned. "I'm not certain a difference of opinion on expanding their business applies," he said. "That happens all the time."

"It does," I nodded, "though perhaps not with such drastic consequences." Norm looked like he was wanting to respond, but I cut him off by continuing. "Down your coffee — we've got to hit the road."

I paid the check and accepted a to-go paper cup of coffee; in short order, Norm and I were headed back down the street toward the small parking lot where I'd left the SUV. Traffic appeared to have tapered off from our earlier walk, though there were still a surprising number of vehicles and pedestrians. It appeared my definition of *dying munici-pality* might need to be updated, especially given how many more cars were packed into the parking lot. I was a bit surprised, actually, for it was clear hardly anyone was using the lot specifically because of the boat ramp. In fact, there was only the one boat parked directly next to the ramp; there were no other empty trailers around, underscoring my assessment.

My eyes went to the boat as we approached the SUV, and it took a moment for me to decide whether it was the same boat that had been there the night of the shooting, I turned to Norm. "That was here on Monday, right?"

"I think so," he replied. "Maybe? I know there was a *boat* here. I'd be hard pressed to tell you it was that one."

"Yeah," I murmured.

"What is it?" Norm asked.

"Something," I replied softly.

Ignoring the SUV for a moment, I walked over to the unplowed boat ramp, and then carefully picked my way down to the where it met the edge of the river. Unsurprisingly, it was a bit icy where the sun hadn't quite reached, but that also worked slightly in my favor: there was no indication anyone had used the ramp since the storm. Turning, I knelt and looked back up the ramp and nodded when I only saw my footprints in the melting snow. Norm stood at the top of the ramp and was patiently watching me; retracing my steps, I nodded at him before moving over to the boat. To my eye, it wasn't much more than a two-bench rowboat that happened to have an outboard bolted to the stern. Coming around to the rear, I could see the tags for the aluminum trailer were current; walking slowly along the side, I found the registration affixed to the boat's bow also appeared to be legal.

Oddly, the trailer was still attached to a fairly new Ram pickup truck; squatting at the front tire of the truck, the accumulated snow around it confirmed it hadn't moved in a while. Standing again, I searched my memory of Monday night and was hard pressed to recall if the truck had been there; I knew the boat was, though, so it seemed like a good assumption to make. Walking around the impressive hood, I squeezed between the fence against which it had been parked and tried the handle to the passenger door; I wasn't surprised to find it unlocked, given the small-town mentality that abided in the state.

I looked at Norm, who had appeared beside me. "We could run the plates," I said. "But since the door is unlocked, and this vehicle appears to be abandoned…"

"I agree," he smiled.

Pulling the door open, I slid into the passenger seat and then popped open the glove box. There was a small plastic sleeve sitting on top of the Owner's Manual which I retrieved; one more piece of the overall puzzle fell into place when my eyes fell on the small proof of insurance card peeking through the clear window of the sleeve: *Leon Angelina*. Sliding back out of the truck, I couldn't help the smile I knew I was wearing. Norm looked at me askance until I handed him the sleeve; his eyes scanned it, then came back to mine. I felt my moment begin to evaporate when I saw his frown.

"Clearly you see a connection here," he said as he handed me back the sleeve.

There were a number of ways to respond to that; the one I chose involved making a call. Retrieving my iPhone, I dialed a number from memory and then smiled broadly when I heard a familiar voice. "Heather, how quickly can your team get back to East Newberry? I think I found the boat that took our shooter upriver…"

NINETEEN

By rights, we should have stayed to oversee the crime scene geeks as they dutifully went to work on the small boat, but the delay in waiting for Heather and the crew to arrive in the first place had threatened our window to speak with Kirk Nevelson's mother. After extracting Heather's usual promise that the case file would be updated just as soon as they finished, I'd packed a still-agog Norm back into the SUV and then put the pedal to the metal in the hopes of getting to Cape Cod on schedule. It wasn't until we crossed the border from New Hampshire into Massachusetts that I realized he'd not said more than five words to me since leaving East Newberry; glancing sideways, I relaxed when I saw he'd nodded off against the passenger-side window. I couldn't blame him, for we'd more or less been on the run for nearly a week. I decided at that point waking him to ask if he wanted to stop for coffee was a bad idea and instead plowed onward toward our destination.

Traffic in Boston was predictably bad; it wasn't a whole lot better once I got off the 93 and began working my way East toward the funny little hook of land jutting into the Atlantic that was Cape Cod. The address I had for Norina Nevelson put her in Chatham, which was just about as far East as you could get on the Cape before pretty much being in the ocean. It was part of the reason I'd planned on overnighting in Boston given the distances involved, especially since Norm had managed to get one of the partners in the law firm Kirk had been using to meet us over breakfast at our hotel on Sunday. *How* he'd convinced them do it was something I chose not to discover.

I'd not been to the Cape in a while; as the highway shrunk lanes and the traffic thinned a bit, I realized my last trip had been with Deidre about a year before we parted ways. A mutual friend from our college years had tied the knot on a sandy strip of beach not far from the Kennedy compound, and we'd made a long weekend of the trip — or at least, had tried to. Vasily had yanked me back to a double homicide just outside of Winslow the morning of the ceremony, another in a long line of poorly timed consulting gigs I'd done over the years for Captain Roberts. De hadn't been thrilled to go to the wedding alone, though she'd been partially mollified by Vas driving down to retrieve me. In hindsight, I wondered if that had been the final straw for my then fiancé.

Traffic began to resemble something close to what we experienced at the height of tourist season in Windeport as I passed the sign for Chatham; I had plenty of time to enjoy the sights as we slowly crawled past homes that fairly screamed beach getaway — though only for those with a few more zeros in their income than the rest of us. The brilliant sunshine poured through the bare limbs of the trees lining the roadway, about the only sign beyond the walkers bundled up in scarves and hats that we were on the cusp of winter. Siri — perhaps sensing I was beginning to grow tired of counting the frost heaves as we went over them — at length finally directed me to turn off the main drag; a succession of side streets soon followed before we finally pulled up to a stately A-frame of a cottage with an impressive amount of ocean frontage. Killing the engine to the SUV, I gently shook my partner from his slumber, then reached into the rear to grab my backpack. It took a moment for Norm to rub the sleep from his bleary eyes before he mirrored my movement and pushed out into the chill of the afternoon.

I paused at the bumper of my SUV, impressed at the small postage stamp of a home. It was painfully clear that the homes on either side had been the result of a purchase-and-tear-down transaction; they filled every square inch of their property in a vain attempt to squeeze every amenity a McMansion could offer into the space. By contrast, the relatively petite cottage harkened back to a time when the population of the Cape was far smaller — and the construction more appropriate to the location. The sides of the cottage were traditional white clapboard and clearly taken care of; the windows appeared freshly washed, with hangars below them speaking to flowering window boxes present during more seasonal parts of the calendar. A short driveway ran from the street to a carport containing a pristine Jeep Wagoneer straight out of the late 1980s; flagstone pavers placed hopscotch style led to a screened in front porch that still had two carved pumpkins from Halloween smiling rather toothily at anyone brave enough to ring the doorbell. Pressing the button, I stood back for a moment to admire the artistically painted tile containing the street number, then turned my attention to the door when I heard the bolt being pulled back.

With a creak that would have risen the dead multiple counties over, the door swung inwards to reveal an older woman of modest height; sandy hair with a few touches of gray was pulled back into a businesslike ponytail, revealing a face weathered from days roaming the beach. A flour-stained apron covered what appeared to be jean shorts and a t-shirt bearing the logo of the Red Sox; the faint smell of something yeasty being baked wafted out on the warm air escaping from the cottage, and I couldn't help an appreciative sniff. Wiping her hands on the front of the apron, bright eyes of blue quickly took stock of myself and Norm, then crinkled with the sheepish smile that slowly appeared.

"I've been meaning to get those hinges oiled," she apologized. "The salt in the air does a real number on hardware around here. You must be Commander Colbeth?"

I nodded. "And this is my colleague, Lieutenant Norm Thomas; thanks for taking the time to meet with us today, Ms. Nevelson."

"Oh, Christ," she chuckled, "no one is that formal out here on the Cape, Commander. Besides, I've never used that name; it's actually Goddard, after my late husband. Regardless, please call me Norina. Won't you step inside? I've got some loaves about to come out of the oven."

"Thank you," I nodded again as we stepped into the cottage. "And I only hear 'Commander' when my boss is angry at me."

"Sean it is, then," she laughed. "Don't mind the mess," Norina continued as she led us through a small sitting room and down a short hallway toward what I presumed was the source of the now borderline divine smell of freshly baked bread. "I've been making Communion loaves for church over the last week or so and haven't had the time to tidy up around here."

While I'd not stopped to do a thorough inspection, there didn't appear to be a speck of dust anywhere, nor the standard piles of bric-a-brac that often accumulated in a home. "I'm hardly one to judge," I said as we entered the cozy kitchen at the rear of the cottage. "My roommate in college often complained about the piles of laundry everywhere."

"I've been to your house," Norm chuckled. "I can't believe that's even *remotely* true."

"Oh Lord," I smiled. "Text Vasily and ask him about the massive argument we had over it. I only started to pick up after myself when I realized he was stealing my swimsuits."

"Swimsuits? Sounds like quite the story," Norina said as she immediately turned and went to the dual ovens on the wall.

I took a moment to reply for the kitchen was something to behold. To my surprise, it had massive windows along one wall with an amazing view of the ocean; there was a large island in the center of the space currently covered in flour and the various pieces of kitchen gear I supposed one might use for making bread. It was angled perfectly so whoever was working at it would be able to partake in the view. Behind the island was a long counter broken only by a sink and a smooth cook-top; the aforementioned ovens were at the far end, next to a large fridge and doors to a pantry. Cabinets in a light oak color were above the counter, and shelves containing other cooking equipment were below, all open to the space. There were two barstools on the far end of the island, and though my natural inclination was to grab one and wave Norm to the other, it would have meant putting my back to the stunning view; instead, by unspoken agreement we took up position perpendicular to the island.

"I swam competitively in college," I finally replied as I watched Norina pull two loaves from the oven and place them on a wire rack to cool. They appeared to be joining about a half-dozen or so already present.

"Oh," Norina nodded as she lifted a dish towel off two aluminum-looking pans sitting on the counter; I could see dough just peeking over the top before she transferred them to the oven. "On scholarship, were you?"

I nodded. "All four years."

"Were you any good at it?"

Norm started and then looked away — but not before I saw his slight smile. For my part, I was a bit surprised she'd not connected the dots. Then again, Beijing was a long time ago now. "I had my moments."

"Good," she replied as she wiped her hands again against the apron. "You mentioned on the phone this was about my son, Kirk?"

"Yes," I replied, my eyes firmly on the bread cooling. "How many loaves do you make, exactly?"

"That is a good question," she said. "I don't always keep track, honestly, but the general formula is that they need one full loaf per service, and there are two services once a month. I guess that works out to about two dozen?"

"Do you always make them in advance?" Norm asked.

"Usually," she nodded. "Far easier than trying to bake last minute, plus I usually get my supplies at Sam's Club. Once you open a bag of flour that big, you really need to use it all up as soon as you can."

"Good point," I smiled. "I hope your congregation appreciates the effort you go through."

Norina shrugged. "I do it for me, honestly. Takes a bit of the edge off of life."

My eyebrows went up a bit, but I decided not to pursue that line — yet. "You didn't take your first husband's name, but Kirk did?" I asked, shifting back to our main reason for the visit.

"It was a bit more complicated than that," she smiled slightly. "I was pregnant with Kirk as a senior in high school. Booger Nevelson is his biological father, though Kirk didn't know his name until he turned eighteen."

I'd seen Norm discretely pull out his iPad from a slot in his backpack earlier; he tapped at it before looking up. "How serious was your relationship with Booger?" he asked carefully.

"I'd planned on marrying him after graduation," she replied. "And after I'd had Kirk. But East Newberry is a small, dowdy little place; Booger knew his prospects were dim if he stayed, so he dropped out of high school as soon as he found out I was pregnant and joined the Army to support me. They shipped him overseas immediately after boot camp."

I had a sense I knew where this was going after doing some quick math in my head. "Afghanistan?"

Norina nodded. "Kirk was three months old when two soldiers turned up on the doorstep of my apartment; my parents had kicked me out for being pregnant, so I was very, *very* much alone when they delivered the news. Worst damn day of my life, honestly. Since we never made it formal, I wasn't eligible for any benefits when he died."

"I'm sorry for your loss," Norm said softly.

Norina shrugged as she began to clear away the material on the island. "It was a long time ago now. The pain is still there, of course; how can it not be? When Kirk took his name, it became almost unavoidable to think about Booger."

"It seems like an odd choice for him to have made," I observed.

"Kirk never liked my second husband," Norina replied before smiling wryly. "I got to the same place myself many years later, but not before it created a rift between us — one large enough that we sort of stopped talking to each other until fairly recently."

"When did he reach out?" Norm asked.

I watched her expression grow thoughtful, then fond. "My birthday, back in May," she said. "It was out of the blue — and he seemed to genuinely want to talk. I think we were on the phone for an hour, maybe more. That led to more-or-less weekly chats, and the promise he was going to visit." Norina sighed. "I must have gotten my hopes up too high, though, for he stopped calling last week."

"What made him want to repair the breach?" I asked, filing away her oblique confirmation of Nevelson's movements and death.

"Two things, mainly," she said as she opened a tin and then spread some flour on the counter. "The first was some kind of deal he was making to create a chain of Pizzeria Angelinas. He needed some advice on how to approach Dad about it."

"I've been through East Newberry a number of times but never tried a slice myself," I said. "From what I understand, though, the restaurant was pretty popular."

"Especially on two-for-one nights," she nodded. "The key to it was our recipe for the sauce, honestly. It's a closely guarded secret that Dad has never shared with anyone."

"Not even you?" I asked, eyebrows going up incredulously. "You must have worked in the pizzeria growing up."

"Oh, I sure did," she laughed as she waved at the counter. "That little bit of unpaid indentured servitude is a time of my life I'll never forget, but at least it gave me some killer skills in the kitchen."

I decided to let the poor choice of words slide. "I take it the franchising was contingent on getting the recipe?"

"Franchise?" she asked, puzzled for a moment. "I suppose that's exactly what Kirk was cooking up, wasn't it? And yeah, I didn't hold out much hope he was going to get anything from Dad. Told him that, multiple times, but Kirk insisted on driving up there nearly every weekend to try and convince him."

I nodded as I checked another box. "Did he ever ask you to intercede on his behalf?"

"I was disowned by the man," Norina replied. "Not much incentive there for me, even if my kid *had* asked."

"Ah," I said. "Understandable. What was the second reason he wanted to reconnect?"

Norina shifted her gaze to the windows. "Kirk was a bit obsessed by the disappearance of his grandmother," she replied. "He was barely a year old when it happened, so he doesn't remember anything about it; I think that's played into his obsession."

"Obsessed? How?" I asked. "I've read the file and know she was supposed to be coming to visit you at the time."

"Booger's grandparents lived in Springfield," she replied. "They were the kindest, sweetest people I've ever known and let me stay with them until Kirk was old enough for daycare — long, long after Booger died. Mom — Kirk's grandmother — wrote me a letter asking if she could come visit; she had something she wanted to talk to me about, so I agreed to see her." Norina looked a bit wistful. "I looked forward to it for weeks, but when she didn't turn up, I assumed it was just another way to twist the knife. Only later did I find out she'd left East Newberry exactly when she said she was going to."

"What do you think happened to her?" Norm asked.

"I've thought about that for years," she replied. "I guess I've settled on the idea she went off the road somewhere between here and there and just has never been found." Norina smiled slightly. "Easier to accept her loss that way, somehow."

I wasn't entirely sure about that but let it pass. "When did you marry your late husband?" I asked.

"1997," she said. "Dudley ran one of the largest private banks in Boston; we met by accident when I delivered some baked goods after he lost his first wife unexpectedly." Norina took on that warm expression once more. "Something clicked between us, and we never looked back. I lost him a year ago to a massive heart attack — but not before we had nearly twenty years together."

"Forgive me, but it's one helluva commute from here to Boston," I said.

Norina laughed. "That it was, but Dudley only did it on the weekends during the summer; I was here full-time from late April until Halloween, then went back to our place in town for the winter. When he died, I chose the cottage and gave Damian our condo on the Charles."

"Damian?" I asked. "Who's Damian?"

"My son," she replied. "With Dudley."

Something tickled at the back of my brain. "He lives back in Boston?"

"Yes," she answered. "Which is just as well, honestly. He tried to live here with me, but he needs more help than is available out here on the Cape." Norina frowned slightly. "The wealthy out here don't truly support any kind of mental health services; I think they feel like it's beneath them to admit they might even have a problem."

That tickling became more of an itch that desperately needed to be scratched. "Did he grow up with Kirk?"

"Not really," she said. "They were about ten years apart in age, so Kirk was out of the house by the time Damian was old enough to miss him. Oddly, though, they were pretty close — more so after the diagnosis."

"Do you mind my asking what the diagnosis was?"

Norina smiled. "Not at all — that's how we keep from stigmatizing people who are brave enough to face their problems publicly. Damian is manic-depressive with paranoid tendencies; it was very hard for him to get through school, but he managed to do it. As long as he stays on his meds and goes to counseling, he remains stable enough to hold down a regular job."

"Is he close to his grandfather, too?" I asked.

Norina's expression hardened. "I doubt it. But Kirk did tell me he was helping out with the franchise thing, though I have no idea in what capacity."

"Which meant he was traveling with Kirk to East Newberry regularly?" Norm asked.

"I believe so, yes. But like I said, I've not talked with Kirk in over a week; same goes for Damian, actually," she added with a frown. "Which isn't like him. I've been so wrapped up getting these loaves of bread done, I'd forgotten he'd not called me like he normally does on Mondays."

I finally scratched the itch. "Is there a chance he shares his location with you?"

"You mean, like his phone?" Norina frowned again. "I'd not thought about that. He does — I share mine with him, too. That way he can keep track of me." She looked at me for a moment. "After my mother disappeared, I never wanted anyone to wonder where I was."

I shot a glance at Norm. "Maybe you could see where he is?" I asked. "It might explain why you've not heard from him."

"Yeah," she said as she wiped her hands on the apron yet again. "One second."

Norina left the kitchen and returned nearly immediately with a sizable leather purse; opening the top, she rooted through it for a few moments before coming up with what looked like a fairly recent iPhone and a small glasses case. Popping the case open, she pulled out a pair of half-moon readers and put them on, then squinted at the front of her phone for a bit. When the frown appeared on her face, I knew another piece of my puzzle had just locked into place.

"This is odd," she said, frowning deeper before she looked at me. "Why is he in Brewer, Maine?"

I glanced at Norm, then turned back to Norina. "Do you have any photos of Damian?"

Norina eyed me for a long moment, and I had the sense that she intuitively already knew where the conversation was headed. It was the clearest evidence yet to my mind that parents were tied into their children in ways that went beyond semantic metaphysics; in my career, I'd witnessed again and again how those instincts had been proven correct, generally under the worst of all possible circumstances. Not having children didn't mean I was somehow immune from such feelings; I still had vibrant memories of the sudden hole being ripped through my heart moments before the call had come in that my mother had passed. I knew it wasn't scientifically provable, but deep down I was certain humans — all humans — were connected in a way that defied any sort of description; it was a connection that often remained hidden until it flared into existence when needed the most.

"Yes," Norina finally said. "Hundreds, actually. Why?"

Keeping my face pleasant, I answered carefully. "It might help explain why your son's phone is showing where it is."

The slight frown on her face told me she wasn't entirely on board, but she nonetheless nodded and then held a hand out. "There are a bunch in the living room."

I nodded and followed her back down the short hallway with Norm right behind me. Norina turned into the space we'd seen as we'd initially entered and made a direct line for the small fireplace in the corner; like any proud parent, a long line of framed photos lined the mantel above, angled perfectly to be seen from just about any spot in the room. Reaching for one toward the center of the line up, she ran a finger over the photo before holding the wooden frame out to me.

"This was taken about a year ago," she said as I took it from her. "Kirk and Damian came for the Fourth."

The frame itself was of the sort we used to stock at our family pharmacy: inexpensive but made to look like exotic wood that had been laboriously cut to the exact dimensions of the eight-by-ten photo it was embracing. Two men had been caught in a candid moment; both were standing beside each other on the far side of the island in Norina's kitchen, clearly assisting in preparing the feast. The deep, verdant blue of the ocean was visible through the windows behind them, as was the nearly cloudless sky of a far lighter shade. While I wasn't a professional photographer by any stretch, I would have expected the abundant light to have washed out the photo incredibly; since the subjects were perfectly in focus and balanced out, color-wise, I assumed some level of retouching had taken place.

It wasn't hard to recognize Kirk; he was standing just left of center, chopping an onion and clearly in mid-sentence. Damian seemed to be watching him intently, possibly because he was completely engaged in what Kirk was saying; the potato he was holding in one hand was half-peeled and apparently forgotten. Now that I had both men in the same photo, their shared genetic lineage was quite evident, especially the high cheekbones that clearly came from Norina. Squinting slightly at the photo, I was relatively certain Damian was the same man that had been lying on Dr. Hamilton's examination table, but a visual match would be hard to validate given the state of the body after its encounter with the rapid response team. Still, I intrinsically knew that the DNA sample I was about to ask for from Norina would come back as a familial match. Looking at the stepbrothers, I quickly reassessed what I *thought* I had understood about the case; handing the photo back to Norina, I found myself struggling to reconcile what Norina had told us about her sons with what had played out in both East Newberry and Brewer. Something was off, and I couldn't entirely put my finger on exactly what it was.

"They certainly look like they were having a good time," I said.

"Considering how they pretty much didn't grow up together, they do get along very well," Norina said as she placed the photo back on the mantel. Turning back toward me, her eyes locked with mine. "What happened to them?" she asked, her tone betraying that she had a pretty decent idea.

"Norina," I started gently, "It seems I have some terrible news about your kids..."

TWENTY

I n retrospect, deciding to stay at the Ritz in downtown Boston might not have been my smartest idea; the drive back to the city from the Cape had been especially brutal, triggering some PTSD flashbacks to the handful of times I'd been forced to drive in Los Angeles. We pulled up at the covered reception entrance to the grand hotel long after the restaurant had closed for the evening, so we'd been reduced to hunting for an alternative out in the city or settling for whatever was still available on the bar menu. Neither of us had seemed interested in extensive foraging, so we'd wound up with burgers and a shared plate of loaded fries; the Sam Adams on draft had been good enough to merit a second sampling, though a third might have made it easier for me to ignore my racing thoughts and actually get some sleep. After tossing and turning for the better part of an hour, I gave up and simply stared at the ceiling until I knew I could go to the gym for a dreary treadmill run. For his part, Norm had been wary of going beyond his single Old-Fashioned cocktail; he continued to be highly embarrassed at how drunk he'd gotten during Vasily's impromptu Las Vegas pool party over the summer, despite its leading to his current relationship with Raphael.

Still, the soft snores coming from his bed told me he was far more at ease than I was, leading to a slight twinge of jealousy.

Once my phone indicated I could escape my insomnia, I tiptoed to the bathroom and quickly changed into my running gear, then quietly exited the room; when I returned a little less than an hour later, Norm was just finishing up in the shower, so I gathered up a clean set of clothes and then swapped places with him once he emerged. On the stroke of seven, we were walking across the lobby to the main restaurant; it had apparently just opened, for there was a short line of hotel guests ahead of us that the host had to work through. Fortunately for my coffee-starved body, the wait wasn't all that long; the nectar of life arrived within moments of being seated at our table by the window with a stunning view of the street. Norm seemed to have sensed that I needed caffeine flowing through my veins before striking up any sort of conversation and waited patiently for me to down nearly half a mugful before speaking.

"So," he began as he fiddled with the spoon the waiter had left for his coffee. "The DNA from Norina is going to match the shooter, isn't it?"

Glancing briefly to make sure we were far enough from other patrons to have such a discussion, I then took another sip of the heavenly robust brew before responding. "I think so, yes."

"That changes things a bit, then," he said thoughtfully.

"In what way?" I asked, intrigued to see where Norm's thoughts on the matter had landed.

"Damian doesn't feel like he could be the shooter," he answered. "I mean, I *know* we found him with shells that matched those used in the pizzeria, but nothing in what Norina told us about her kids makes me think he could have pulled this off."

I felt myself smile slightly. "I agree."

Norm put his spoon down. "So why was he in Brewer, and how did he get there?" he asked, before pausing. "And who did the actual shooting?"

"I can answer part of that," I said as I drained the last of my coffee. Norm saw my look of longing cast toward his still-full mug and carefully moved it out of easy reach. "I am relatively certain we are going to find Damian's prints on the boat from East Newberry."

"That only tells us that he was on the boat at *some point*," Norm replied.

"True," I nodded. "Proving the timing is going to take some legerdemain, but in the end, I think we'll have enough evidence to prove he boarded in East Newberry."

"Legerdemain? Isn't that a little outside of the State's Standards and Practices manual?"

"I've not read it yet," I lied.

Narrowing his eyes at me, Norm finally took a sip from his mug. "I see. Well, regardless that means there has to have been someone else involved, someone to pilot the boat on the roundtrip to Brewer."

"Exactly."

My companion began to get annoyed. "*Fuck*, Sean. Just spit it out already."

"But you are so close," I smiled.

"Clearly I've not had as much coffee as you, yet," he sighed. "Who is this third person?"

"Leon Angelina."

Norm nearly did a spit-take with his coffee. "How the *fuck* did you get there?" he asked. "And how the *hell* does the timing work out?"

"I'll have to check the file again," I hedged, "but Heather noted that the backpack found with Damian — or, more accurately, 'the body alleged to be Damian' — had a few days of food and water. I would submit Damian was dropped off long before the shooting took place in East Newberry."

"Why?"

"This is just informed speculation," I hedged again. "However, my sense is that various pieces of this mess were set on the proverbial chess board well in advance of the shooting. Damian, probably unwittingly, was playing the role of shooter-in-hiding, unaware that someone would turn him in later the way they did."

"That's pretty cold," Norm observed. "Especially if your assumption is correct."

"Agreed."

"What are the rest of the pieces?"

I held out a hand and started to tick them off. "The pizzeria suddenly offers a special on a night of the week they don't ordinarily run it," I began. "Kirk and Damian had been visiting their grandfather just about every weekend for the last few months. Kirk appears to have been shot sometime on Sunday and stuffed into a fridge; I would submit that would be fairly close to when Damian is shuttled up the Penobscot."

Norm frowned. "You think he killed Kirk?"

"No," I shook my head. "But he may have been led to believe he was involved in it."

"Enough to agree to flee the scene," Norm said slowly. "Only to be outed by an anonymous tipster a few days later and conveniently killed before he could be interviewed."

"Exactly." I waited for a moment. "And, perhaps most importantly, the majority of the victims in the pizzeria appeared to be trying to get out the *front* door, not the *rear*."

Norm's eyes widened. "Do ballistics support the shooter being at the rear of the pizzeria?"

"Heather was waiting for the Feds to drop their data to the state, but her unofficial read on it was that might be the case." I glanced toward the waiter and meaningfully held up my mug; he immediately returned and refilled it for me before moving to the next table to take their order. "I've worked enough mass shootings to recognize how people panic in such situations, though. I don't think we need to wait for the confirmation."

I watched Norm roll the idea around in his head. "So, your take is that Leon killed Kirk for some reason—"

"Yes," I nodded.

"—and then commits mass murder to cover the whole thing up?"

"Yes."

"*Fuck*," he breathed. "That is super messed up. And how on earth did he expect to get away with it?"

"We'll have to ask him," I smiled. "I was planning on swinging by the hospital on our way back to Windeport."

"I'm in." Norm eyed me again. "What the *hell* did Kirk do to piss Leon off enough to go through all this trouble?"

Movement at the front of the restaurant caught my attention, and I smiled slightly when I saw the tall, solidly built gentleman in a tailored suit scanning the room. "I believe we are about to find out," I said once the guy saw us at the table and began moving in our direction.

Norm turned slightly. "Would you look at *that*," he said appreciatively.

"Tsk, tsk," I teased. "Raphael's gone barely a week, and your eye is already roaming."

"I was referring to the suit," he whispered though the slight flame that appeared on his cheeks said otherwise.

It took a moment for the suit to work his way across the room; as he neared the edge of our table, I realized he was incredibly young, with model-worthy looks; frowning, I wondered if that meant the law firm had actually sent us one of their paralegals instead of the promised partner. Still, I put on my best smile when he arrived; up close, it was clear he was quite nervous, underscoring my original assumption.

"Lt. Norm Thomas?" he asked as he held his hand out to me. "Gareth O'Keeffe, O'Keefe and Garmin."

"I'm Commander Sean Colbeth, actually," I smiled as I stood and shook. Nodding to Norm, I smiled a bit wider. "That's Lt. Thomas, but as you can see, it's easy to confuse the two of us."

O'Keefe seemed unsure if I was kidding or not, and decided I was; a sheepish smile appeared as he shook Norm's hand. "Sorry. I should have looked you up online before I drove out here, but there wasn't time. May I join you?"

"Please," I said, indicating with a hand one of the open chairs. "We've not ordered yet."

"Thank goodness," he breathed as he sat down beside Norm after tossing his overcoat into the last empty chair. "The MBTA is doing work this weekend on the Red Line, so I had to leave pretty early to get here on time." He glanced at what appeared to be a very high-end watch. "I apologize for being late."

"It's truly not a problem," I replied. "We appreciate you're agreeing to meet with us on a Sunday."

"Of course. I understand you have questions about the work we're doing for Kirk Nevelson?"

"Yes," I nodded. "How long has he been a client?"

"Since the beginning," O'Keeffe smiled. "My partner and I put out our shingle right after law school, so I guess that's five years?"

"Forgive me, but isn't it unusual to start your own firm like that?" I asked. "I thought most lawyers began their careers working for other, more established lawyers."

"That is the typical path, yes," O'Keeffe nodded. "Micheline and I weren't interested in dealing with any of that political bull crap and decided to bypass it."

"Still," I persisted, "I'm impressed you had the resources to launch something so soon after graduation."

"We found the right sort of banker," he smiled.

I began to nod. "Dudley Nevelson."

"Exactly," he smiled wider. "Fortunately, our work in this area is quite profitable; we were able to pay off the startup loan three years in."

"What is your area, exactly?" Norm asked as the waiter reappeared.

There was a brief pause while the three of us quickly scanned the menu to make a selection, and then O'Keeffe replied. "We specialize in converting established businesses into franchises."

"Any sort of business?" I asked.

"Pretty much," he nodded. "There are a few exceptions, of course, but for the most part just about any idea can become a marketable concern. We do the legal work to get the parent organization set up, then assist any franchisees with creating their own org to run what they bought."

To my ear, it sounded a bit like a barely legal Ponzi scheme, but it seemed best not to make that observation. "I presume Kirk Nevelson was attempting to spin off his grandfather's pizza business?"

"Exactly," O'Keeffe replied.

"Pizza places are a dime a dozen," Norm said. "What made his version attractive to franchise?"

"Have you ever *had* Pizzeria Angelina pizza?" O'Keeffe countered. "I drove up to Maine when we were in the investigative stage of the process and sampled the menu. Nothing out there compares with their recipes, especially the red sauce they use in every dish. It's one of a kind and could be sold all by itself."

"I haven't, actually," I admitted. "But I did hear that Leon Angelina was quite reluctant to part with the secret recipe for the sauce."

"There was that," O'Keeffe sighed. "Old Leon was a bit of a curmudgeon and had no sense of what Kirk was trying to put together. I can't tell you how many trips Kirk and I have made to East Newberry just to beg Leon to reconsider his position."

"That would seem to have torpedoed the whole idea, then," I said.

"Until last week, I would have agreed with you," he replied. "In fact, Kirk was in the process of closing down his activities with us."

"What changed?"

O'Keeffe shrugged. "All I know is that Kirk called a week ago to tell me Leon had relented and wanted to talk through the options again. He and his brother, Damian, planned on spending the weekend in Maine to finalize the deal with their grandfather; I expected to get the low down on Monday when he returned to Massachusetts, but never got the call. I assumed that meant the plan had crashed and burned completely."

You could say that, I thought. "Have you heard from Kirk since then?"

"No," O'Keeffe replied. "That's not unusual, though. His day job keeps him pretty busy; so does mine. Until your colleague reached out to me, I'd not realized Kirk hadn't called."

"Have you sold anyone on this concept yet?" I asked.

O'Keeffe's eyes momentarily widened with shock, but he regained his composure quickly. "Not officially, no," he replied. "How could we? There was nothing to sell as yet."

"Other than the idea," Norm emphasized. "One that could have a paid waitlist, perhaps?"

O'Keeffe's cheeks flamed slightly. "I don't appreciate what you are intimating," he said. "Yes, we have a list of individuals who are interested in the concept, and before you ask, yes, they have to put down a good faith deposit. I can assure you it's standard practice in this field; we are providing completely legitimate services to entrepreneurs."

"Maybe," I said. "Then again, I can't be the only one curious how such a relatively small firm managed to become profitable so quickly."

"Legal work isn't exactly inexpensive," O'Keeffe said.

"True," I nodded.

O'Keeffe made a show of looking at his watch. "I'm afraid I have to go," he said as he stood. "It's been a pleasure. If you have any further questions, you can reach me through our lawyers."

My eyebrows went up. "Lawyers hiding behind lawyers," I said. "That's not a good look, Mr. O'Keeffe."

Our guest yanked his overcoat from the spare chair. "Good day, Commander. Lieutenant."

I tried not to smile as I watched O'Keeffe march out of the dining room; turning, I saw Norm was trying not to laugh. "You sure pushed his buttons, Sean," he said.

"Unintentionally," I agreed. "I think we got enough out of him before he clammed up, though."

"Agreed," Norm nodded. "It also fits with what we know about Angelina and how he ran the pizzeria."

"It does indeed," I said as three plates of food arrived. Eying the extra dish, I then looked up at Norm. "Well, eat up. We might not get a chance to stop again for a bit."

He rolled his eyes. "This is gonna be a long day, isn't it?"

"You have no idea," I laughed as I speared a sausage from O'Keeffe's plate. "Especially since we have to solve a mystery in Glenn Hills before we can get to the main event."

"*Solve* it?" Norm asked. "I feel like we've barely begun looking into it."

"Oh, Norm," I admonished, "you really do need to learn how to keep up."

"Fuck," he breathed. "Just, *fuck*. I think I was happier as a beat officer."

"Hardly," I laughed.

Twenty-One

I'd known that Suzanne would be back at Leslie's house in New Hampshire on Sunday; seeing her Subaru Forester sitting in front of the ranch-style home would have normally lifted my spirits immensely, but that morning I felt a slight pang of regret over how the next thirty minutes were going to play out. My mood felt as dark as the foreboding clouds that had formed and then dogged us all the way back from Boston, clouds that portended yet another major snow event. As I pulled the SUV up beside the Forester and parked, a not insignificant part of me wanted to turn right around and make haste to get back to the safe confines of my bungalow long before the storm had a chance to break; fortunately, my professionalism took over, though it wasn't lost on me that Norm's eyebrows shot up when I reached over to the glove box and retrieved my sidearm from the safe.

"Expecting trouble?" he asked, his eyes firmly planted on the Glock as I slid it into the holster on my belt.

"No," I replied. "Just making this official."

He looked through the window beside me at Suzanne's car. "What, exactly, are we doing here?"

"Closing the case," I said as I pushed open my door. "And getting some answers."

Norm's face drained of all color. "I... I'm not sure I like the sound of that," he said. "Given who all is here at the moment."

I smiled wryly as I stepped out in the frigid air. "I assure you, everyone we need is here now."

"That's what I'm afraid of," he said softly as he exited the SUV.

Ignoring him, I walked across the plowed pavement and focused on the little things as I approached the front porch; my boots squeaked slightly on what little snow was left of the surface, a reminder that the remnants from the last storm hadn't quite been wiped out yet. Looking up, I saw the aeronautical-themed weathervane fastened to the side of the brick chimney, the large wrought iron arrow clearly confirming the gathering storm had, indeed, followed us up from Boston. A handful of pigeons had gathered on the apex of the shingled roof and were judging us as we went up the short steps to the front door; pausing, I realized they were just two short of a full jury. Somewhere in the distance, the shriek from a raptor as it went after prey pierced the air; given my frame of mind, it sounded nearly as bloodcurdling as anything I'd experienced in those horror movies Vasily had subjected me to.

My hand was on the knob for the storm door when the inner door was pulled open; Suzanne's smiling face appeared, then frowned slightly. Pushing open the outer door, she leaned in for a kiss. "I thought you were in Boston."

"We finished our inquiries there," I replied, smiling myself. "I wanted to get another look at this scene so I could close out this case, too, and since it was on our way back to Windeport...."

Suzanne eyed me for a moment; it gave me a chance to take in the fact that she was dressed similarly to the first time we'd seen her at Hammersmith's home, wearing jeans and an old flannel shirt. This time around, she'd tied her long, black hair back with a bright yellow kerchief. "If I'd known you were coming, I would have saved some of the cleaning for you."

"I would have called," I continued as she stepped aside for us to enter. "But you know about the cell coverage."

"Yeah," she nodded. "I think there's a modest connection about four miles down the road."

"I'd noticed," I nodded again, noting Norm's shift in expression. It was apparent he'd suddenly realized why I'd pulled to the side of the road a number of times on the drive up to the property.

"Well," she smiled warmly. "I can't say I'm upset to see you."

"Same," I replied.

"What did you want to see?" she asked as we went up the short set of steps to the main level. Pausing at the top, she looked a bit chagrined. "If you are looking for forensics again, I might be in trouble. This time around I *have* been touching things."

"I don't think that will be a problem," I said and then nodded in the direction of the den. "I'd like to start in the den, if you don't mind?"

"I'm done in there already," she replied. "Go right ahead; I'm going to finish up in—"

"I'd prefer if you'd join me, Suzanne," I said calmly.

Suzanne looked at me for a long moment, then slowly began to nod. "You've figured it out, haven't you?"

"Yes," I replied simply. A quick glance at Norm revealed his extremely shocked expression, but to his credit, he remained silent and let me continue to lead. Holding out my hand toward the den, I continued. "Lead the way, if you would?"

Nodding, Suzanne took point and quickly moved down the short hallway; the three of us entered the den and found it far different than the last time we'd been there. Cardboard boxes were stacked irregularly everywhere, containing the contents that had once been on the shelves behind the desk and along the other walls; the desk itself had also been cleared, revealing the sizable rectangular wooden surface that had been hidden beneath the blood and clutter. Taking up position at one particular corner of the desk, I took a long moment to gaze around the room; with just about everything packed, what little trace of Hammersmith's personality I'd seen earlier had been completely eradicated. Through the window, I could see a small column of grayish smoke rising into the cold air, evidence that, well, *any* evidence of Suzanne's ex-husband was in the process of being destroyed.

Suzanne took a few steps into the center of the room, then turned to face me. Her face had long been an open book to me, though it was also clear that my own recent obsession with her ex-husband had apparently shrouded a few key passages. Her expression was expectantly calm, almost as if she had known from the beginning such a moment between us would come. Raising her chin slightly, Suzanne seemed to brace herself before speaking.

"This feels a bit like that first week we met," she said carefully. "If I recall correctly, you read me my rights before we got too far back then."

"I did," I replied. "As you may be aware, though, I am currently outside of my jurisdiction."

Suzanne's eyes widened for a moment. "I suppose you are."

"I am, however, an active consultant for the Glenn Hills Police Department," I continued as I began to walk around the massive desk. Running my finger along the rounded edge of the surface, I paused at a corner. "My report to them will be conclusive and fully documented."

"Of that I have no doubt."

"How they act on the information I give them, I have no way of knowing," I said as I leaned down to inspect the corner of the desk. Turning, I looked at her. "Do you understand?"

Suzanne looked thoughtful. "I do."

I nodded. "Did you ever find your sweater?"

That seemed to catch her off guard. "My—what?"

Standing again, I eyed her carefully. "Your purple sweater. The one you had at the meet." I paused for a beat. "The one I gave you for Christmas," I added softly.

"I... never had a chance to call the facility," she replied. "I'll do it on Monday."

"Probably not worth the effort, really," I said as I glanced meaningfully out at the burn pit.

Slowly, she nodded. "Probably not."

I moved behind the desk and looked at the now-empty bookshelves; I had to admit, the cleaning had been exceptionally thorough as there was no trace of the blood or dura matter that had once been present. "Leslie was dead when you visited him on Sunday," I said quietly before turning back to her. "Wasn't he?"

It wasn't lost on me that Norm's already white face had gone ashen. "Sean—"

I waved him off. "If you are uncomfortable, please feel free to step out."

Slowly, Norm shook his head. "I think it might be best if I stay."

I nodded and returned my gaze to Suzanne; the answer was in her eyes before she spoke. "Yes."

"I've not gone through all of the social media and other video from the swim meet — yet," I continued, keeping my eyes firmly locked on hers. "You could save me the trouble and confirm what I suspect already."

Slowly, she nodded. "You had that break between the four hundred fly and the four hundred medley," Suzanne said. "The one long enough for a full-body massage?"

I smiled slightly. "Not something I normally would do," I said. "But my personal doctor told me it might be beneficial for someone of my age, especially since I would be going straight from that to the warm-up pool. That gave you, what, about an hour?"

"Slightly more," she nodded again. "Under other circumstances, I'd have been upset that you'd not noticed I was missing."

"You made sure I was distracted," I said. "Well played."

"I'm a doctor," she said, smiling slightly despite the tension that had developed in the room. "We learn that early, especially when giving shots."

I moved around to the front of the desk and stopped about where I thought the rug had been bunched up. "This is where he was, right?" I asked, looking at her again. "In front of the desk?"

Suzanne nodded. "Lying that way, yes," she replied.

"Why were you here?" Norm asked, finally finding his voice. "Did he call you?"

She looked at him. "No," she answered. "He doesn't — *didn't* — have a phone; once he moved up here, he became something of a hermit. I actually got an old-fashioned letter from Leslie back in August; there was some sort of legal snafu from the divorce that left me as his primary beneficiary. He had paperwork I needed to review and then sign and asked me to come take care of it."

"Why not send the package to you?" I asked. "If not directly, to a lawyer of your choosing? Seeing him again wasn't necessary."

"No," she nodded, "but I knew we were going to be at the swim meet. I decided I wanted to face him one final time." Suzanne paused. "I'm not the same woman I was when we were married; I felt like I needed him to see that."

"You could have told me about this," I said.

"And you would have counseled me to not do it."

"With good reason."

Suzanne's temper flared. "I don't think you have the moral high ground here, especially since you were running an off-the-books investigation into Leslie."

"I don't profess to," I said. "Still, the point remains: you were here close to when Hammersmith died."

"He was already dead," she reminded me.

"From having hit his head on the edge of his desk," I said. "Right about there, I think."

Suzanne nodded. "I don't think it had been more than an hour prior to my arrival," she said. "From the way the rug was bunched up, I believe he tripped over the toolbox that was here and lost his balance."

I folded my arms across my chest. "The paperwork was on the desk?" I asked after a moment.

She nodded again. "Right on top. He had no idea I was coming that day, which tells me something. I found it after I realized there wasn't anything I could do for him; turns out, the fucking idiot wanted me to *sign away* my rights to his retirement funds — most of which had been funded *by* me when we'd been married."

I looked out to the burn pit. "So, you burned it?"

"Yes," she nodded. "Along with anything else I could find that looked like it pertained to his estate." Suzanne looked around the room. "It seemed somewhat justified."

"There will be copies of everything filed with Probate," Norm said softly. "Destroying what you found wouldn't stop the court from proceeding as he'd wished."

"There is only the original will he wrote while we were married," Suzanne smiled mirthlessly. "The one *I* filed for *him*. Leslie was an idiot and never updated *anything*, even after the divorce."

"Why did you move him?" I asked. "You could have just left him here, on the rug. It would have been ruled an accident — especially since I suspect the wood from this desk will match what the coroner found in the head wound."

Suzanne continued to look out the window. "I could have. I *should* have," she added before turning back to me. "But I was a bit... annoyed... when I found the paperwork."

I felt myself frown. Moving to the rear of the desk again, I waved at the bookcases behind it; my movement brought her attention back to me. "What we saw here speaks to more than annoyance," I said, my voice tight.

Suzanne's nostrils flared. "What do you want me to say?" she demanded. "Was I pissed? Yes, I was. Infuriated. White hot, in fact."

"You *moved* the body," I said; anger infused each word, anger that, once again, I'd left myself open to a massive blind spot — or, worse, had willfully ignored the signs that something was going on right under my investigator nose.

"Yes."

"Then literally beat what was left of your ex-husband to a bloody pulp," I continued. "That's not just anger. That's something else entirely."

"Sean—"

I felt betrayed and knew it was reflected on my face. "Your prints aren't anywhere because you borrowed gloves from the kit I keep in the SUV — though I also think if we try hard enough, I'll be able to match the smudges on the door and the cabinet out by the fire pit to you."

"That just confirms what I told you," Suzanne said.

"Does it?" I replied icily. "Because all of this feels just a bit too premeditated to me. Forensically, there's no way to know for *sure* whether Hammersmith died there on the rug or because you struck him over the head with the stool while he was sitting behind the desk — a stool that is now conveniently missing. About the *only* thing you have going in your favor is the angle of the blow that Lou thinks killed him; it's *more* likely he got it slamming into the desk as he fell." I paused and tried to get my heart rate back under control. "Even that isn't conclusive, Suzanne. There's *nothing* here that proves or *disproves* anything." I paused again. "And it's just enough wiggle room for a prosecutor to make a case."

"I didn't kill Leslie," Suzanne said firmly. Her face was flushed, and in turns looked both horrified at what was happening but also not the least bit contrite. "You have to believe me. He was dead when I got here."

I came around to the front of the desk again. "It's not a matter of whether I believe you or not — it's what the evidence says to an impartial jury," I said coldly. "Something that I cannot be when it comes to you, Suzanne. Not now." I paused. "Not... ever."

She looked like I had struck her across the face, which I suppose I had, verbally. "Sean—"

"You fucking *used* me," I said, my voice so low that I caught Norm leaning toward me to hear.

Her eyes began to glisten. "That's not—"

I lifted my hand, and she stopped. "It's probably better if you leave it right there. For both of us."

I turned away and started for the door, then paused at the threshold; there was one last piece of unfinished business, and though I was reluctant to address it, I knew the kind of person — the kind of investigator — I was demanded it. Without looking back at Suzanne, I took a breath and then plunged forward.

"When were you planning on telling me you were leaving Windeport?"

The silence that followed felt unusually heavy; after a long moment, Suzanne finally spoke. "After the property fully transferred to me. Late spring, maybe; I've already begun the process of merging my practice to the statewide group run by Maine Medical. It'll take a bit to square everything away."

I nodded. "That doesn't really answer my question," I said as I turned toward her. "And yet, it does."

Suzanne looked at me, her eyes pleading. "I wouldn't expect you to understand, not completely," she began. "But I had hoped you'd join me."

My eyebrows went up. "You want me to *leave* Windeport?"

"Yes," she nodded slowly. "Haven't you had enough heartbreak there? Don't you deserve a fresh start?"

"My *life* is in Windeport," I said, surprising myself with the forceful response.

"Your life could be with me."

I looked at her. "I thought it already *was*," I said slowly, suddenly seeing everything from a new angle. "Though I'm not sure how to handle the notion that while you could never move in with *me*, you're more than happy to have me move in with *you*."

Suzanne's face faltered. "That's a nuance without distinction."

"No," I replied as something cold and hard settled about my heart. "No, it's not."

She took a tentative step toward me. "You're obviously hurt and not thinking straight—"

"That's the first thing you've said that I agree with," I replied as I turned and left.

Twenty-Two

To his credit, Norm managed to keep his own council for the entirety of our drive to Bangor from Glenn Hills; it was just as well, for I had absolutely no idea what to say if he'd pressed me in any way over what had taken place with Suzanne. By rights, any insights I'd had into the Hammersmith case should have been memorialized in the files and handed back over to Bartram, something I knew I was in no position to do — not now, and probably not ever. The long drive northward had in one sense been a godsend, then, allowing me to both ignore my responsibilities as a consultant as well as nurse my wounded soul. And wounded it was, for weighing heavily upon it was the serious doubt that Suzanne had ever been completely open with me about *anything* in the time we'd been together. I knew in my heart she hadn't killed Hammersmith — I'd more or less told her that — but in the end, the investigator part of my brain was rightly reminding me *anyone* was capable of murder under the right sort of circumstances. If what Suzanne had described didn't fall under that category, I wasn't sure what would.

About the only thing I felt capable of doing was packing away everything I was feeling so I could focus on the current task at hand; when signs appeared that we were nearing the Dysarts exit just south of Bangor, I took a small measure of pity on my companion and pulled off of I-95. Considering how late it was — and guiltily remembering we'd not had anything since our breakfast at the Ritz many hours earlier — it seemed prudent to recharge before facing the final act with Leon Angelina. The illuminated low fuel light on the SUV's dashboard may have also contributed to the decision, another indicator I'd been more than a little preoccupied.

Entering the restaurant felt like walking through the front door of your favorite relative's house; the fragrant smells from the kitchen were enough of a distraction for me that it took a moment before I realized Norm had gotten us seated. His earnestly worried expression finally cut through the fog that had been surrounding me like some sort of protective magical spell; reaching for the mug of coffee that had appeared out of nowhere, I smiled wryly.

"Hell of a day," I breathed as I brought the mug to my lips.

Norm nodded. "How are you doing?"

"I don't know," I sighed. "I really don't."

"Understandable," he nodded again, then paused. "Look, Sean, you don't have to answer this—"

"She didn't kill him," I said. "It was an accident."

Norm looked a bit relieved. "Is that what you're going to put in the file?" he asked cautiously.

"The truth," I replied, "is not something to be trifled with. I'll write up what we know and what we found. It'll be up to Bartram and company to decide what to do with the information."

"What if it gets interpreted incorrectly?"

I toyed with the napkin in my lap. "It won't."

One of Norm's eyebrows arched upward. "You've met Bartram; hell, he was *this close* to arresting her initially. Anything you put into that file will be far more damning than what he had before."

"It's a risk," I smiled wanly, "but Suzanne knows a good lawyer."

Norm frowned. "I applaud your morality here, but, *fuck*," he breathed. "How can you be so calm about this? Suzanne's your—"

"I'm not calm in the least," I replied honestly. "And as for the rest, I suspect our relationship is about to go through a rocky patch." I dropped the napkin and reached for the spoon that had arrived with the mug of coffee; tapping it against a finger, I finally allowed myself to acknowledge out loud what my heart had been screaming for most of the drive. "One that it likely won't survive."

He looked at me. "Fuck."

"I couldn't have said it better myself," I sighed again before smiling gamely. "It's not the first time I've lost someone I love in the most unexpected way. You'd think it would get easier, wouldn't you?"

Norm reached across the table and took my hand. "It never does. And it never will."

"Yeah," I nodded. "I suppose not. Come on, let's order; I want to get through the rest of this day as fast as we can, for there's a case of Samuel Adams waiting for me back at the bungalow that I am quite anxious to crack open."

Norm cocked an eyebrow. "That would not be the best approach, Sean."

"Didn't say it was," I smiled.

As late as it was, I ordered the pork chop special and Norm had a steak large enough to serve a family of four. The ache in my stomach was more or less satiated by the time we returned to the SUV, but its companion in my heart wouldn't let up. Pulling out of Dysarts, I tried unsuccessfully to set aside my inner emotional turmoil and wound up settling for simply having it recede slightly into the background; recriminations over how I had handled the situation in New Hampshire would simply not allow me to completely ignore what had happened, and the effect it was going to have on my personal life. Suzanne was, frankly, my *everything*; after that odd Christmas where she'd disappeared for a week, we'd forged something special that I'd plowed my soul into. Looking back on it now, I wondered how my heart had ignored the cracks that had developed over the summer; our reunion on Carpenter's Island had made it seem like the final corner had been turned, but clearly I'd instead wandered further into the labyrinth, completely unaware of the minotaur awaiting me deep in the maze that was our relationship.

First Deidre, now Suzanne, I sighed as I pulled onto I-95 and sped toward Bangor General. *I might be a brilliant detective, but I suck when it comes to understanding those closest to me. The ones I care for the most. I can't keep doing this! But how do I break out of the cycle?*

The exit I needed appeared suddenly, causing me to glance down and see that I was doing twenty over the posted speed limit. To his credit, Norm appeared unconcerned as he flipped through pages on his tablet, but I could also see his right hand was white with the effort it took to hold onto the passenger door handle. Slowing down, I berated myself for letting my personal situation completely occupy my attention; the remainder of the drive to the hospital was as borderline legal as I could make it given the late afternoon traffic. I had no idea, frankly, that there even *was* a rush hour in Bangor, but it was clear I had landed right in the middle of it, exacerbated by roads that had been narrowed with snowbanks from the last storm. Parking at the hospital proved to be a similar challenge, with almost a third of the surface lot hidden beneath a manmade glacier that had been created when the lot had been plowed. Stuffing the SUV into the first slot I could find, I grabbed my backpack from the rear and hopped out into the chill of the early evening; adjusting the pack as I locked the truck up, I glanced over at Norm and found myself thankful he was going to be by my side for what was coming next. Some major part of my investigative mojo had been stolen by the events in New Hampshire; mojo I wasn't certain would readily return.

A quick enquiry at the reception desk revealed Leon Angelina remained a resident of the intensive care unit, an unsurprising situation given how serious his wounds were. Unwilling to contemplate the cost of such an extended stay, though, I instead wondered as I lifted the phone to request access if I would encounter the same duty nurse who had been less than enthusiastic about granting my initial interview request. I was therefore quite relieved when a young nurse who appeared barely able to shave — let alone stick a needle into anyone's arm — appeared when the door to the ward swung open.

"Commander?" he asked, his voice cracking mid-syllable. "The patient is actually awake since we've just done another round of blood-work. You probably won't have a better time to speak to him."

"Thank you," I said as we followed him in. "We won't take long."

"You won't," the kid replied. I had to look twice to ensure he wasn't being sarcastic. "He's going back into surgery at the bottom of the hour."

"Why?" Norm asked as we continued down the aseptic hallway. "I thought he had already undergone that."

"So did the doctors," the nurse said. "Privacy regulations prevent me from getting into specifics but suffice it to say Mr. Angelina is leaking somewhere and they need to stop it."

"That sounds... not good," I said as we entered the main space. There was far more activity at the Nurse's Station than during my last visit, commensurate with the number of lit chambers surrounding it. I didn't like what that meant but chose to stay on task.

"Honestly? It's not." The nurse paused and then lowered his voice. "I don't think he's expected to survive the night, even if the surgery is successful."

"Does his family know?" Norm asked after shooting a glance at me.

"We got ahold of his daughter, yes," he nodded. "She's on her way, but..." he trailed off.

Damn, I thought.

The nurse continued across the space and pulled open the glass door to the small room; the only light on was the one above and behind the bed, and that had been set to the lowest possible setting, casting hardly more than a pale white shadow across Angelina. The same stack of portable machinery was arrayed to either side of the bed, though I'd have been hard pressed to know if they were performing the same services as during my prior visit. Angelina himself was sitting upright, his torso leaning against a stack of pillows; while he looked alert, his face was only a shade removed from the waxen pallor cadavers took on. Cables ran to both of his arms, and the oxygen tube had been replaced by a transparent mask covering his nose and mouth. I'd spent enough time dating a doctor to know that was not a good sign — that they were attempting to pump up his oxygen levels by force feeding air to his lungs.

Angelina's eyes were surprisingly wary, though, as we approached his bedside. "Fuck," he rasped. "Why are you here?"

I looked at the nurse. "Could you wait outside?"

He looked at me, then Norm. "Hospital policy prevents me—"

"Get *out*," I said flatly. "*Now*."

The kid nodded and scurried back through the doorway; I waited for Norm to slide the door shut behind him before returning my attention to Angelina. "You weren't completely honest with me when we last spoke," I answered at length. "So, I'm back, trying to get a few answers before you become unavailable to me."

Those eyes narrowed. "Idiot doctors," he finally breathed, each syllable a struggle.

"Medicine is a science, not magic," I said as I came around to stand on his left side; Norm took up position on his right, holding his tablet at such an angle that it could get both audio and video of our conversation. Like me, he'd come to the same conclusion that this might be our only chance. "Though, honestly, there have been times when I've thought the two are one and the same."

Angelina closed his eyes for a moment. "What d'you want?"

"Before we get into that, just a reminder that I explained your rights to you the first time we spoke. Do you still consent to talking with me without legal representation present? Or would you like me to call someone for you?"

Those eyes remained shut. "No."

"No, what?" I asked. "No, you don't want to speak to me? Or no, you don't want us to call someone?"

"I ain't got nothing to say."

I nodded, though he couldn't see it. "I'm surprised," I replied. "Since you'll be dead in a few hours, I'd assumed you'd want to set the record straight. I hear clearing the soul like that often allows one to rest easier when the final darkness descends."

Norm flicked a shocked expression at me but kept silent. Angelina took a deep, halting breath, but also kept to himself.

"It won't matter, I suppose," I continued, looking at my nails nonchalantly. "I've got everything I need to prove you killed your grandson and your wife, as well as had a hand in killing your other grandchild."

Angelina's eyes snapped open; I didn't look at Norm as I could easily feel the waves of incredulousness coming off of him.

"Shall I tell you a story?" I asked Angelina, holding his gaze. "One that involves no small amount of family drama?"

"I never liked stories."

Glancing out the glass window of the door, I could see the nurses at the station were watching us intently save for the one who had escorted us in; he was on the phone. The guilty way he was avoiding looking in our direction told me we had very little time, so I looked back at Angelina. "Maybe in the interests of alacrity, I should skip right to the salient parts."

Angelina considered me as I walked to the end of the bed, then walked back to his side.

"I've known quite a few strong women over my lifetime," I began, smiling as a parade of them flashed in my mind's eye. That Suzanne was at the end of the parade wasn't much of a surprise. "And I suspect that your wife, Beryl was one of them. I imagine she actually ran the business side of your pizzeria — balanced the books, placed the orders, did all of the dirty work to keep the lights on each month."

There was a tiny flicker in Angelina's eye, nothing more.

"When she discovered she had cancer, I'm guessing she realized she needed some sort of contingency plan to keep the pizzeria going when she couldn't be there to make it happen. But I also suspect she was a realist and knew East Newberry was dying, and the Pizzeria was dying along with it."

"We've always been successful, no matter what," he said haltingly.

"Whose idea was it to sell the business?" I asked. "No — don't answer that, for it was likely Beryl. She laid it all out for you, didn't she? Showed you the numbers, explained how it would work — she even started to spruce up the restaurant, didn't she? So any potential buyers might see its best foot forward."

He just glared at me, which came off poorly given his situation.

"I don't yet know what the final trigger was," I said as I leaned over the edge of the bed and got closer to his face. "Maybe you didn't like the idea in general, or perhaps the thought that she'd accepted her fate openly rubbed you the wrong way. Whatever it was, it led to you shooting her in 1988—"

Those eyes narrowed at me, and I found myself nodding that they'd not flown open in shock at the accusation.

"—and then used her planned renovations to the lobby to cover it up. That was inspired, actually, though, honestly, you should have followed through and completed the work to the rest of the space."

"My wife left me," Angelina managed to say.

"I'd buy that if we hadn't recovered her body from the Penobscot," I said, getting some small measure of satisfaction when his eyes flicked wider for a moment at my disclosure. "Unfortunately for you, your method of disposal meant Beryl was nearly perfectly preserved for our medical examiner." I paused again as I leaned away. "Perfectly. Preserved. Including the bullet you shot her with."

"I don't... own a gun," he breathed. My eyes flicked to the small monitor over his head and saw that his blood pressure had gone up a few points.

Interesting.

"Do you think I'd be here if that were true?" I asked dramatically, knowing we'd not located a handgun yet. "Seriously?"

The eyes were becoming a tell, and I smiled darkly when I saw them open slightly wider. That, and his heart rate ticked up enough to tacitly confirm what I was saying. There seemed to be some merit to having a suspect wired up to equipment, though I knew it was something that would never be allowed in our criminal justice system. At least, not yet.

I dusted off my hands. "With Beryl out of the picture, you were free to go on running the business the way you wanted, with no fear of having to give it up. And that worked well for a few years, I'm sure — right up until your daughter refused to take it over from you. Who could blame her?" I asked rhetorically. "Especially since the town was fading. Suddenly, Beryl's idea wasn't so outlandish, was it?"

Angelina looked away.

"We've looked at the financials," Norm interjected. "You've barely been able to make ends meet for the last decade, with negative cash flow for the past three years. At this rate, there won't *be* a business to sell to anyone other than a creditor by next Christmas."

The silence built for a long moment, then I continued.

"Somewhere along the line, your grandson, Kirk, figured out how bad things were and appeared with his own version of the plan — only this time, you'd not have to sell the business. Only the name — and the items on the menu. And that was the sticking point, wasn't it?"

Angelina looked at me. "Th' sauce recipe has been in the family since they arrived in New York."

"I'm sure," I said. "Kirk had to have explained how that was the lynchpin of the franchise agreement, though. Without the sauce, Pizzeria Angelina was just another cookie-cutter pizza joint."

"It wasn't his to give," Angelina rasped. Blue had begun to tint the edges of his lips.

"From what I've seen, Kirk had to have been pretty damn persistent. Trudging up to East Newberry every chance he got, working on you to reconsider. At some point, he doubled down and began to bring

Damian, thinking — incorrectly — you'd break under the impassioned pleas from your grandkids. I suspect he'd pretty much given up, though, until you called him and said you'd changed your mind."

"I never—"

"Never called? Or never changed your mind?" I replied, cutting him off. "Records prove the former, and I'm sure Kirk didn't know the latter. And that miscalculation cost him his life. As well as Damian's." I waited a moment, sorting through how to proceed; out of the corner of my eye, I saw an orderly appear at the nurse's station. "When he arrived last weekend, he had to have been extremely excited; I suspect he had no clue you were planning on killing him."

"I didn't—"

I held my hand up. "I'm going to cut to the chase. We have the gun, and matched bullets taken from your wife and your grandson to it," I said, trying to sell the lie with a bit of force. "You tossed it after you left your *other* grandson to die in Brewer — neither move was very smart."

Angelina just looked at me, slack jawed.

"Here's what I know," I continued. "You threatened Kirk, trying to get him to back off. Damian didn't understand what was happening; maybe he went for the weapon, maybe you threatened him, and Kirk stepped in. However it happened, Kirk wound up dead and Damian was convinced he'd had a hand in it." I eyed the orderly in the outer area; he'd started toward me, with the nurse who had granted us access behind him. "From there, it was all according to plan — you stuffed Kirk into your fridge, took Damian up to the barn in Brewer with a bag of supplies you'd already packed and then told him to wait for you. Then you returned to East Newberry."

"That's... crazy!" Angelina exclaimed. His breathing was ragged and nearly painful to witness, and for a moment, I felt guilty for pushing him — right up until I reminded myself of how many people had died as a result of his actions.

"Crazy was running a pizza special on Monday that drew all of your longtime customers into the restaurant — friends, neighbors, pillars of the community — and then mowing them down like they were cattle." The shock in his eyes was all I needed to continue. "Oh yes, we know *exactly* what happened that night. And once you were done killing everyone, you had one last task to perform — you dragged your grandson back out of the fridge and made it look like he was just one more victim."

There was a knock on the glass door, which I ignored.

"Somewhere in there, you realized you needed to be wounded yourself in order to sell the story to the cops; that's when I think you discovered just how hard it is to purposefully self-inflict a gunshot wound — especially from a semi-automatic." I smiled slightly. "It was true you were shot by the killer — you just left out the fact the killer was *you*."

The door slid open. "Commander—"

"I'm almost done," I replied without looking to the speaker.

"We need to get Mr. Angelina to surgery—"

My glare to the orderly effectively silenced him, but I knew I was out of time. Turning back to Angelina, I watched his drawn face carefully as I played my final card. "We found the gun," I nearly whispered. "With your prints on it, Leon. You can go to your grave knowing that."

What little color was left in his cadaverous face drained from it, though the resulting alarms from the various monitors surrounding Angelina underscored it was a Pyrrhic victory at best. Still, the ever so slight slumping of his shoulders was enough of a confirmation for me that I felt my job there was done. If the nurse could be believed — and the dropping stats on the monitors seemed to support him — I wasn't sure Angelina would live long enough to see traditional justice served. I wasn't one to leave things in the hands of a deity, but in this case felt strongly that something quite severe would be meted out if and when Angelina arrived at the Pearly Gates.

"He's all yours," I said to the orderly as Norm and I headed for the open door.

"You know the way out," the nurse who had escorted us in said. It was a statement, not a question.

Ignoring him, I hovered at the edge of the doorway and looked directly at Angelina one final time. "This isn't what your wife would have wanted, was it?"

Angelina slowly shook his head. "No. I should have... listened to her..."

"Yes," I said simply. "Yes, you should have."

I turned and walked out of the ICU; Norm was right behind me but put a hand on my shoulder once we were clear of the doors to the ward. "I didn't realize Heather's team had recovered the gun — that info wasn't in the file."

"We didn't," I shrugged. "But now I know where to look."

EPILOGUE

y mood was as bleak as the desolate late November landscape in Windeport when the Thanksgiving holiday rolled around; as my staff scurried around taking care of last-minute items before closing the office for the holiday, I found myself standing at the tall window behind my desk staring at the hill behind the high school and not feeling particularly motivated about anything. The mug of coffee in my hand was quietly steaming into the air; another shot of caffeine in a long line that had begun the evening I'd returned to my bungalow after our final interview with Leon Angelina. And it *had* been final; I'd barely walked through the door before my iPhone had buzzed with a text message that the body of our lead suspect was headed to Augusta for a perfunctory postmortem. The six-pack of Sam Adams in the fridge had suddenly seemed like an indulgence I didn't deserve, so I'd popped a K-Cup into the Keurig instead and watched the starlight dance on the water in the harbor until it was time to head to morning practice.

Sipping at the mug, I pondered the current text message that was sitting on the screen of my phone; my cousin, Charlie, had extended her usual invitation to join her and my nieces for Thanksgiving Dinner, but for the first time in years I'd found myself unable to accept. The farm had always been a welcoming space for me, especially during some of my darkest moments right after the passing of my mother. Suzanne's absence beside me at the table wouldn't have gone unnoticed or unremarked upon, though, and for whatever reason was something I simply hadn't wanted to deal with. So, instead I'd hunkered down in my bungalow with a sad excuse of a frozen turkey dinner and a slate of equally as terrible NFL games, then watched the stars dance against the dark sea before slipping between the sheets of my very lonely bed. I'd been ignoring every text message from Charlie since. Staring at the dead trees reaching their empty branches to the overcast afternoon sky, I was still trying to come to terms with the oversized and rather outlandish sign that had gone up on the pharmacy building a few days earlier; it wasn't much of a stretch to deduce the merger with the Maine Medical physicians group had been in the works far longer than Suzanne had led me to believe, yet one more indication of just how badly far off I'd been about the woman I'd loved.

Still love, I corrected mentally. *After all of this, I* still *fucking love her.*

My eyes followed a random red squirrel that appeared beneath one of the trees; as it sat there, considering its next move, I thought about the appropriately generic form letter I'd received telling me that Suzanne's practice had become part of a larger network — and the small note at the bottom assuring me my primary care physician would not be changing. The letter had been the longest amount of contact I'd had with her since our crash-and-burn moment in New Hampshire; we were civil when we saw each other at the IGA, of course, but it also wasn't lost on me that the two of us appeared to be keeping exceedingly unusual hours just to avoid such a happenstance. Windeport being the size it was meant that should have been nearly impossible, but we managed somehow to pull it off.

Looking at the mug for a moment, I frowned that it was once again empty and made my way back to my prized coffee machine for another refill. As the machine began to sputter into life, I leaned on the counter and chastised myself yet again for purposefully overlooking just what had *not* been going on between us for the past couple of months. Sure, Suzanne had begun spending the random night at the bungalow, but it had always been with an overnight bag; when had she stopped leaving a change of clothes or two at my place? Or, for that matter, why hadn't I said anything about her not inviting me back to her apartment? I'd laughed off her washing my cache of workout gear that had long hung in her master bedroom closet, but now I realized her handing me that duffle bag was another step toward removing me from her life.

In retrospect, it now seemed our rapprochement in August had been anything *but*.

No, that's not entirely fair, is it? I thought as I waited for my coffee. *There* was *something there in August — it just evaporated when her ex-husband rode back onto the scene.*

Grabbing the mug from the Keurig, I wandered back to the window and wondered what I'd tell Vasily; so far, I'd managed to deflect questions about his wedding in January, but I knew sooner or later I was going to have to face the music. While I was clearly planning on attending, I just didn't know how to broach the fact that I was going to be flying solo, especially since Suzanne had just as much a hand in the planning of the affair as I had. At that particular moment, I wasn't feeling big enough to be professional about the situation; if anything, I wanted her excommunicated from our friendship with the guys on the West Coast, but that was far beyond my reach (and, frankly, kind of petty).

Face it, Sean, I sighed, *you're actually feeling petty right now. And why not? She ripped your heart out twice in three months. Anyone would feel betrayed to have it happen just* once.

Spinning on my heel, I went back to my battleship of a desk and considered briefly sitting back down and completing the insane number of administrative duties that came with being a department head for the State of Maine. I'd had my share of paperwork when I'd served as Police Chief for Windeport, but the bureaucracy in Augusta had turned the process into a fine art, one that I was not sure I wanted to experience that afternoon. I decided to split the difference and do the timesheets for the staff, mindless busywork that would allow me to avoid answering Charlie for just a little bit longer – perfect for what was shaping up to be a truly Black Friday. Somewhere along the line, I lost all track of time for when I finally glanced out the open door of my office, I found the lights over the cubicles in the squad room had been turned off; what little chatter I could still hear seemed to be coming from the pair of officers at the far end who had drawn the short straw and were on duty until midnight. One of the few positives of no longer working for the Village was not having to worry about the cruise ship that had appeared in the harbor that morning — or the requisite number of tourists that would be flooding the streets during the Thanksgiving long weekend.

Exiting the system used by our Human Resources operation, I discovered I still had the Angelina case file open on my desktop; despite it being officially closed, I'd been going over the details for a planned interview with the *Bangor Daily News* that Captain Roberts had arranged as some sort of coda to the affair. My role as Commander, Major Crimes made me the public face of such investigations despite having only worked one small part of the case; still, weeks later, the mass shooting in East Newberry continued to dominate the media. Jimmy was hoping my smiling visage would provide enough closure to get the journalists to move on.

Good luck with that, I snorted.

My eyes quickly flicked over the final page of the case summary, the one noting that the semi-automatic had ultimately been found in the bottom of the barrel of tomato sauce in the back of Pizzeria Angelina's pantry; why it hadn't been searched by any of the various agencies that had worked the scene was a subject a new task force was going to be looking into over the coming months. For my purposes, the prints that had been lifted on the exterior as well as the removable lid had come back to Leon Angelina, though what prints we'd found on the gun had been degraded enough by the acidity of the sauce that a match to anything had proven impossible. Ultimately, it hadn't been necessary —

nor was the discovery of the Glock with matching striations to the bullets that had killed both Beryl and Damian. As we had suspected, Angelina had dumped it into the river while boating back to East Newberry; divers managed to recover it just about a mile downstream from the barn where Damian had been hiding. Finding both guns made for a tidy little bow around a case that had wreaked such havoc, and not just in East Newberry.

I shut down the case system and logged out of my MacBook; my trusty laptop had not survived its encounter with the Apple Store and had been replaced by the latest model. The anti-Apple brigade that was central I.T. hadn't been happy with my *fait accompli*, if the one-on-one meeting their director had demanded with me were any indicator. Running my finger over the logo on the cover, I wondered if my days on a MacBook were ultimately numbered.

Sliding the laptop into my backpack, I pulled my gun out of the safe, took a look around the office as if I were leaving for the final time then shut the lights off as I closed the door behind me. The cubicles had gone completely silent by that point; passing Norm's office, I smiled at the hope he was enjoying some much-needed downtime with Raphael in Washington, D.C. His boyfriend's case had spawned a sub-investigation that had delayed his return to Maine, much to Norm's chagrin; he'd been waxing poetic about Charlie's blueberry liquor and had been majorly bummed to not be able to share it with Raphael. Striding down the long hallway to what had originally been our reception area, I paused at the door and turned back to look at the empty walls; for the decade I had worked as Police Chief, my predecessors had hung there in a long row, judging my every move. Now that they were gone, I was surprised to find that I missed them; that, in fact, their presence had been far more preferable to those in Augusta who had since taken over. Taking the gig as head of Major Crimes was beginning to look like a career mistake, though I was unsure of how, exactly, to rectify it.

The parking lot outside of the office was empty save for my SUV; I unlocked the door and slid behind the wheel, tossing my backpack into the well for the passenger seat. As I pressed the button to start it up, my eyes flicked down Main Street in the general direction of the pharmacy building; the abomination of a sign announcing the new practice glowed brightly against the dark of the brick, presenting a forced cheerfulness that belied what had actually happened. No lights were visible in the apartment above, which wasn't much of a surprise; I assumed the estate of Suzanne's late husband had finally been settled, allowing her to take full possession of what I now knew was something of a dream house for her. While it had been a nice location, I'd spent too many years living along the ocean to have my horizon limited by towering mountains — something Suzanne had plainly not picked up on.

Backing out of my spot, I pulled around and turned onto an unusually deserted Route One; the lot in front of the IGA was similarly quiet, making my quick dash in for weekend supplies extremely quick. Perhaps more depressing was the empty carport of my bungalow; I'd become accustomed to seeing a particular Subaru Forester sitting there, so being able to pull beneath the canopy myself felt amazingly awkward. Grabbing my groceries from the back seat, I pushed the SUV door closed with a foot and trundled everything into the house; the warmth of the interior enveloped me like a hug I didn't know I needed, so I stood there for a long moment relishing the feeling.

Packing away my groceries took hardly any time; as I pulled a casserole I'd made that morning from the fridge and put it into the oven to warm up, my phone pinged again with another missive from Charlie. Knowing I couldn't avoid her any longer, I tapped back a two-word response and then tossed my phone on the counter as though it were radioactive. Suddenly finding myself at loose ends — and wanting to put some distance between me and my iPhone — I fled the kitchen and wandered down the hallway toward my room with no specific purpose in mind. My traitorous heart, though, had other ideas, for I quickly found myself standing at my dresser, holding the small velour box I'd taken great pains to hide from the world what felt like a lifetime ago. Staring at the box, I couldn't tell if my hands were shaking as I held it, mostly because my vision had started to blur; blinking away the crushing sense that my life had taken an incredibly unexpected turn, I cracked open the top and glared accusingly at the diamond I'd picked out for Suzanne.

It certainly wasn't the gemstone's fault that I was a complete idiot when it came to relationships, but a part of me needed something to blame; since it was inanimate, there was no chance it could fight back, which paradoxically, seemed a bit unfair. Twisting the ring in the muted light coming in from the window facing the harbor, I felt the tears begin to roll down my cheeks much as they had the day Vasily had announced his departure for California. Everyone I cared for seemed to ultimately leave me: my mother, Deidre, Dad, Vasily and now Suzanne. Was it me? Was I the one driving them away?

What the *fuck* was wrong with me?

My pity party was interrupted by the cheerful two-tones of my doorbell. Startled, I nearly dropped the ring from my hands but recovered fast enough to snatch it from disaster. Sliding it back into a drawer, I wiped at my face before hustling down the hallway, mind racing at whatever emergency had just landed on my porch. It wouldn't have been the first time my time off had been interrupted by an unexpected appearance of a uniformed officer at my home, but when I pulled open the door and saw the duo standing there, I felt my mouth drop open.

"Vas?" I said, the incredulousness clearly audible in my voice. "Alex? What the hell are you doing here?"

Vasily's boyish face cracked into a sly grin. "Does family need a reason?"

"No," I replied as he pulled me into a hug. "Of course not," I nearly stammered as I felt myself handed off to Alejandro, who nearly crushed me with a second hug. "You should be in California," I added lamely, still in shock.

"We're clearly not," Alex said, arching an eyebrow that disappeared beneath his mountain of black curls.

"Yes," I nodded, still not sure what was going on.

"May we...?" Vas asked as he inclined his head toward the bungalow.

"Shit," I said. "Yes -- yes, come on in. I've got dinner in the oven — the guest room's not ready, but go ahead and put your luggage in there—"

"I'll do just that," Alex said as he grabbed two suitcases I'd not seen and began rolling them down the hallway, but not before he gave Vas a meaningful look. "I'm going to clean up a bit, too."

"Sounds good," Vas nodded, clearly getting whatever message his fiancé had given him.

"Beer?" I asked as we went the opposite way toward the kitchen.

"Sure."

I tacked toward the fridge and removed two Sam Adams, popped the tops from each and then handed him a bottle. Leaning against the counter, I took a sip of the bitter hops and eyed my best friend. "Charlie told you," I said after a moment.

"Last night," he nodded, then pulled off the beanie he'd been wearing. Despite his having already told me about suffering a rather severe concussion while pursuing his last major case, I wasn't prepared for the short cut he was sporting; it had yet to grow out enough to hide the slight scar from where he'd apparently also required stitches. I frowned slightly at how both he and Alex appeared to have undersold just how injured he had been. "We booked the first flight we could get after she revealed you were burying yourself in work to avoid dealing with it."

"Me?" I smiled wryly. "Would I do that?"

"In a heartbeat," he said before taking a long drag from his bottle. "So I won't ask how you're doing, especially since your red-rimmed eyes are speaking volumes."

"Yeah, probably wise," I sighed. "I'm not even sure I'd be able to answer, anyway."

"Have you seen her?"

"Here and there."

"But not talked to her?"

"Talked? About this? No."

Vas eyed me. "Do you *want* to talk to her?"

I thought about that for a moment, and as my vision began to blur once more, I heard myself answer: "Despite everything? More than *anything*."

I felt Vasily pull me back into a hug. "We'll figure this out, Sean," he whispered to me as what was left of my self-control finally let go. "Together."

ACKNOWLEDGMENTS

This novel had the unfortunate timing of coming into existence during a period when my professional life was in serious turmoil; while I've long tried to keep my two worlds separate, as more and more of that turmoil bled into the prose I was creating, I decided to lean into it and see what sort of adventure it would lead me on. I had zero idea it would result in yet another nuclear bomb going off in Sean Colbeth's life, nor did I realize the depth and breadth of soul searching my main character would indulge in as he dealt with unexpected waves of buyer's remorse for having accepted a position with the State of Maine. I mean, *seriously*? Where did *that* come from?

Sixteen books in and my characters continue to surprise me.

And while I didn't expect the major twist that happens in the final act, overall I think the story still plowed new territory through a set of unusual cases that resolved in a satisfactory if not unexpected way; this is the first time I've let Sean work more than one problem at a time, which is a bit overdue since Vas pulled it off all the way back in *Pariah* (something I'm sure he'll use to rib Sean as soon as this comes out). Those two are a matched set, no question — even if they can't see it themselves.

Speaking of new territory, something extraordinary happened after *Mirage* was published. While it has done exceptionally well as a novel, it also appears to have become something of a gateway for new readers to discover my Windeport Universe. To those of you who have recently joined me, a million thanks for supporting my writing — and telling your friends about me. As an author, I cannot underscore how much it means to me that there are fans out there fully invested in how these characters evolve; I only hope the events in this story don't destroy your confidence in me. (If they *do*, please remember: I am a sucker for happy endings — and there are more books to come in this series. Enough said.)

And finally, to my wife **Paula**: you've long supported my efforts as an author, but this time around, found yourself pressed into service keeping me sane while the rest of my world turned upside down. That quiet support reminded me of what was *truly* important — and that I am far more than the guy who slings code for a living. Thank you for being you, and for restoring my faith in *me*.

—C

September 2, 2024

About the Author

Born and raised in Maine, Chris has spent nearly three decades as an IT nerd, writing just about everything other than a novel in the process. That changed in early 2019 when he was advised to find a way to wind down from his day job; sifting through his options, he recalled a childhood ambition to become a writer and quickly found himself weaving an entirely new world from the comfort of his laptop. *Belie* is his sixteenth book, part of the series featuring Sean Colbeth and Vasily Korsokovach.

Despite his love for the Northeast, the author escaped the cold for Arizona, where he currently resides with his beautiful wife and a Staffordshire Terrier rescue who insists on being walked as frequently as possible.

For all of the latest information, including hints about upcoming books in both series and an exclusive reader newsletter, please visit the author's website at https://chrisjansmann.com

instagram.com/chrisjansmann

facebook.com/christopherjansmann

mastodon.coffee/@chrisjansmann

amazon.com/author/chrisjansmann

bookbub.com/authors/christopher-h-jansmann

goodreads.com/chrisjansmann

www.ingramcontent.com/pod-product-compliance
Lightning Source LLC
Chambersburg PA
CBHW021146310726
48971CB00002B/504